THIS
IS OUR
STORY

ASHLEY ELSTON

HYPERION

LOS ANGELES   NEW YORK

First Edition, November 2016
3 5 7 9 10 8 6 4 2
FAC-020093-16327
Printed in the United States of America

This book is set in Adobe Garamond Pro
Designed by Maria Elias

Library of Congress Cataloging-in-Publication Data
Names: Elston, Ashley, author.
Title: This is our story / Ashley Elston.
Description: First edition. | Los Angeles : Disney-Hyperion, [2016] |
Summary: "When a hunting accident claims a boy's life, his best friends
all come under suspicion"—Provided by publisher.
Identifiers: LCCN 2015047500 (print) | LCCN 2016016801 (ebook) |
ISBN 9781484730898 (hardback) | ISBN 9781484731864 (ebook) |
Subjects: | CYAC: Mystery and detective stories. | Accidents—Fiction. | Death—Fiction. |
BISAC: JUVENILE FICTION / Mysteries & Detective Stories. | JUVENILE FICTION /
Love & Romance. | JUVENILE FICTION / Law & Crime.
Classification: LCC PZ7.E5295 T47 2016 (print) | LCC PZ7.E5295 (ebook) |
DDC [Fic]—dc23
LC record available at https://lccn.loc.gov/2015047500

Reinforced binding
Visit www.hyperionteens.com

SUSTAINABLE FORESTRY INITIATIVE Certified Sourcing www.sfiprogram.org SFI-00993

THIS LABEL APPLIES TO TEXT STOCK

For my mom, Sally

A ten-point buck and a dead body make the same sound when they hit the forest floor. It's hard to believe a person could be mistaken for an animal, but it happens more than you know.

We know these woods. We've spent as much time here as anywhere else. Every hill and valley, every place the deer forage for food and rest in the heat of the day, is mapped out in our heads. We know exactly where the shot comes from when we hear it. Stealth no longer necessary, we tear in from every direction, each wanting to see the kill first.

But that excitement evaporates at the sight of Grant's body twisted in odd angles over a downed tree. The impact of the bullet knocked him completely out of his boots, which are still upright several feet away.

We gravitate to one another, standing in a tight pack several yards away from him, momentarily scared to get any closer. One by one, our guns slip through our fingers, thudding softly on the blanket of leaves covering the ground.

And one by one we move closer to Grant.

Stunned, we stand in a circle around him, our bodies covered in camouflage, each of us blending into the next.

No one goes near him. No one bends down to check his pulse. There is a small hole in the center of his chest and blood pours out of him and soaks into the ground and there is no question—Grant Perkins is dead.

Two of us drop to our knees, crying; another seems unable to move at all.

But one of us studies the guns piled on the ground.

"That's not a buckshot wound. He got shot with a rifle."

All eyes go to the Remington—the only rifle in the group.

Concern for Grant is over quickly; the sorrow turns to panic and every finger quickly points to someone else and shouts of "I didn't do it!" ring through the air. We all handled that rifle and we know it could point back to any one of us.

The amount of booze and pot and pills still flowing through our systems will guarantee that this is seen as a crime, not just an accident.

We push each other.

We cuss each other.

We threaten each other.

We are imploding.

I watch my friends, who are more like brothers, and know this won't end well for any of us.

A buzzing sound on the ground beside Grant quiets everyone. His phone, set on vibrate, rattles in the dead leaves. No one moves to touch it, to answer it, to make it stop. We all just stare at Grant.

Single file, the ants begin to claim his body. Birds swoop into the nearby trees, waiting for a clear shot at him. We will look guilty if we wait too long to call for help. We will look guilty no matter what. We need to do something—call someone—but we're paralyzed.

I study each person in the circle, faces tear-streaked and numb from either the shock or the alcohol or the drugs. Or maybe all three. I weigh strengths and weaknesses.

Only one of us pulled the trigger, but we all played our own part in his death. They will find marks on Grant that don't fit with an accidental shooting. They will find marks on us that shouldn't be there either. The last twenty-four hours will have them talking about more than what happened during this early-morning hunt.

"So no one is owning up to using the Remington," one of us says, more a statement than a question.

Do any of us remember which one of us was holding that gun a few minutes ago?

Silence as loud as a freight train fills the space, and we stare at Grant to avoid looking at each other. Or looking guilty.

"If one of us goes down for this, it'll be as bad as all of us going down for this," I say. "We can't let that happen."

All eyes are on me. One look is blank, like my words aren't registering, while others are nodding, ready to agree to anything that will keep them out of trouble.

There is only one way out of this, and it has to be together. We all have to agree.

"This was just an accident. A horrible accident," one of us mumbles. "Whoever used the Remington should just admit it. There's no reason to drag us all through this."

"Even if it was an accident, whoever did this could still go to prison," another of us says.

Our actions this morning would be viewed no differently than if Grant had died while we'd been driving under the influence.

Negligent homicide.

"Look, I know we're all scared shitless right now, but we'll be fine. There's no reason for anyone to ruin his whole life over this," I say.

There's one person who hasn't spoken at all, and I realize just how fragile this plan is. We all have to agree or the whole thing will fall apart. He looks down at Grant and then back at the rest of us and finally says, "We're in this together. We stick together."

I lean forward and the other three do the same. Hovering over poor, dead Grant, I say, "Okay, this is our story . . ."

OCTOBER 20, 7:55 A.M.

REAGAN: They're here

They look calmer than they should, given the huge amount of trouble they're in. The fact that they've been ejected from that private school of theirs—just two weeks after Grant was killed—should have knocked them down a notch, but instead the opposite seems to be true.

They are as cocky as ever.

The loud pre-school madness falls to a hush as the boys make their way down the hall. It's just like something you would see in the movies.

There's only one public high school in our small Louisiana town of Belle Terre. It's in the old Garden District and is named after William B. Marshall, who had done something incredible for our town, though I'm not really sure what it was. Marshall is very regal, with its façade of brick and stone, surrounded by huge trees that have been here for ages. It's really one of the prettiest buildings in town.

But it's still considered second-rate by those who attend St. Bartholomew's.

Or St. Bart's, as it is more commonly known. St. Bart's is very exclusive. And very private. I always thought no matter how bad those kids screwed up, they wouldn't get in trouble, but apparently, they don't take kindly to students who are under suspicion for negligent homicide . . . even if their families donate ridiculous piles of money to the school.

There was some question as to whether our school would take them when they got the boot from St. Bart's. There was an emergency parents' meeting over the weekend led by a few vigilant moms who did not want these boys in our school. But they are in our district, and until they are actually convicted of a crime, they have a right to attend school.

So here they are.

This has been their school for only a matter of seconds, and yet they already own it. The four of them walk shoulder to shoulder, most people moving out of the way to let them pass, dressed in khakis and button-downs like they're still accountable to some dress code.

My fists ball at my sides as I try to control the rush of anger that flows through me.

Reagan scoots down to my locker and watches them too, her chin resting on my shoulder. "Which one do you think did it?" she asks.

I shrug. "Does it matter? It's not like they'll get in any trouble even if it comes out." The words leave a vile taste on my tongue and an even deeper hole in my chest.

"Sure they will. They can't get away with this," she says. I'm glad she can't see me roll my eyes.

"Well, I'm sure we'll get some good scoop when we get to work this afternoon," she adds.

"Yeah, if they got kicked out of St. Bart's, then something must be happening with their case. Isn't the gym at St. Bart's named after John Michael's grandparents?" I ask, nodding toward the boy on the far right side.

"Who knows? But today will be ex-ci-ting!" Reagan says *exciting* in a high-pitched singsong voice. And then she leans back against me, hugging my shoulders. "Sorry, I know this is hard for you."

"It's fine. And you're right, work should be . . . interesting."

Most people our age have to work a drive-through or bag groceries, but Reagan and I scored jobs as paid interns in the district attorney's office. No weekends and we're usually off the clock by five. And to make it even sweeter, we qualified for work passes, so we're done with school by lunch.

We are the envy of the teenage workforce.

Favors were called in for us to get these jobs, though. I got my spot because my mom has been a secretary for one of the assistant district attorneys for the last twelve years and he knows how bad we need the money. Reagan's cousin's brother-in-law is the district attorney, Mr. Gaines, and even though he's barely a relative, he agreed to hire her as a favor to her dad. Reagan wants nothing more than to go to design school right out of high school, but her dad is insisting she consider "more worthwhile pursuits," hence the job at the district attorney's office. No one has the heart to tell him he's fighting a losing battle.

You only need to look at Reagan once to know she doesn't fit the mold for some nine-to-five job. Her sketches come to life in bold patterns and fabric combinations that shouldn't work but do. Walking the halls with her every day feels like getting a sneak peek at what future runways will showcase.

"With me in Morrison's office, and Camille and you both interning for prosecutors, we should know all the dirt before anyone else. Maybe they know who did it. Maybe they're just keeping it quiet for now," she says.

"Maybe," I answer.

Reagan, still perched over my shoulder, lets out a soft purr. "Don't kill me for saying this, but damn . . . Henry is seriously hot."

I shrug my shoulders, making her chin bounce. It's hard for me to see any of them as anything other than Grant's killer. One of these boys killed their friend and refuses to admit he did it.

Even though they're new to our school, we already knew who these boys were. It would be impossible not to know them in a town our size. But that doesn't mean we run in the same circles. Not even close.

Only one of the boys makes eye contact with those he passes; the others stare straight ahead as if they are oblivious to us. His name is Shepherd Moore—Shep to his friends. I turn away before he has a chance to find me watching them.

"Come on, they're not worth getting a tardy over," I say, dragging Reagan in the opposite direction as she gawks at the boys over her shoulder.

• • •

The worst part of this job is the filing. I've decided there is some evil fairy that must live inside the *Qu–Rh* drawer, the only drawer with any extra space, just to torment me. She waits until I leave for the day, after the filing tray is empty, and then spitefully pulls the most random pages from almost every file in every drawer.

No matter how much filing sucks, it's got to be better than whatever Reagan is doing. She works for Mrs. Morrison, head of the administration department. It's the pit of paperwork hell over there.

Our parish is big but mostly rural. The district attorney governs the parish, and his offices are in Belle Terre. But even though Belle Terre is the largest town in the parish, it's still pretty small, so the DA's office is actually in the same building as the courthouse and the police station.

It's a really old building, older than the high school. The courtrooms, judges' offices, and administration offices, where you can pay your water bill or tax bill or file a complaint, are all on the main floor. The district attorney's offices take up the second floor, and main filing rooms and storage are on the third floor. The jail is in the basement.

I'm sitting on the rough tan carpet, drowning in paper, when I get a text from Mom:

> Even if you're not done filing, come back to Mr.
> Stone's office. I need you to cover the phones.

Mom must be in need of a smoke break. I push to my feet. Anything's got to be better than this. My first stop on the way back to the second floor is Camille's cubicle. She's an intern like me, but she attends the local community college. Camille always has the best gossip, since she works for the secretary of the DA.

There's only one thing buzzing through the halls today, the only thing anyone wants to know: Will there be charges filed against the boys who shot Grant Perkins? I know everyone wants to believe that information like this is carefully guarded and that only those who should know do, but that's not even close to being true. The DA's office is no safer from gossip than the cafeteria at school.

I perch on the edge of her desk and ask, "Any word yet?" She has no idea how interested in this case I am, so I try to play it cool.

Camille is looking through some files in the top drawer of a filing cabinet. She peeks at me over her shoulder, then scans the area, making sure no one is nearby, before joining me at her desk. "The case was referred to our office today. The police have no idea who pulled the trigger."

My mouth drops open. Mr. Stone, the ADA Mom and I work for,

said this was a possibility—a worst-case scenario, but still a possibility.

"Seriously? How can they send it to us if they don't know who did it?" The shrillness of my voice has her looking at me funny.

Camille shrugs. "There's a lot of pressure coming from Grant Perkins's dad to arrest someone. He was in here this morning. Two of the other boys' dads have been in today, too. Gaines is in a panic. Every one of these dudes helped put him in this office—including Mr. Perkins—and they're all here to call in their favors."

"Oh God! So what's he going to do?"

Camille motions for me to lower my voice, then says in a near whisper, "I don't know if he knows yet. The loudest one right now is Perkins, obviously. The other parents are trying to do damage control."

I hop off her desk and start to leave, but Camille calls me back.

"You owe me info now. Make sure you share if you hear something."

I nod and turn away. Just as I'm about to head into Mr. Stone's office, a blur of orange and red and blue that can only be Reagan barrels down the hall.

"Sorry," she says as she skids to a stop in front of me, catching us both before we fall down. She's breathing like she's run a 5K and her eyes dart up and down the hall.

"What's wrong?" I've known Reagan since we were young and she's always been a little dramatic, but this seems over-the-top even for her.

"Stone got it. Stone got the River Point Boys case," she says in between labored breaths.

"Are you sure?"

She nods. "Gaines just left Morrison's office. Told her to get everything up here to Stone. She's pretty shocked, too. We all are."

It's no secret the assistant district attorney Mom and I work for shouldn't be the automatic first choice for this case. He's older and on his way out. In his day he was fierce, but those days are long gone.

She steps in even closer, until our noses are just inches apart. "Gaines had to recuse himself. The hot one—Henry—his dad gave a bunch of money to his campaign. Well, they all did, but Henry's dad gave the most. He's too close. He could have given it to the attorney general and let them handle it, but he didn't. He's keeping it here. It's weird. And insane that he gave it to your guy. Word is he wants this case to go away and he thinks the fastest way for that to happen is to turn it over to Stone."

She squeezes my arm and asks, "Are you going to be able to handle this?"

I nod, not trusting myself to speak, then she's gone as fast as she appeared, and I'm left in the hall, still trying to digest this latest news.

"There you are," Mom says as I step into her office. I study her face while she digs around in the bottom drawer of her desk. After so many years working long hours plus the half pack of cigarettes she smokes a day, she looks older than she really is. From pictures, I know she used to have long, dark hair like mine, but it's mostly gray now, and pulled back in the ever-present bun.

I drop down in the chair next to her desk. Her office is small, with barely enough space for her desk, a couple of filing cabinets, and a small table and chair. I glance through the door on the other side of the room and find Mr. Stone, leaned back in his chair, eyes closed and head-phones on.

There's a good chance he doesn't even know he's gotten the case yet.

A knock on the door makes me jump.

Mr. Gaines, the DA, steps inside, his tall figure taking up most of the space.

"Mrs. Marino, I need a moment with George," he says to Mom. He nods to me and I smile back, then start shuffling papers around Mom's desk so I look busy.

Mom alerts Mr. Stone and he sits up in his chair, probably embarrassed at being caught in such a relaxed state.

"Come on in," Mr. Stone calls out.

Mr. Gaines shuts the door and it takes everything in me not to press my ear against it.

"What's going on?" I ask. I don't dare let on that I know about the case. Mom is a stickler when it comes to office gossip, and Reagan has more than one strike against her in Mom's book right now.

Mom takes a deep breath. "I hope this doesn't mean what I think it does." She twists her hands and then busies herself at her desk. I know she wants to sneak out for a cigarette right now, but there's no way she'll leave until Gaines does.

Mr. Gaines is in there a while, and nervous energy seems to be bouncing back and forth between Mom and me. I've alphabetized the files on Mom's desk, shredded about two inches' worth of documents in the shred pile, and watered all the plants.

Thirty minutes pass before the door opens.

Mr. Gaines leaves without sparing us a glance.

Mr. Stone leans against the door frame and lets out a deep breath. "The district attorney has decided to put the River Point case to a grand jury." He pauses a moment before continuing. "And he wants us to present it."

From the first day I started, Mr. Stone referred to any case he had as "ours," since it is a group effort to get him through it.

"Is there enough evidence against them to even make a case?" Mom asks in a whisper.

Stone shrugs. "Doesn't sound like it. The picture the DA painted for me is this is a wild but essentially good group of boys who partied a little too hard and against their better judgment went hunting that morning. He wants Grant Perkins's death to be classified as an accident, but there's that pesky part about them being drunk and negligent." He says the last part scornfully. "The victim's family isn't as willing to sweep this under the rug and are threatening to make a big stink, which Gaines doesn't want since he's up for reelection next year. The other boys' families have contributed to Gaines's campaign, so he's in the 'difficult position' of making everyone happy."

He says *difficult position* with enough disgust that we all know what he means—Gaines doesn't want any of the boys to get in trouble, no matter what the evidence shows.

"Gaines said he's too close to both sides so he's going to leave it up to the grand jury to decide if there was a crime committed. He thinks this is the only way to appease everyone, but he wanted to make sure I understood that I wasn't to 'press too hard' on this."

And that's the thing about a grand jury—they *only* hear from the prosecutor presenting it, so if Stone presents a weak case, this whole thing disappears and no one will be arrested for Grant's death.

Mom moves closer to him and squeezes his arm. "We'll be behind you no matter what."

He nods at Mom, then glances toward me. "Kate, I understand the boys involved in Grant Perkins's death transferred into your school today."

"Yes, sir," I answer.

He fumbles around in his suit pocket, finally pulling out whatever he was searching for and holding it up for Mom and me.

It's a picture I've seen a thousand times.

In the image, there are five guys, all dressed in camo, holding rifles and standing behind a sign that says *River Point Hunting Club*. The woods behind them are alive with the reds, oranges, and yellows of fall foliage. They look happy and carefree, just as boys with bright futures and privileged backgrounds should look.

But one of those boys is dead now.

"Have you ever seen any of these boys in any social situation? Maybe at a football game, school dance, or anything like that? Ever dated any of them?"

"I've met a few of them but never hung out with them at a party or anything. And I've never dated any of the River Point Boys."

And technically, that's the truth.

Mr. Stone ponders this a moment. In a town this size, everyone pretty much knows everyone else, so there's never any true separation. He finally says, "Steer clear of them at school. Don't talk to them. Don't talk about them. Things are different now that I have this case and you work for me. Until this is over, keep your distance from them. Are we clear?"

"Yes, sir. Very clear."

Mom and I follow him into his office. He sits in his chair and gazes at the wall. Most would assume he's lost in thought, but I know he's looking at us the only way he can.

Mr. Stone does a good job faking it for others, but with us he lets his guard down. He has macular degeneration, which means everything in his central line of vision is blurry, but the edges are in focus. So basically to see something clearly, it has to be in his peripheral vision. His disease is getting progressively worse and there isn't a cure.

The DA is aware of his condition, but pride has stopped Stone from telling Gaines how bad it's gotten. This job has been Stone's life, not leaving any room for a wife or kids. In fact, Mom and I are the closest thing he's got to a family, and he spends most holidays at our kitchen table. I'm not sure Gaines could actually fire him over his deteriorating vision, but Stone knows he would be more or less put out to pasture and he says he's just not ready to go out like that.

"Gaines already subpoenaed the grand jury. We're set for Tuesday,

November eighteenth. This case will be in front of them in four weeks, so it looks like all of this will be over soon enough."

I swallow hard and examine each face in that picture, wondering which one of them pulled the trigger.

Just as Mom's about to speak, I say, "But you're not going to do what Gaines wants, right? I mean, you have to try to find out what really happened."

Stone leans forward, resting his elbows on his desk. "I've got three options: present this the way Gaines wants so that it disappears quickly and quietly, try to convince a grand jury to indict all four for negligent homicide since they were all hunting while under the influence, or dig a little deeper and try to find out who pulled the trigger."

I'm nodding my head at his last suggestion. I'd even be okay with the second option. Mom directs a confused look at me and I school my features. I'm not normally this enthusiastic when it comes to Stone's cases, and I don't really want to explain why I care about this one.

"We'll be making an enemy here if I push too hard. These boys' parents are powerful, and going against them could turn out badly."

He's going to throw the case, I can feel it. I consider any argument I can make to change his mind.

And then he surprises me when he says, "Damn, if it doesn't piss me off, though, that he's given it to me to lose."

Relief rushes through me. It's not over yet. "Yeah, it sucks he didn't give it to that new guy . . . what's his name? Peters? This will probably be the last big case you get."

Mom lets out a gasp. I may have gone too far.

Stone cocks his head; his pupils roll around trying to find a spot where I'm in focus. And then he smirks.

Yes!

"Okay, then, Kate, let's see what we can do with this heaping pile of shit Gaines just dropped on us. It'll be next to impossible to indict them *all* for this, so for the next four weeks, we see what we can dig up. Within the hour, we'll have all the evidence that was collected and copies of the police interrogations from the morning of the accident. Apparently, there was a big party at River Point the night before, so we're getting some videos with witness statements from some kids who were there. The findings from the coroner are expected next week." Mr. Stone leans closer to Mom and me, his voice dropping when he says, "Just so you understand, I'm only going to try to push this case through if we have hard evidence and a clear perpetrator. We need to be at the top of our game. Because if we pull this off, Gaines is going to be gunning for us all."

They call us the River Point Boys.

We are never called by our individual names. That's what we wanted, so that's what we got. This way, the focus is on the piece of land where Grant died, not on any one of the four names that potentially pulled the trigger.

The picture of us in front of the River Point Hunting Club sign was taken last year, last hunting season. Grant is in the center, holding the Remington—the rifle that killed him. He's got a big smile on his face, his friends—his brothers—on either side.

If any one of us, other than Grant, had been holding that gun, our story would have fallen apart. Regardless of who pulled the trigger, an image of one of us holding the Remington would have been the only proof the public needed.

We all got a copy of that picture in the same rough wood frame as a gift from Grant's mom. She liked doing that—taking pictures of us, then printing and framing them so we could all share in that memory.

I've kept every one . . . lined them up from first to last. You'd think the last one would be hardest to look at, but it's the first one that strikes a pain straight through me every time I glance at it.

In the picture, we're dripping with mud from head to toe, arms thrown around each other, and we're grinning like idiots. It was one of the first weekends we spent together—just the five of us. We took a trailer full of four-wheelers to the Mud Nationals and it was the best weekend of our lives. We rode over every trail and raced through every mud pit and camped high on a ridge where we cooked hot dogs and talked through the night about everything from girls we liked to the same unreasonable expectations all of our dads seem to have.

I look down the line of framed pictures, stopping again on the one of us in front of the River Point sign. The one that's been posted with every news story about us.

That was a good weekend, too. One of the last before the drinking and the pranks got out of control. Before a lot of things got out of control.

And then I get to the end of the line. I printed and framed this one myself, since there's no way Grant's mom would have. It was taken the day before he died. Age isn't the only difference between this picture and the one from Mud Nationals. There's a hardness in our expressions and a distance between us that wasn't there before.

Seeing all of these moments in time, lined up in chronological order, makes it really easy to see when things went wrong.

Pulling my phone out, I look at another image. One I can't frame. One that reminds me who Grant really was.

We are lucky the police can see us on that day a year ago, happy together. Before things changed.

Who could look at that picture and think we meant him any harm?

2

REAGAN: Did you hear? Grant Perkins was shot hunting this morning at River Point

KATE: WHAT???? Is he ok????????

REAGAN: I heard he died ☹

REAGAN: Are you there?

REAGAN: Kate???

REAGAN: I tried to call you. Call me back.

I'm boxing up all the old files on Stone's desk to make room for the mountain of paper and folders and evidence that was just delivered for the River Point case.

A felony case like this one, with no clear perpetrator, can't move forward until the prosecutor proves there is enough evidence to bring someone to trial by going in front of a grand jury. In four weeks, hopefully Mr. Stone will be standing in front of twelve jurors, asking them to believe one of these four boys committed negligent homicide.

But even if he can prove who pulled that trigger and get the grand jury to indict, there's still the hurdle of a judge or another jury finding him guilty. And knowing how well-connected these boys are, my bet is whoever did this may never see the inside of a jail cell.

I throw the lid on the box, then kick it. I hate the legal system. Hate it. I've learned that not all who should go to jail do. And not all who should walk free will. The facts of a case and the innocence of the accused are only as strong as the person presenting them. And if you have enough money and connections, there's little to no chance you'll ever get in any real trouble. A slap on the wrist, some community service, and it's back to life as usual.

Lately, Mr. Stone has been given the cases no one else wants, like the third-offense drug possessions and the ones for domestic violence and child abuse. It's so unbelievably hard seeing how the system can fail the women and kids who come through here.

But now, we've got the biggest case in the parish. Mr. Gaines's intentions couldn't have been any clearer when he threw this case our way.

He gave it to Stone to lose.

By the time our shift is over and Reagan drops me off at home, I'm worn-out.

Mom and I live in the small side of a duplex in an old area of town. It's not a bad area, just an old one . . . and not the kind of old area that gets revived. The house is quiet and dark when I make my way inside, since Mom will be working late tonight and probably every night for the foreseeable future.

It's just been Mom and me for a while. My dad bailed when Mom found out she was pregnant with me; then he turned back up a few years later. Mom and I were sitting at the table in the kitchen, eating spaghetti, and he just walked in like he'd only been gone five minutes instead of five years. We played house for about three months before he took off again. I wished he had never come back. It was one thing when he just ran from the *idea* of me; it was another to know being with me every day wasn't something he wanted.

There's only one picture of Dad and me, and it's hidden in the bottom of my desk drawer in my bedroom. Mom doesn't know I have it and I have no idea why I've kept it all these years, but I feel like I should have some proof that he existed. Sometimes I try to think back to the day that picture was taken, remember what we were doing just before someone, probably Mom, asked us to look at the camera and smile. But there's nothing.

And then there was a series of Mom's boyfriends, some good, some bad, some really, really bad, but none who hung around for long.

Mom has sworn off men since the last one convinced her to invest all our savings into some crazy business idea he had and then skipped town when the business went bust.

I pop a frozen pizza in the oven and sit at the table so I can tackle my homework, but I'm distracted. I check my texts—no new messages. My finger hovers over the screen of my phone and I try to talk myself out of what I know I want to do. I'm all but torturing myself by going back and rereading the conversations. After holding off as long as I can, I scroll down until I get to what I'm searching for, the text from Grant that never fails to bring a smile to my face:

GRANT: Truth or dare?

ME: Truth

GRANT: Dang I was hoping you were going to say dare

ME: ?? Why? What craziness were you going to have me do?!

GRANT: I can't tell you now. You picked truth.

ME: Well then ask me something
and I'll tell you the truth

GRANT: Ok. If I dared you to come to a party
with me Saturday night would you say yes?

ME: :)

ME: Yes

GRANT: Truth or dare?

ME: Dare

And then I scroll down to the last message Grant Perkins sent me. The one that scrapes out all happiness and leaves me hollow inside.

The one he sent the night before he died.

I'm sorry. Please give me a chance to explain.

I run my hand across my eyes, wiping away the tears that have formed there. I was so mad at him I couldn't see straight. I was going to surprise him, meet him earlier than we had planned, but I was the one who was surprised instead when I saw him with another girl. It's not like he was cheating on me, because we weren't dating. In fact, pretty much our whole relationship had consisted of late-night texts, but something was there between us. Something new and exciting. I thought we both wanted to take the next step.

Then I saw him with her. His arm across her shoulders, his words in her ear, and the smile on her face because of something he said.

That should have been me.

I took a picture of them. Stared at it for what seemed like forever. Sent it to him in a moment of weakness hours later, just before I was supposed to meet him at that party—the party at River Point—with a message asking how could he have been talking to me all this time and not have told me he was with someone else.

It was a while before he responded. A simple *I'm sorry. Please give me a chance to explain.*

I couldn't bring myself to respond because I knew any excuse he gave me, I would take it. And I wasn't ready to sacrifice my pride so quickly.

I was going to wait a day. Or two. Then respond. Make him sweat it out.

But then he was gone.

If I could change anything, I wouldn't have ignored his last message.

I throw my phone across the table and move to the couch and turn on the TV, anything to distract myself.

And of course, the first thing to flash across the screen is a copy of the picture Mr. Stone showed me earlier. The news stations found out the River Point Boys were slumming it in public school and thought this deserved the top story of the night. Everywhere I turn, there is the image of the River Point Boys.

One of those boys shot Grant.

I stare at the screen until they move on to the next story—the protesters who have gathered outside one of the older buildings downtown. Reagan and I passed them this afternoon when we left work. A local construction company renovated the building for some sort of downtown renewal project but apparently charged way more than they should have. The project is millions over budget and it's not even finished yet.

Everything about this town is so screwed up.

· · ·

Because of block scheduling, there was no way to know yesterday if I was going to share any classes with the River Point Boys.

Three of the four of them are already seated along the front row of my English class when I get there.

And just like yesterday, they're all dressed like they're going to church.

I sacrifice my usual seat, which would put me right next to them, and choose one in the middle of the room.

John Michael, Shep, and Henry are just feet away.

From their recurring appearance on the news, I feel like I know them. I mean, the reporters love bringing up the fact that Grant was killed on John Michael Forres's family's land. I know how long it's been in his family. I know how many acres it is. I know the layout of the cabin.

And Shep Moore. Arrogant, cocky Shep. He was with Grant when I met him that first time. The news has told his story a hundred times: his family is in the oil and gas business, and when natural gas was discovered in North Louisiana, Mr. Moore's business skyrocketed.

Then there's Henry Carlisle—the bad boy. I've heard rumors about him since grade school. He's the richest in the group, and also the one most likely to buy his way out of trouble. I heard he's been busted drinking and driving by the cops four times, one of those before he even had his license, but he's never been arrested. Or that's what some of my friends who have friends at St. Bart's say.

Shep turns around and I'm caught staring at him. We watch each other a second or so, and confusion or anger, I'm not sure which, flashes across his face.

My eyes drop to my desk. God, I'm so stupid. I shouldn't even be sitting this close to them.

The bell rings and Mr. Stevens quiets the classroom chatter, which is unsurprisingly louder than usual, since we have such notorious guests.

"As you are all aware, we have some additions to our class. We'll skip the normal introductions since we are all very aware of who they are and why they're here," Mr. Stevens says.

There are a few embarrassed laughs, but mostly everyone is silent. I wish now I could see the boys' faces rather than just the ramrod posture of their backs.

Just as Mr. Stevens is about to turn toward the board, Henry raises his hand.

"You've got something to add, Mr. Carlisle?" Mr. Stevens asks.

Henry leans forward in his desk. "You think you know us, but we know you, too."

Shep reaches over and grabs his arm, but Henry brushes him off.

Mr. Stevens leans against his desk and with a wide flourish of his arms says, "By all means, please tell us what you think you know."

Shep pulls Henry close and whispers something to him. They have a quiet fight, with muted words and jerky movements, before Henry finally pushes him away.

"You're a judgmental, condescending asshole because you're stuck teaching in public school. Didn't you apply for a job at St. Bart's and they laughed your ass right out the door?"

There's a shocked silence, and then hoots of laughter explode through the room. Henry turns around to the class and shoots us a grin.

Mr. Stevens picks up the phone, probably calling the office, his face red with rage.

John Michael looks nervous, his eyes darting around the room, while Shep seems pissed.

"Mr. Carlisle, you are needed in the office. Take your things, since I don't foresee your return."

Henry salutes Mr. Stevens and says, "Best news I've heard all day." He slides his books off the top of the desk and is gone seconds later.

It takes another minute for Mr. Stevens to quiet the class. When he starts writing our assignments on the whiteboard, no doubt adding in more than he planned since the class turned on him, Shep spins around and scans the room. I'm not sure what—or who—he's looking for, but his eyes stop on every person in class.

Including me.

I hold his stare for a count of five before I have to look away.

. . .

Mom's area is empty; I'm sure she's off sneaking a cigarette somewhere, so I make my way to Mr. Stone's office.

"I'm here, Mr. Stone. What do you need me to do today?" I ask, then glance at the "to be filed" basket behind his desk and cringe. The pile is at least two feet high.

Mr. Stone is shuffling his papers around his desk. "Come on in, Kate. I've got something I need help with."

I move into the room and suck in a sharp breath when I see Logan McCullar, the fourth River Point boy, frozen on the screen behind him.

Logan is the tough one of the group. From what I've heard, if there's a fight, he's the one throwing the first punches.

Mr. Stone glances up, taking an extra few seconds to move his eyes into a position where I'm in focus.

"What's wrong?" he asks.

I point to the monitor. "Nothing, I just didn't expect a face to be staring at me over your shoulder."

He swivels around, almost like he forgot what was on the screen behind him. "Oh, yes. This is what I need help with today."

I inch closer.

"Sit down."

Once I'm in the chair in front of his desk, Mr. Stone says, "Your mom told me about the photography award you received. Congratulations."

It takes me a second to switch gears. "Oh, thank you."

Mr. Stone leans back in his chair and his eyes drift to the ceiling. Mom told me a while back that his eyes tire easily from constantly trying to decipher the blur of color and movement in his central line of vision, so that's why he takes to staring at the plain white ceiling—so he can give his eyes a break.

"I knew you were into photography, but I've never asked you what type of pictures you like to take."

I squirm like I usually do when people ask me to talk about the thing I love. It always sounds so weird when I try to explain what I see when I look through the lens.

"I take candid images of real life, ordinary things, and try to find something extraordinary about it. I want every image I take to tell a story."

A small smile touches his lips. "Tell me about the last photograph you took. Paint the picture for me."

It doesn't even take a second for the image to come alive in my brain.

"Well, I was at the park, just watching the kids play. There weren't that many kids around since it was a little chilly out. But then I saw this mom pushing her little girl in the swing. The mom was clearly tired—her hair was a mess and there were huge bags under her eyes—and it seemed like the last thing she wanted to do was stand there and go through the same motion over and over. But the little girl, I guess she was maybe three or four, was ecstatic. I mean, every time she got that push, her face lit up. For me, it was so interesting to see two such different emotions—joy and exhaustion over the same experience."

Mr. Stone seems pleased with my answer, although I have no idea why. "Have you narrowed down which college you'd like to attend? I know you were looking at several that have good photography departments."

I can't stop the smile. "There are a few I'm really interested in. I'm getting my portfolio together and trying to work out the financial stuff."

"What type of photography would you like to do once you're finished?" he asks.

I cock my head to the side. "I'm not interested in taking baby portraits or wedding pictures. I'm leaning more toward photojournalism. You know, like when something huge happens and there's that one image that sums it up—the sorrow or the happiness, the heartbreak, the loss, or the utter joy? That's what I want to do. I want to find those moments."

Instead of boy bands covering my walls, I've plastered a copy of every image I've ever seen that moved me. Reagan and my other friends think it's depressing, since most of the images were taken during natural or man-made disasters, but they're just looking at them wrong.

He stays in his reclined position and his eyes close. "Obviously, you know the trouble I have with my vision." He takes a deep breath before continuing. "I expect this to stay between us, but part of the problem is I'm losing the ability to make out details. I can see the large objects, like a face, but I'm struggling with expressions. Do you understand what I mean?"

I nod but then say, "Yes, sir," when I remember his eyes are closed. "Can you still read?" I ask before I can stop myself.

Just when I think he isn't going to answer, he says, "It's getting challenging. Your mother has been a lifesaver."

I know Mom spends hours reading documents into a recorder so he can listen to them instead of reading them. I thought it was because his eyes needed the rest—but apparently it's worse than that.

"There are video statements taken from the scene and interviews with witnesses that I need you to watch and then help me see what you do. Paint me that picture. Tell me the story. You obviously are very perceptive about the small details that others would miss, and your mom is swamped with everything else. Are you up for this?" he asks.

Hours and hours of watching the River Point Boys and others talk about their last moments with Grant. Can I handle that? Can I turn down this chance to peek behind the curtain and discover what it was really like between them? See a side of Grant I didn't know? Maybe this is the closure I need. Maybe hearing about him, finding out what happened that night, will help ease the near-constant ache in my chest.

"Yes, sir. I can handle it."

"Great. Let's get started."

The others don't know what to make of us.

They study us.

They fear us.

They want to be like us.

We made a decision coming in: we stick together, we don't let anyone in, try not to show any interest at all.

We learned to keep our mouths shut the hard way. We thought refusing to give a statement at the scene would make us look like we were trying to hide something, but we should have waited for our parents to arrive and made sure we had a lawyer there.

We are asked over and over by our parents and the lawyers if there was anything we said that could be used against us later.

We tell them no. We don't know anything. We don't know who did it. There was nothing to say other than that.

They know one of us is lying. One of us pulled that trigger.

And when we're alone with our parents, they beg us to give up the one who shot Grant. They tell us to protect ourselves, our future. They bribe us, threaten us . . . anything to get the truth. The truth about what was going on at River Point.

But they don't really want that truth. None of them want to think their son is guilty of negligent homicide . . . or any of the other things going on out there.

They're worried one of the others will break and put all of the blame on their son.

I'm worried about that, too.

3

AUGUST 29, 9:45 P.M.

GRANT: What's up

KATE: Taking pics at the regional debate and wishing
I was anywhere but here. What about you?

GRANT: At River Point and wishing
the same thing

Mr. Stone's finger hovers over the button that will resume the video of Logan. "What we're watching today are the segments from their statements at the scene about the gun. There were five guns found at the scene—four shotguns and a rifle. The officers knew Grant's wound was made by the rifle, a Remington 700 XCR II. It was later confirmed by the medical examiner."

"How did they know that? Is there a difference between a wound made by a rifle and one made by a shotgun?"

"Yes." Mr. Stone leans forward, turns to the side so he can focus on the pad of paper in front of him, and sketches a crude drawing of a shotgun shell. "A shotgun shell is filled with lead shot, or pellets, and they spread out when fired, so the wound would be wide with lots of little entry points from each pellet." Then he draws a picture of a bullet. "A rifle has a single bullet that pierces whatever it hits. The entry wound would be the size of my pinkie finger and then would blow out the back side of whatever it hit. So anyone familiar with guns would know just by looking at him that he was shot with the rifle."

"Wait. If there was only one rifle and they know Grant was shot with the rifle, why don't we know who did it?"

He drops the pencil and leans back in his seat again. "No one is admitting to using the rifle, but one or all of them know who did."

"But aren't there fingerprints on it? Or gun residue?" Mr. Stone has not had a case like this since I started working for him, so this is all new. And it doesn't help that my entire knowledge of forensics comes from television.

Mr. Stone pats my arm and gives me a small smile. "The Remington was found in a pile with the shotguns when the police got there. They all participated in target practice the evening before and each one of them shot the rifle that killed Grant, so all of the boys' fingerprints were on the weapon and they all tested positive for residue on their hands, including Grant Perkins."

"Oh God."

Mr. Stone motions to the frozen image of Logan. "The boys were separated at the scene and were questioned until their parents got there and shut it down. Luckily, the officers were equipped with body cameras, so we have footage of each interview. The clips we're reviewing now are when the boys were asked about the Remington. I've grouped them together. I've heard these parts of the tapes so many times today that I could recite the words. I'm not interested in the words. I'm interested in how they look while they say the words."

I nod and just before he presses play to start the video again, I ask, "Do I just blurt out what I see? Wait until it's over?"

"Describe the scene as it happens. I don't want you to make assumptions. I want facts. What are his hands doing when he speaks? Where are his eyes? Is he looking at the officer? Are they darting around the room? What is his posture like? Just the facts, do you understand?"

He presses play and Logan comes to life.

I start off a little unsure. "He's sitting in a wooden desk chair. Looks like he's in some sort of home office."

"How's his posture? Paint the picture, Kate."

I scoot my chair closer to the screen and imagine I have my camera in front of me.

Logan's voice startles me.

"I don't know what else you want me to tell you. We were hunting, just like we do every weekend."

"He's slouched in his seat. Hands are on the arms of the chair. He looks relaxed but . . . not really."

Mr. Stone shakes his head and pauses the video. "'Not really' doesn't work. Why doesn't he look relaxed?"

I stare at his frozen image. "Well, even though his body is reclined, he's gripping the arms of the chair. His knuckles are almost white. His shoulders seem tense, too. He's got lines across his forehead."

Mr. Stone nods and pushes play again.

The officer rolls out a map of the property and lays it on the desk in front of Logan.

"He glances at the map but then looks away," I say.

"Logan, point out on the map where you were hunting this morning."

"He's leaning forward and looking at the map. He seems to be studying it before he finally points to a location."

"So let's think back to this morning. Everyone is about to walk out the door. Each of you grab a weapon. There were four shotguns at the scene: two Brownings, a Winchester, and a Benelli. And then there was a rifle—the Remington. The only rifle. So on the way out to hunt, what gun did you pick up?"

Logan sits up a fraction in his chair and tilts his head forward. I relay every move to Mr. Stone at the same time I listen intently to his answers.

"I grabbed my Browning."

"Do you remember what gun the other boys grabbed?"

"He throws his head back a bit and squints his eyes."

"No."

"Who grabbed the Remington?"

"His eyes are all over the place."

"The Remington was Grant's gun."

"But there's no way Grant shot himself. Someone else was hunting with his gun. Who was it?"

Logan looks directly at the cop, no flinching, no wavering. "I don't remember. All I know is it wasn't me."

The monitor goes blank for a few seconds; then a second face fills the screen.

John Michael Forres.

An officer is offscreen, just like with Logan, but the voice is different. Less hostile.

I study John Michael, noting everything for Mr. Stone. It looks like he's in a bedroom. He's sitting in an oversize chair and I can see the corner of a bed in the background.

"His eyes are red-rimmed like he's been crying. His nose is red, too. And now that I think back, Logan's eyes were dry."

"Son, all this can be over quickly. We can see how upset you are. Talk me through it. You're in front of the gun case. I got a good look at the collection of guns there and it's mighty impressive. Lots to choose from. Which gun did you hunt with this morning?"

"I used my dad's Browning."

"Okay, good, son. You're doing really good. Did you get a good look at what the other boys chose? Did they use their own gun or one of y'all's?"

"He looks shaky. And kind of out of it. Like he's in a daze or something."

"John Michael, can you hear me, son? Do you remember what gun your friends were hunting with?"

"His eyes snap back into focus. He holds his hands out in front of him and his eyes close. Maybe he's trying to picture it in his head?"

"I grabbed Dad's Browning. I can't remember what anyone else grabbed."

"He opens his eyes and drops his hands."

"You don't recall anyone using the Remington? We know it was an accident. I'm sure the DA will understand that. We really need to know who used the Remington."

"John Michael's shaking his head back and forth."

"The Remington was Grant's gun."

I sit up straighter. "He sits up and looks directly at the officer, just like Logan did, when he answered that."

"John Michael, I didn't ask whose gun it was. I asked who used it. I know you boys are close. Everyone probably borrowed from everyone else all the time. It wouldn't be a big deal to borrow a gun on the morning of a hunt. I just need to know who borrowed it."

"John Michael is squeezing his eyes closed and his face is all scrunched up."

"It wasn't me. I don't remember what anyone else was hunting with."

And the screen goes dark again, then shows Henry Carlisle. Same camo outfit as the others, but he's sitting on a barstool. Behind him are several stuffed deer heads hanging on a dark, paneled wall.

"Henry's hair is sticking up all over the place like maybe he's been running his hands through it over and over. His left leg bounces, fast, like he's nervous. It's making his whole body shake." I'm not sure why, but I don't mention it's a far cry from the arrogance he showed in class today.

"Henry, I've known you and your family a long time. I know you boys think even if you didn't pull the trigger, you'll all be in trouble because of the drinking and the drugs, but I'm giving you my word. Just tell me what happened this morning. Let's start with you showing me where you were hunting."

"Henry leans forward. Seems to study the map more intently than Logan did."

"I was here, right by a big pecan tree."

"All right. How'd you get there? Walk? On a four-wheeler?"

"Walked."

"He's really chewing on that lip. Surprised it's not bleeding."

"And what gun did you take out in the woods with you?"

"I had my Winchester."

"What about your friends? Run across any of them when you were walking to your spot?"

"No. I didn't see anyone else."

"He runs his hands through his hair again. Leg is still bouncing."

"You didn't see anyone else? Maybe someone using the Remington?"

"He's blinking pretty fast, eyes are darting around the room."

"The Remington was Grant's gun."

"Wait, his eyes go straight to the officer, too, when he said that."

"Henry, that's not what I want to hear. I want to hear who used that gun. I want to know right now. This isn't a game, son. A boy was killed this morning. Who used the Remington?"

"Henry chews his bottom lip every time the man says 'Remington.'"

Mr. Stone gives me a quick nod and pride flushes through me like I've cracked some big clue.

Henry's voice shakes when he says, *"I really don't know. All I know is it wasn't me."*

"They all have the same answer?"

"Just wait. There's one more," Stone says.

And the screen flips to the last River Point boy—Shep Moore.

Shep is sitting awkwardly on a couch, turned sideways so he can see the officer who must be sitting next to him, but his legs are still planted on the floor. He's staring straight at the officer, and a wave of disgust rolls through me when I look at him.

"The first thing I think when I see his face is he's calm. Calmer than the rest."

Mr. Stone pauses the video. "What makes you say that?"

I study Shep's face. He's attractive, but then again, they all are.

"I'm not sure what it is. He seems sad. It's in his eyes. I don't know. The rest of them were fidgeting around, eyes darting or angry faces or crying faces. But not his. He just looks different."

Mr. Stone waits a second, then starts the video again.

The voice offscreen is different. *"Where were you hunting this morning?"*

"Right near deer stand number seven."

"He didn't even glance at the map the officer was holding out to him."

"Okay, what gun were you using?"

"He relaxes against the back of the couch a bit."

"I had my Benelli."

"Did you see anyone else on the way to your stand? Do you know what gun they were using? Did you see anyone with the Remington?"

"No. No. And no."

"He barely blinks."

"You're telling me you didn't see anyone else or notice what any of the other boys were hunting with? I don't know if I believe that. You're a smart guy. Surely you notice things like that. Just tell me who used the Remington."

"Shep's staring at the ground now. His shoulders are sagging. He looks defeated."

He takes longer than the other two to answer. *"The Remington was Grant's gun."*

"He didn't look at the officer. He was the only one who didn't."

"Yeah, Shep, we know that. Grant's dad gave him that gun on his last birthday. We've already verified that. But I need to know who used it this morning. You can tell me. Was it you? Were you the one who borrowed that gun? I've known these families for years, and those boys have been friends with each other since they were babies—you're newest to this group. If it was you, they're gonna throw you under the bus, son. Best to tell me now."

"Shep's looking back at the officer now. Staring straight at him."

"It wasn't me. I used my Benelli."

And the video ends.

I lean back in my chair. From the news, I knew the police were having a hard time getting the full story out of the boys. They made it sound like it was because they were drunk or high and they were all really foggy on what happened, but I knew there had to be more.

"They all have the same story. Like practically word for word the same story. The police have to know they're hiding who did it." I feel uneasy. Sick even. They were his friends. His best friends.

Mr. Stone shakes his head. "Of course they know, Kate. Gaines asked me not to push too hard on this case—you can guarantee he asked the same of the police. The DA is up for reelection next year and the sheriff is up the year after. They did their jobs—they turned over what they had and nothing more. We have a few interviews, the analysis on the guns and scene. They threw in some pictures from the wildlife cameras scattered throughout the property, but there was nothing on them but some deer and other animals."

"What's a wildlife camera?"

He flips a series of grainy pics across his desk. "They're cameras mounted in trees that take pictures of whatever crosses in front of them. They have motion sensors. Mr. Forres has five of them, but they're scattered throughout the woods. They let the hunter get a feel for where the deer are. These are some copies of the images taken from those cameras."

"But none of the cameras showed any of the boys hunting that morning?" I ask.

Mr. Stone shakes his head. "No. It would have been nice if they did. One of those boys picked up that Remington before heading out to hunt, and it would make my job a lot easier if I had a picture of the boy using it."

I'm having trouble wrapping my head around all of this. "Is it unusual for one of them to hunt with a rifle and the others with shotguns?"

Stone shrugs. "No. It's personal preference. That rifle was Grant's and apparently he hunted with it all the time."

I sit back in my chair, letting it all sink in. "So what do you think is going on?"

"We know they all had alcohol and/or drugs in their systems when they left that camp to go hunting. One of them was negligent with a gun. Whether he mistook Grant for a deer or was just horsing around with a loaded weapon, the end result was, Grant Perkins was shot. They had to know that act is punishable with prison time after going through hunter safety. I believe they are prepared to protect each other no matter what, and I would guess they know the district attorney is on their side. Those boys' families aren't just donors but old family friends."

He pauses for a moment, his eyes going to the ceiling. "Finding out what really happened that morning is going to be like swimming upstream. And don't expect anyone to throw us a rope. We're going to be completely on our own."

I swallow down the lump in my throat. "Do you think we can do it?"

Stone tilts his head to the side. "The trick now is going to be figuring out where the weak link in that group is. That's why I'm asking you to look so closely at these videos. If one of them breaks, I think the whole group will fall apart. If that happens, we may have a chance."

We all mourn for Grant in our own ways. Some of us tell "Grant" stories over and over while others look physically pained every time they hear his name.

But no one talks about the rifle. No one asks who used it. No one asks who pulled the trigger.

We all handled that gun. We all fired that gun.

We all know that any one of us could go down for this if the other three decide that's what needs to happen.

It is the secret that binds us.

The clock is ticking. We have to hold it together for a couple of weeks. Then this will be over and we can find our new normal.

Right now, the others feel strong. They trust our parents and the lawyers and believe the DA when he says everything is under control. They don't believe there is anything to bring us down.

But I know it's going to get worse before it gets better.

4

SEPTEMBER 2, 12:02 A.M.

KATE: If there was only one food left
on earth what would you want it to be

GRANT: This is what you're thinking
about in the middle of the night?

KATE: I'm hungry. But too lazy to
go to the kitchen.

GRANT: Easy. Shrimp. I love shrimp

KATE: Well ok. Looks like there's no
future for us. I'm allergic to shellfish.

GRANT: A world without shrimp or a
world without Kate?? How do I pick?

KATE: I see how you're gonna be

GRANT: Ok I pick a world with Kate. But
you're not allergic to French fries are you
cause that might be a deal breaker

It's early; the pale morning light is just barely making its way through
the tiny slits of the wide metal blinds. I love being on campus before

anyone else. Really, I love getting to the media arts room before anyone else.

Since Marshall is the only public high school around, it's pretty big. And we have one of the best media arts programs in the state. We not only keep the school's website current and put together the yearbook, we also maintain all of the school's social media accounts, create highlight videos from big events, and publish a monthly newspaper.

An hour from now, this room will be full of people, some of them my closest friends. Reagan will be arguing over fonts for the page headers in the yearbook while Mignon fights Mrs. Wilcox tooth and nail for extra space for her special-interest pieces in the newspaper. Alexis will take over the computer to edit her video footage and get it ready to be uploaded to the website.

But right now, it's quiet. And all mine.

I stare at the long whiteboard on the back wall. It's full of images the other two staff photographers and I have taken so far this year: candids of football players and cheerleaders, math bowl participants and drama club members, and everyone in between. If there's one thing that's really important to me, it's that everyone be represented.

Scanning the list of upcoming events, I put my name next to the few I can cover while I'm not at work: a Shakespeare in the Park play next Thursday night, the cross-country meet on Saturday morning, and the fall food drive Sunday afternoon. The others can cover the rest.

I settle in at the computer, ready to edit the images I took at the Key Club mixer, but my mind wanders, as it's done in quiet moments over the past couple of weeks since Grant died. My eyes drift toward my phone. My weakness. My addiction.

I don't really need to reread the messages anymore since I know them all by heart now, but, as with any addiction, I can't seem to stop myself.

Just as I'm about to unlock my phone, the metal door flies open and hits the back wall, scaring me so bad I almost fall out of my chair.

"Sorry, I didn't know anyone was in here."

My stomach drops. It's Henry Carlisle.

Mr. Stone's words echo in my ears: *Steer clear of them at school. Don't talk to them. Don't talk about them.*

Should I leave?

Henry studies me, quickly sizing me up, and then pulls a large trash can into the room. It's on little metal wheels that squeak so loud that I feel it in my teeth. Again, he's dressed exquisitely, in pressed dove-gray pants and a crisp, white button-down. Reagan is right, he's gorgeous, but there's something dark underneath that layer of cool good looks.

I turn my back, prepared to ignore him. But all I can picture is the interrogation video I saw yesterday. His hair in spikes, his knee rattling so hard I imagine it was sore the next day. Today, he's a million miles from that disheveled boy in camo.

It's on the tip of my tongue to ask him how many times his leg has shaken like that since Grant Perkins died. Was it just the one time in interrogation, or is it every time they flash his face across the TV screen?

But I resist. And keep my mouth closed.

Henry chuckles quietly as he empties all the small cans scattered around the room into the big trash can, like he's in on some private joke. I'm assuming this early-morning janitorial work has something to do with his getting sent to the office from English yesterday. He doesn't look like the type who would perform this chore at home, much less at some public school he openly loathes.

I didn't notice it at the time, but after reading back through the texts from Grant at least a hundred times now, he hardly ever mentioned the other four boys individually. Whenever he talked about them, it was always *the boys. I'm hanging out with the boys . . . The boys are coming*

over later . . . I was with the boys last night. So it's strange to see just one of them, away from the group.

Henry moves to the other side of the room, the trash can grinding along behind him. Swiveling in my chair, I see him easily over the computer screen. The light from the window has gotten stronger and it backlights him perfectly—his white shirt nearly glows. His light brown hair falls haphazardly across his forehead; his lips are full and his nose precisely straight. My hands itch for my camera. Here is this perfect specimen, dressed to kill, dumping garbage.

I reach down and slip my hand in my bag. Just one shot. Just for me.

With a quick glance, I change the settings to silent mode and inch the camera out from behind the screen, just far enough that the lens has a clear shot of him. I click once then pull it back. Even though the sound of the shutter was a mere whisper, I feel like it was as loud as a cannon. He doesn't even flinch.

Maybe I can grab one more.

By the time Henry makes it around the room, I've gotten about eight shots from different angles.

Just as he opens the door and I think I can finally breathe, he turns around quickly and says, "Personally, I think the one of me changing the trash bag will be the best one, but let me know once you check them out. I'm always looking for a new profile pic."

Heat floods every inch of my face as I sit there, frozen, looking at him. He smiles a beautiful smile and then leaves the room, laughing all the way down the hall.

I tiptoe to the door a little while later, making sure he's really gone before I upload the images to my laptop. No way I'm using the school computer for these. I'm beyond humiliated that he busted me, but when I view the images, I don't care how embarrassing it is. I click on the first one I took, the one in front of the window.

Is this the portrait of a killer?

His face is partially shadowed, but I can make out the grin. If I hadn't been trying so hard to be secretive, I would have seen it immediately. But somehow I'm glad I didn't. This is my favorite part about photography—discovering something new that I didn't see when I first took the picture.

As I stare at him, I think about the nervous boy sitting on that barstool with all those dead animals behind him. It's like they are two different people.

But which one is real?

Thankfully, I push Henry and the rest of the River Point Boys out of my mind by the time the warning bell rings. On the way to first period, I duck in the bathroom but stop cold when I hear a gut-wrenching sob. It's not unusual to find a girl hiding out and crying in one of the stalls, but this sounds different. Like someone is in serious pain.

I turn the corner to see if I can help and find Julianna Webb standing outside the stall door, pleading with the girl inside.

"Bree, please come out," she says through the crack. "It's going to be okay."

"It's never going to be okay. Never!" Bree screams, so loud it makes me jump back; then she bursts from the stall and runs toward the door. Julianna starts after her, but Bree shouts, "Leave me alone!" just before fleeing the bathroom.

Julianna leans back against the tile wall, the color drained from her face. I've gotten to know Julianna pretty well ever since we were partnered together in debate last year. This is the same look she would get just before having to go onstage to make our argument.

"Who was that?" Since I feel like I've photographed every person in this school at least once, it's surprising to see a face I don't recognize.

"Bree Holder. She just transferred here from St. Bart's, but I've known her since middle school."

I forget that Julianna used to go to St. Bart's. "What's wrong?" I ask.

"That horrible picture is back online," she says.

She doesn't even have to clarify. I know the ones she's talking about. "Is Bree one of the girls in that picture?"

"Yeah. She came here thinking it would be better to start over somewhere new, but it keeps popping up. Some asshole just stopped her in the hall and told her it's up on some website called Girls Gone Crazy. She lost it. She's always been so shy. It's killing her that people are passing that photo around. What's worse is she doesn't have any memory of it being taken and has no idea who did it."

I can't help but cringe. "Oh my God, that sucks," I say.

Julianna pushes off the wall. "I'm going to call her mom and let her know Bree is upset. I'm really worried about what this is doing to her."

"How are the other girls doing?" I ask just before Julianna leaves the bathroom.

"Not good. It's been really rough for all of them. I really hope they find out who took that picture."

. . .

"How was school?" Mr. Stone asks the second I shut the door and take what has become my usual seat next to his desk. He's leaned back in his chair, eyes resting on the ceiling.

"Good," I answer. There's no way I'm mentioning getting busted taking those pictures of Henry. I deleted the shots—well . . . all but one . . . I couldn't bring myself to trash the one by the window.

"What do you need me to do today?" I ask.

I thought it would be a nightmare to work on this case, but I've found it's exactly what I need. I need the person who shot Grant to be caught and prosecuted. I need Stone to sway the grand jury into indicting one or all of those boys. And I'm glad of any way I can help the process along.

He swivels around in his chair and grabs a large box on the floor behind him and puts it on his desk. "Help me see what I'm missing with the boys from that morning. The interviews with the River Point Boys aren't that long. Then there are the videos of the witnesses from the party the night before."

The party where I was supposed to meet Grant.

"Okay. Am I looking for anything in particular? Or just something that seems weird?"

Mr. Stone thumbs through some papers on his desk. "Anything that throws negative light on them, even if it doesn't have to do with the shooting, can only help us. There was a lot going on that night—some fights and all-around bad behavior. This case is a tricky one; almost every person who gives their version of events, whether it's the River Point Boys or the witnesses, was drinking or high that night, which makes their testimony unreliable, but it might lead us to something else we can use. Your mom has you set up next to her desk. My plate is full right now with this stuff the detectives on the case sent over." Mr. Stone rummages around in the box, pulling out random paper bags labeled with their contents. "I've got Grant's clothes and his wallet among other things." Then he pulls out a black bag. "And his phone."

The sight of his phone makes my knees buckle. Has he examined it yet? Has he read through the conversations we had over the last several weeks?

"Wha . . . what did you find on the phone? Do you need me to look?"

He shakes his head. "No. Not much here. I'm getting the idea that Grant had an unusual sense of humor. Most of his contacts are listed under nicknames or initials, so it's hard to decipher who he was actually talking to."

"What do you mean nicknames?" I ask. I would give anything to know what my nickname was.

He lets out an awkward sounding cough-laugh. "Some of the more colorful ones are Big Juicy, Pit Stains, and someone called Blunt Roller."

Okay, so maybe I don't want to know what my nickname was.

"I've got a list of the numbers that make up the text messages and calls sent and received in the forty-eight hours before his death. In between everything else your mother is working on, she's matching up these ridiculous names to real people with the help of a list the phone company sent over. There are some discrepancies between the call log on his phone and the records from the phone company, so it looks like Grant was also in the habit of deleting calls. But the really interesting thing is that phone records show a call made the morning of the hunt, but it's not on the log in his phone. The number matches the contact name Booty Call 3, so that's no help determining who it is. The name on the account with the cell phone company for that number is a big accounting firm in town that does business with the River Point Boys' families. In fact, several different numbers in Grant's contacts are all under this one account. Needless to say, we've asked them to tell us who uses these numbers—we're assuming the phones are used by the children of some of the employees there—but they're dragging their feet getting back to me. Just help me with the tapes for now."

I backtrack out of the room to the area where Mom is working, shoving my shaking hands deep in my jeans pockets. At some point they're going to match my messages to my number . . . Oh God, my number that is in Mom's name. I cringe when I think about Mr. Stone and Mom reading them. I know he said it's not a big deal if I talked to any of them before, but I'm sure they're going to wonder why I didn't tell them exactly how often I texted with Grant.

"Over here, Kate," Mom calls from her desk.

I didn't notice it before, but on the table next to her desk sit a screen, headphones, and some sort of microphone. "Are you ready to start?" she asks.

"I guess. What is it I'm supposed to do?"

I follow Mom to the small table and she motions for me to have a seat; then she cues up a video. "You won't be watching the entire interview, just the sections Mr. Stone has flagged. This one is a portion of John Michael Forres's interrogation."

She hands me the microphone and the headphones. "This will record both the audio from the video plus any comments you make, so just jump right in when you want to say something. Don't worry if you accidentally talk over the boys or the officer—he's listened to these tapes a hundred times by now."

She points to a button on the keyboard. "Just press this when you're ready to start and then this button when you're done. The rest of it is all ready to go."

Mom moves back to her desk while I put the headphones on. They are noise canceling, so instantly I'm thrown into my own quiet little world. John Michael's face is frozen on the screen, and it's almost like we're having a staring competition. I press play and John Michael's voice surrounds me, and suddenly it's like we're all in the same room, John Michael, the officer, and me.

Here we go.

TRANSCRIPT OF THE OCTOBER 5 INTERROGATION OF JOHN MICHAEL FORRES BY DETECTIVE FONTENOT, WITH BODY LANGUAGE COMMENTARY BY KATE MARINO

DET. FONTENOT: So it seems like your place is the place to be.

KATE: John Michael shrugs.

JOHN MICHAEL: I guess.

DET. FONTENOT: You're the one with the camp. You're the one with the vehicles and all the toys, right?

JOHN MICHAEL: Yeah.

DET. FONTENOT: Man, I'd get tired of everybody using all my stuff all the time. Inviting people to my house, trashing it. That must get old.

KATE: He shrugs again.

JOHN MICHAEL: I like it. What good is having all that stuff if you can't enjoy it with your friends?

DET. FONTENOT: Sounds like you provide more than just entertainment. I hear you can get anything you want at your place . . . pot, pills . . . you name it. Is that right?

JOHN MICHAEL: I have no idea what you're talking about.

DET. FONTENOT: Okay, we'll play it that way . . . for now . . . John Michael, take us back to the beginning of yesterday. When did y'all get to the camp?

KATE: He relaxes just a bit in his chair. Shoulders drop, grip on the chair loosens. Eyes are red as well as his nose.

JOHN MICHAEL: Shep and I got there first. We rode together in my car. We unloaded some stuff . . . our clothes, some food . . . some . . .

KATE: His expression changes. Looks nervous.

DET. FONTENOT: Booze? Y'all unloaded some of that, too, right?

KATE: He coughs and worms around in his chair. Looks uncomfortable.

JOHN MICHAEL: Anyway, it was still early. Logan, Henry, and Grant were about a half hour behind us.

KATE: He's shuffling around in the chair, eyes darting around the room. I've never seen anyone so fidgety.

DET. FONTENOT: So everyone gets to the camp, all the stuff is brought inside, everyone is gearing up for a big night. So what next?

KATE: Another cough.

KATE: Another twitch.

KATE: Another turn.

JOHN MICHAEL: We decided to do some target practice. Grant wanted to make sure his sights were zeroed in for the hunt the next morning.

DET. FONTENOT: Where did you do the target practice?

JOHN MICHAEL: On the back of the property, we have a range set up. We rode the four-wheelers back there. Shot off a few rounds. Headed back to the camp.

DET. FONTENOT: Whoa, whoa. Let's walk through it. Whose four-wheelers?

KATE: He rolls his eyes.

JOHN MICHAEL: Mine.

DET. FONTENOT: Y'all were shooting at targets? Was that it?

JOHN MICHAEL: Yes.

DET. FONTENOT: What guns did y'all use?

JOHN MICHAEL: We just shot Grant's Remington.

DET. FONTENOT: You each fired that gun?

JOHN MICHAEL: Yeah.

DET. FONTENOT: We had an officer ride around the property. We found where y'all were practicing. Y'all were shooting at more than bull's-eyes.

KATE: He throws his head back against his chair.

JOHN MICHAEL: We were going to give it back.

DET. FONTENOT: You were going to give it back . . . full of bullet holes? Who shot it?

KATE: He blows out a deep breath, looks straight at the officer.

JOHN MICHAEL: We all took a turn shooting it. It was just a prank.

DET. FONTENOT: Seems like there were a lot of pranks that went on at St. Bart's.

KATE: He shrugs.

JOHN MICHAEL: I'm not sure what you're talking about.

DET. FONTENOT: There have been a lot of parents calling our office, and your name, Grant's name, hell, all of y'all's names have been thrown around. They're pretty pissed off.

KATE: He chews on his bottom lip.

JOHN MICHAEL: I really don't know what you're talking about.

DET. FONTENOT: So y'all are shooting things, drinking, taking pills, smoking joints until how late? Midnight? Two a.m.? Dawn? What all do you have in your system right now?

KATE: He looks really uncomfortable. Actually, he looks like he's about to either vomit or pee on himself.

JOHN MICHAEL: I don't know.

DET. FONTENOT: You don't know, huh? 'Cause once we get a blood test on all of y'all, it's gonna tell us everything we need to know. Might as well fess up now.

JOHN MICHAEL: A little of everything. I don't know.

DET. FONTENOT: And y'all didn't see anything wrong with picking up a gun and going hunting?

KATE: He's squinting his eyes now. Obviously not liking where this is going.

DET. FONTENOT: Just like you didn't see anything wrong with all the drugs and drinking you let take place on your family's property. What else did you let happen there? Maybe one of your friends asked you to keep quiet about him using the Remington and promised you he'd be quiet about all the bad shit that happened at your place. And since most everyone who parties out there is underage—how mad is Daddy going to be if he goes down for the stupid behavior of you and your friends? I think he's got enough on his plate right now as it is. Or maybe you were using too much of your own product? Maybe you were careless with your daddy's gun?

UNKNOWN VOICE: His parents are here and requesting a lawyer be present for any more questioning.

KATE: He leans forward. His eyes dart around.

DET. FONTENOT: Do you want a lawyer?

KATE: He nods his head. Looks relieved.

JOHN MICHAEL: I want a lawyer.

SEPTEMBER 8, 10:52 P.M.

GRANT: What's up?

KATE: Editing some pics I took at Columbia Park

GRANT: Where's that?

KATE: Near Highland. My favorite place.

GRANT: I should check it out if it's your favorite

KATE: Make sure you sit under the big oak tree in the back corner. It's the best spot.

The best fried catfish in town is prepared in a ten-foot-long trailer that's parked in front of an abandoned strip of old stores on the edge of town. Mom and I discovered this place when we were meeting someone to test-drive a used car several years ago. The same car we share and that I'm driving now. Mom has hours of work in front of her, so I thought it would be a nice surprise to pick up her favorite dinner for her and Mr. Stone.

John Michael's interrogation tape is still fresh in my mind. It took me a few minutes to get up the courage to ask Mr. Stone what they had been shooting at the practice range. Thoughts of dead rabbits and other small defenseless creatures littered my brain but it turned out not to have been as gruesome as that. Weird, but not gruesome.

They had stolen the stuffed mascot from the junior class at St. Bart's—the one used in the Battle of the Paddle game—and shot it full of holes.

Everyone in town knows about St. Bart's annual Battle of the Paddle game and the prank war between the juniors and seniors that leads up to it. There are more vandalism complaints in the two weeks before the game than the entire rest of the year. There was a car that had cow manure stuffed down the air vents, some senior girls who had paint-filled balloons thrown at them outside the movies, a house that had gotten egged, and a junior's car that someone covered in plastic wrap, among other things.

Since St. Bart's isn't big enough for a regular football team, the Battle of the Paddle is more like a pickup game. No pads or helmets. No real tackles. Junior class plays the senior class. Winner gets to hang an old wooden paddle—it's a paddle some military person used in the Civil War when this area got flooded or something like that—in either the junior or senior hall for the rest of the year.

I pull into the parking lot, and wave to Pat, who's manning the fryer. Once I'm out of the car, I skirt around the small crowd at the picnic tables and work my way to the back side of the trailer.

"Hey, girl. Haven't seen you in a while. How's your mama?" Pat asks when I get close. Pat is a tall black man who played two seasons with the Dallas Cowboys before an injury to his back took him out of the game. Even though his hair is now mostly gray and there are wrinkles around his eyes, he's still built like a tank. There's barely any room for him to maneuver around in the cooking trailer.

"We've been busy, just like you," I say, and nod to the group of people on the other side of the trailer.

"Your mama works too hard. Just like me," he says with a laugh.

"I agree. But I don't see either one of y'all slowing down anytime soon."

Pat does a hundred things at once. He batters catfish fillets, turns the ones in the fryer, mixes up his secret sauce, and takes orders, all while carrying on a conversation with me. He fills a Styrofoam box up with catfish and fries fresh out of the fryer and ladles several plastic cups full of the sauce he knows Mom and I adore. He slides it all to me while I offer money I know he won't take. We're getting far more food than what usually comes in one of his to-go orders.

"It's bad enough you let me cut in line, but I'm going to quit coming if you don't let me pay you. It's not right."

He gives me a smile and a wink. "You'll be back and you know it. Best catfish in Louisiana."

Mom and I haven't paid for a meal in over a year since Mom helped him out when he got caught running this business without a license. She made some calls, pulled some strings, and helped him go legit.

"Well, it's not right," I say.

"Tell your mama don't work so hard."

I roll my eyes. "If she won't listen when I tell her that, she's sure not going to listen to you."

I grab the bag with the fish and sauce. "Thanks, Pat! You're too good to us," I say and turn back toward the car. My eyes graze across the crowd on the other side of the trailer but stop suddenly on a small group not far away.

You can't stare at faces for hours without burning every detail about them into your brain. I recognize them immediately.

The River Point Boys stand together in a tight circle on the other side of the parking lot against the backdrop of their expensive vehicles. I gaze at them as if I'm in a trance. I analyze their movements just like I would for Mr. Stone.

They are almost shoulder to shoulder, their heads bent forward. Whatever they are saying, they don't want anyone to hear them. Henry and Shep, the tallest of the four boys, stand across from each other, and by the jerky motions of their shoulders, I'd say they're arguing over something. What are they fighting about? Logan nods along with both of them, his thick, dark red curls bobbing back and forth. Reagan calls him "Ginger-licious" and I have to agree. John Michael stands there, seemingly absorbed with whatever they're saying, his eyes darting back and forth between Shep and Henry.

I study Shep. The uptight attitude he shows at school is intensified by stiff shoulders and a scowling expression. He's attractive, but in a rough sort of way. His dark hair is shaggy like he's missed his last haircut, and it always looks like he needs to shave. Even though Henry would be considered the hottest guy in that group, there's something about Shep. But then I remember the few texts he sent me after I met him and Grant, and I can't stop my lip from curling up.

Any pleasant thought I have about him evaporates. His personality drops his hotness down to subzero.

"Whatever is happening over there, Kate, you need to stay a hundred miles away from it," Pat says, breaking my concentration.

I turn to him. He's stopped working and is watching me.

"Do you know who they are?" I ask.

He nods. "Everyone knows who they are." Pat glances in the direction of the boys and shakes his head, like he's disgusted. "Been meeting out here almost every night. Stupid boys, like no one they should be

concerned with would spot them here. Hell, just before they showed up yesterday, the chief of police and his wife were picking up dinner."

I get why they would think they were safe. It's in the middle of nowhere, definitely off the beaten path, but they didn't take into consideration how many people come out this way to get Pat's food. Or rather, how many people from the courthouse come out this way because Mom told them about Pat's food.

"Okay, I'm leaving. 'Bye, Pat, and thanks again for dinner."

I turn away from Pat, heading back to my car, and questions run like wildfire through my head. Why are they driving way out here to meet? What are they talking about? Or arguing about?

I back out of my spot and notice Pat checking on me, making sure I leave. I wouldn't put it past him to call Mom and tell on me if he thought I was up to something I shouldn't be. I turn out of the parking lot but stop once I'm hidden behind some overgrown azalea bushes. Grabbing my camera, I fire off several quick shots of the group. Henry is gesturing wildly while Logan rocks back and forth on his heels, like he's just waiting for the second they're all going to tear into it. John Michael hasn't moved an inch. But Shep is the one who surprises me. From this angle, I get an unobstructed view of his face. And he looks pissed. Very pissed.

One more shot, zoomed in close.

I study them. Study their body language. From a distance, they are four boys in a tight circle, but looking closer, it's easy to see the divide. Shep and John Michael are on one side and Logan and Henry are on the other.

The group is split right down the middle.

I finally pull away and Mr. Stone's words bounce around in my mind. *The trick now is going to be figuring out where the weak link in that*

group is. If one of them breaks, I think the whole group will fall apart. If that happens, we may have a chance.

So which side has the weak link?

. . .

Mom and Mr. Stone are thrilled to see me bearing food when I get back to the office. Mom clears off a corner of his desk and I unload the bag with Pat's fried fish.

"Who wants a drink from the vending machine?" Mom asks as she reaches for her purse.

Mr. Stone holds up an enormous water bottle. "Thanks, but I'm fine."

"I'd like a Coke, Mom."

She leaves, and I skim the top of Mr. Stone's desk. The tall pile of files, the box with Grant's personal belongings, and pictures of the boys litter the area. My mind wanders to Grant. Just like it does every day. I wonder who else is fighting for him. Who is going to make sure justice is carried out for him? Right now the focus is on the River Point Boys and whether or not a case can be made against them. When you watch the news, Grant's name is hardly mentioned. The utter fascination is with the four boys who walked away from that hunt.

"I saw the River Point Boys while I was getting food from Pat." I'm not sure what makes me blurt this out.

Mr. Stone pauses, a piece of fish midway to his mouth. "They were there getting food?"

"No. They were across the parking lot. They were just there."

His forehead scrunches up. "What were they doing?" he asks.

I shrug. "Looks like they meet there just to talk." I'm very conscious about how I answer him. I really don't want to give him anything but

cold facts, without adding in my personal feelings or opinions, but I want him to understand how weird they were acting.

Mr. Stone leans back in his chair. "That's interesting."

I glance at the door, making sure Mom isn't about to walk back in. She wouldn't want me involved with this case outside of the office. "And Pat said they've been meeting out there almost every evening."

That just sort of hangs in the air a minute. Finally, Mr. Stone says, "Very interesting."

We eat in silence another minute or so before he says, "Let me know if you see anything else that seems . . . odd."

I nod and am about to ask if he wants me to actively search them out, but Mom comes back in the room.

Mr. Stone digs into his food. We're just about done eating when he says with a smile, "Kate, this was a wonderful treat. Pat's food is some of my favorite. Feel free to surprise us with it anytime you wish."

I'm pretty sure I just got his permission to spy on the River Point Boys.

Some of us are starting to panic.

Some of us are a little too cocky.

Some of us are as clueless as the police.

But we are all paranoid. No one wants to use his phone or meet at each other's houses when we need to talk.

So with a single text message that lists a time, we all know to meet here, in the middle of nowhere.

Today's meeting is because one of our dads wants us to take a lie detector test.

It can be private, no one needs to know the results, he said.

In case things go wrong in the grand jury, there's no reason for all of the boys to get in trouble, he added.

Every one of us acts like he's for it, because really, the only one who would be against it is the shooter, right?

But then other events of the night find their way into the conversation—the drugs, the fights, the missing money—and we know silence is our best weapon.

We're fighting about the same things over and over. It doesn't change the fact that one of us going down would be as bad as all of us going down.

We all look at each other, each of us trying to figure out who it is. Only one of us knows the truth.

And I'm going to make sure it stays that way.

6

SEPTEMBER 15, 3:05 P.M.

GRANT: What's up?

KATE: I'm buried under paper in the filing room. I could die up here and it would be days before anyone found me.

GRANT: Are you already at work?

KATE: Yeah, I have a work pass. But don't be jealous. Days like this I'd rather be in school than here.

Reagan and I walk down the hall toward science lab. "Okay, so Halloween is in three days and I'm still not sure about our costumes," she says.

"Are you going to tell me what we're going to be yet?"

Halloween is Reagan's thing. Every year since eighth grade, she's come up with costumes for us. She likes it to be a surprise, but most years she's given in and told me what we're going as weeks before Halloween. Reagan is being more secretive than normal this year.

She flings her arms up in the air, and a swish of iridescent fabric billows around her. "I feel like we have to kill it this year. I mean, it's senior year. I had an idea but I don't know now. I think it might be boring. I'm not sure I can do boring."

"You can tell me what it is and I can give you my opinion," I say in a singsong voice as we push through the double doors and drop our bags on the table.

"Maybe I can put glitter in the blood," she says, almost to herself.

I turn toward her. "There's blood?"

She looks at me, scrunching her face up. "No," she says. "I'm changing it."

I shake my head and laugh. "Whatever. You're the expert. I'll just wait until you tell me what to put on."

Julianna walks through the door a few minutes later and I motion for her to stop by our table.

Reagan and I both say, "Hey."

She smiles at us. "Hey, what's up?"

I pull out my phone. "We need to schedule a time for the group cheer pics for the yearbook. Can y'all do next Wednesday during lunch?"

Julianna is the head cheerleader and it's easier to make plans with her than it is to try to track down the cheer sponsor.

"Yeah, that should be fine. I'll tell everyone to bring their uniforms and we'll be ready during the second half of lunch."

"Okay, good." We both add it to the calendars in our phones; then I ask, "Hey, how's Bree?"

Julianna tilts her head to the side and frowns. "I don't know. I tried calling her but it goes straight to voice mail. I heard her parents took her to the ER when she had a panic attack," she says in a whisper.

Reagan asks, "Do you know the other two girls in that picture?"

Julianna shakes her head. "Not really. I mean, I know who they are, but I don't know them. They came to St. Bart's after I left. All three of them are seniors, but Bree is gone, one is getting homeschooled now, and the other one is still there." She scrolls through her phone and shows us a post from a guy at St. Bart's. "St. Bart's thinks that picture was part of the prank war, so they just announced this year's Battle was the last one because things have gotten so bad. It's a shame. The game was so fun to watch."

Reagan's face scrunches like she's smelling something bad. "Ew. Who would do that for a stupid prank war? It's sick."

"So they think it was a junior who did it?" I ask.

Julianna shrugs. "I think so. The seniors were pretty hard on them this year, so the school thinks the juniors took that picture to retaliate."

She starts to walk to her table in the back but stops and says, "The last time I saw Grant Perkins was at that game. Weird to think he's gone."

My hands start to shake, so I press them together in my lap. That was the last time I saw him, too. That's where I took the picture of him, walking off the field with that girl. We had planned to meet later that night at the party after I got done taking pics at the science bowl. But I got Miranda, another photographer, to cover for me so I could go to the game.

"Did you know him pretty well?" Reagan asks.

"Yeah, I went through elementary and middle school with him. He was sort of a screwup, you know. Always getting in trouble and clowning around, but no matter what he did . . . you still loved him." She stares off into space, lost in her memories. "He was just so fun to be around. He had a weird sense of humor for sure, but he was so full of life it was impossible not to be completely charmed by him."

I want to ask her questions about him. I want to know everything. Anything. But my throat is locked up.

Julianna smiles. It looks a little sad. "And Grant made the winning touchdown for the seniors." She shakes her head. "Sorry, not trying to be all weird about the guy who died," she says just before slipping away from our table.

Reagan looks at me and I can tell she knows I'm about to lose it. "Your eyes look funny. Are you okay?"

I shrug. "I'm fine."

She raises one eyebrow and I know she doesn't believe me, but she doesn't push.

Reagan knew Grant and I had been texting, but she didn't know just how much. Or that I had completely fallen for him. She knows I was upset when I heard the news—she even went to the funeral with me, and there was no hiding the tears from her. There were so many people there we had to wedge ourselves somewhere in the very back, and we never even got close to Grant—thank God—or his family, or the River Point Boys, although I heard they were all there.

Everyone was there.

It's not like I set out to hide my real feelings for Grant from her, or from our other friends. Truthfully, I thought Grant would get tired of talking to me and move on to someone else, so the fewer people to witness that embarrassment, the better.

"It really sucks what happened to those girls. Freaking St. Bart's. I bet if they find out who did it, they won't get in any trouble just because of who their daddies are," she says.

My hands curl into such tight fists I can feel my nails digging into my palms. As much as I hate to admit it, she's probably right.

• • •

I drop my bag just inside the office and Mom jumps like she's being shot at.

Her hand flies to her chest and she says, "Good grief, Kate. Are you trying to put me in an early grave?"

I laugh and pull her in for a hug. Mom and I are not touchy-feely people, but it's been a hard day and I'm craving some human contact.

"I'm not sure I can fuss at you now that you've hugged me so tight," Mom says.

I pull back and look at her. "You can't fuss at me at all, and you know it."

She shakes her head and nods toward the door. Mr. Stone is at lunch, as he usually is when I first get here. She closes the office door, gestures for me to sit in the chair next to her desk, and plops a legal-size printout in front of me.

"This is the list of contacts from Grant Perkins's phone."

My stomach bottoms out. My eyes focus on the words, and I realize the typed names in the first columns are the nicknames from Grant's phone. The second column is the numbers associated with those nicknames. And halfway down, the third column is filled in with handwritten names. Those must be the real names matched up to the nicknames.

I scan the numbers quickly until I find mine. It's the last one labeled with a real name, and the nickname beside it is just three letters: FWS.

FWS?

What does that stand for? My initials are KGM: Kathleen Grace Marino. Not even close.

"I know you said you'd met Grant, but I was still a little surprised to see your number listed here. And why is it listed under FWS? What does that mean?"

I can't tear my eyes from the paper. "I don't know," I mumble.

"Don't know what? Why you're under those initials? Or why you were in contact with him before he died? Mr. Stone asked you if you knew any of these boys, but you made it sound like they were practically strangers."

I shake my head and force myself to look at Mom. "I met him at the library a few weeks before he . . . died. We talked. He asked for my number."

Mom leans back in her chair. "Did you go out with him?"

Shaking my head, I answer, "No." And that's the truth. "I've only seen him in person one time, at the library. We just texted." I wait a beat before I ask. "Have you seen his phone? Read his messages?"

Heat blooms across my cheeks. I'll be mortified if Mom or Mr. Stone reads the messages. It's not like what we talked about was bad . . . it was just personal. Talking to him was easier than it should have been.

"No, I haven't seen the phone yet. Mr. Stone wants me to go through and match the contacts with real names first. Imagine my surprise when I'm working down this list and run across *your* number."

I sink down in my seat. "Sorry. I should have told you."

"Yes, you should have."

"Is this going to cause a problem? I mean, can Stone get in trouble if I was texting Grant before he died?"

"No. We can't help that and it's not bad the victim was a friend of yours. I shouldn't be surprised—from the number of contacts in his phone, it seems like he was texting or talking to half this town."

For some reason, that comment hits me right in the gut.

"It would look bad if you had been at that party the night before he was shot or if you are texting or communicating or hanging out with the other four boys now. You weren't at the party, were you?"

I shake my head. "No."

"And you're not texting or hanging out with those other boys, are you?"

"No. Definitely not."

Mom looks at me, her eyes narrowing. "Are you okay with all of this? If he was your friend, maybe you shouldn't be involved."

I swallow hard. "Mom, it's fine. I'm fine. I'm glad I can help."

She watches me closely and I struggle to look normal, like this is no big deal, even though I'm crumbling inside. "If I find that this is too much for you, I'll pull you off immediately, no matter how much Mr. Stone needs you."

I take a deep breath in and nod.

She picks up the printout and mumbles, "What a mess this case is turning into."

. . .

I told myself I wasn't coming back. But Pat's words have been like a tiny breeze that drifts in and out of my consciousness. *They've been meeting out here almost every night.*

I'm parked across the street, my car hidden behind an abandoned semitruck. The parking lot is full in front of Pat's, but the other side is empty. Glancing at the clock, I promise myself that if they don't show in the next ten minutes, I'm leaving.

Leaning back against the headrest, I tick through the case against the River Point Boys. Time is running out. So far, we've got next to nothing on any of them. There's the Remington, but everyone's prints were found on it, including Grant's. Someone used that gun, but none of them are talking. All four boys admit to running up to Grant after they heard the shot. They all came from different directions, and when questioned as to where exactly they had been hunting, they all named a different part of the property. They had all been drinking and some of them had been smoking pot, but if anything, that helps them with the whole *I don't remember, Officer* thing they have going on. Mr. Stone should get the coroner's report tomorrow afternoon, and hopefully, maybe, that will show us something the police missed.

Six more minutes. Six more minutes and then I'm leaving.

I scroll through my phone, but instead of looking at the messages from Grant, I pull up the ones from Shep. He'd texted me a couple of times and he seemed funny and nice, but then things went downhill. Fast.

SHEP: What's up

ME: trying to decide which pics to turn in for this grant I'm trying to get for college

SHEP: What are the pics of

ME: Regular people but trying to make them look not regular

SHEP: I have an excellent eye. Send me some pics and I'll tell you which one is the best

ME: You really want to see the pics I took?

SHEP: Well I'd really rather see pics of you

ME: Of me?

SHEP: Yes u. Show me what you look like right now

SHEP: But take your shirt off first

ME: Now you're getting creepy

SHEP: I wont show anyone else. Promise.

ME: You're disgusting

SHEP: Just one pic. It's no big deal

And that's when I took a picture of my hand flipping him off, telling him this was the only picture he was ever going to get of me.

Thankfully, except for the laughing emoji, he didn't text again.

I throw the phone on the seat of the car, my blood boiling just like it was when I first got those messages.

One more minute. I crank the car, ready to give up, when a black Tahoe pulls into the far lot. Logan pulls it in a tight circle until the front of the car is facing the street. I duck down in my seat, hoping he doesn't spot me. A tiny stream of smoke filters out of the driver's window.

Henry pulls in a few seconds later, lining his Range Rover up next to Logan so they can talk without getting out of the car.

I glance at the clock. Six ten. I was here around six thirty last night and they were already well into their conversation. I grab the camera from the passenger seat and take a few images.

Time crawls as I wait for the other boys to show. Logan and Henry seem relaxed, leaned back in their seats, talking through their open windows. Logan has already thrown one cigarette out of the window and lit a second one. Six minutes go by before a silver BMW pulls in next to Logan's Tahoe. John Michael. And then a jacked-up red Jeep with the top off shows up. Shep.

The gang's all here.

Shep pulls off to the side, and they all get out of their vehicles and move into the same tight circle as the night before. The sun is sinking low in the horizon, so I adjust the camera's setting for the low-light conditions. I zoom in and fire away.

God, I wish I could hear what they're saying.

I get a good shot of Logan and notice a long thin red mark, almost like a new scar, running down his neck.

What is *that* from?

And then I'm on John Michael. There are some serious dark circles and bags under his eyes. That boy isn't getting any rest.

Within minutes, the shoving starts. Shep pushes Henry so hard Henry bounces against the back of John Michael's car. I zoom out to make sure I get everyone in the image. Henry launches himself at Shep and they end up in a tangled knot. Logan pulls at Henry, and John Michael yanks Shep back until they are separated.

Shep stands rigid, like it's taking everything in his power to maintain control. But Henry's body language is different. He's relaxed as he straightens his shirt and throws Shep a mocking grin.

Henry moves close to Shep, saying something that has Shep diving at him again, but Logan steps in, stopping him. Protecting Henry. With a final shove, Logan and Henry get into their vehicles and peel out of the parking lot, dust and gravel billowing in their wake. John Michael puts a hand on Shep's shoulder, bends his head close, and says something to him that makes Shep nod. I can almost see the tension leave Shep the more John Michael talks to him. John Michael pulls something out of his pocket. I focus in on it and it's a joint. He offers it to Shep, but Shep shakes his head. John Michael shrugs and stuffs it back in his pocket. They stand there talking for several minutes until they both head back to their own vehicles. John Michael pulls his car close to Shep's Jeep, says something else that makes Shep laugh, then drives out of the parking lot. But Shep doesn't leave. His hands grip the top of the steering wheel, and through my lens I notice there are a few cuts on his knuckles that are almost healed. And if my lip-reading skills are accurate, he lets out a few expletives before dropping his head.

From this angle, I have a clear shot of his profile. I zoom in close and it's like I'm sitting right next to him in that Jeep. His dark hair falls forward, and my fingers itch to move it out of his eyes so I can get a clear shot of them. The click of the shutter fills my car as I pray that I'm able to capture the absolute despair on his face.

He looks completely dejected. Defeated.

He looks as bad as I feel. From somewhere deep down, the desire to reach a hand out and comfort him is overwhelming. And it seems, through this lens, that I almost could. But then I remember his messages and I want to slap his face instead.

His head starts to turn slowly. I'm fascinated by the movement until he's looking directly at me. I drop the camera quickly and duck down in my seat.

Did he see me? My heart rate spikes and I can feel the blood pumping in my veins.

I'm not sure how long I stay hunched down in my seat, but when I finally raise my head, Shep's gone.

TRANSCRIPT OF THE OCTOBER 5 INTERROGATION
OF LOGAN MCCULLAR BY DETECTIVE ROSS, WITH
BODY LANGUAGE COMMENTARY BY KATE MARINO

DET. ROSS: Last night was a little more than a celebration, wasn't it? You've got a nice little side business going on, don't you?

LOGAN: I have no idea what you're talking about.

KATE: Logan sits on the edge of his chair. Shoulders are hunched.

DET. ROSS: How much money did you clear after LSU beat A&M last night?

KATE: His eyes pop up, looking at the detective.

LOGAN: I said I have no idea what you're talking about.

DET. ROSS: A little birdie told me there's more going on out at River Point than a bunch of spoiled kids drinking and messing around. You can't run a sports betting operation like that without people getting really interested in what's going on out there.

LOGAN: I don't know who your "little birdie" is, but they're full of shit.

KATE: He picks at his thumbnail, won't look at the detective.

DET. ROSS: Want to tell me how you got that cut across your neck?

LOGAN: Cut myself shaving.

KATE: His hand goes to the cut on his neck. It's thin and slashes down from below his left ear to the center of his throat. Does not look like a shaving nick.

DET. ROSS: You're a regular comedian. Okay, let's talk about last night. Everybody's having a good time. Partying, feeling good about winning that football game of yours. Were there any problems inside your group?

KATE: He dips his head to the side. He's smirking a little.

DET. ROSS: I'm taking your silence as a yes.

LOGAN: You can take it any way you want to.

DET. ROSS: There was a fight. We found evidence of trouble. Broken table, broken glass. And poor Grant's got some pretty ugly marks on him that have nothing to do with the gunshot wound.

KATE: This silence is awkward.

DET. ROSS: Tell me who was fighting with Grant.

LOGAN: I don't know what you're talking about.

KATE: He's looking at the ground. Hands clenched in his lap.

DET. ROSS: Sure you do. There's always one guy who rises to the top. The leader. The one who makes the plans, or decides what everyone else will be doing. The one who made the decision not to tell us who was using the Remington.

LOGAN: There's no leader.

DET. ROSS: I know you're trying to protect your friends, but you're only hurting yourself. Who's calling the shots? Because I know it's not you.

KATE: His eyes squint. He looks pissed. Insulted.

LOGAN: Man, you don't even know what you're talking about.

DET. ROSS: You just follow along and do what you're told, right? Which one of those boys told you to sit here and play stupid? Because there's no way you don't know which one of them fired that Remington this morning and put a hole in Grant Perkins's chest.

KATE: Logan glares at the officer.

DET. ROSS: You said it wasn't you, so who was it?

LOGAN: I don't know.

DET. ROSS: Are you afraid of what will happen if you tell the truth? Maybe your friends know all about that little side business. Maybe if you rat them out, they'll rat you out. Are you keeping your mouth shut to save your own ass?

KATE: He shifts around in his chair. Rubs his hand across his face. Smirk is gone.

UNKNOWN VOICE: Parents are outside. No more questioning without a lawyer.

DET. ROSS: Logan, you're eighteen. Is that how it's going to be? You afraid to talk to me? Just like you're afraid of your friends?

LOGAN: I want a lawyer.

7

SEPTEMBER 26, 10:03 P.M.

GRANT: Where do Marshall girls hang out
on a Friday night?

> KATE: When you're friends with a future fashion
> designer, you find yourself in Dallas looking
> at fabric FOR HOURS. Why?

GRANT: Damn. Was hoping I could
run into you.

> KATE: I would have liked that. A lot.

The door to Rhino Coffee chimes when I push it open, and several people turn toward the entrance. The delicious aroma of coffee floats through the air; an indie rock station plays in the background.

I'm in my happy place.

Scanning the room, I see Reagan is already in our usual spot, but I stop at the counter first to place my order. I'm tempted to pull the *"I'll have my usual,"* since we've been hanging out here every Wednesday night for years, but it would be devastating if the barista looked at me like she had no idea who I am.

"What can I get started for you?" she asks with her usual smile.

"Large chai, please."

I carry my steaming cup of goodness to the back corner and drop down on the big fluffy couch next to the chair Reagan's perched in. She's totally absorbed in her sketchbook and jumps about a foot when I tap her leg.

"Holy crap! You freaking scared me to death," she says.

I laugh when I notice her brightly patterned outfit. I've never known Reagan to wear Spandex before. "Those pants are hot."

She stretches her legs out. "These are my new yoga clothes. Just finished a candlelight meditation class at Breathe Yoga. You didn't think I'd wear all black like everyone else, did you?"

"No. God forbid you not stick out." Taking a peek at her pad, I revel in her artistic genius. At first glance, it looks like the dress she designed is two pieces, a cropped top and a flared short skirt, but it's an illusion. An intricate lace design covers the neck and shoulders, and it's somehow fun and sexy at the same time.

"Oh my God, Reagan. You have to make this and wear it to Winter Formal."

Her face scrunches up; she's definitely her toughest critic. "You think?"

"Absolutely. Josh won't know what hit him."

Reagan rolls her eyes. "He probably won't even ask me."

I shove her arm. "Whatever. He totally will. And his eyes will pop out of his head when he sees you in this."

"Whose eyes are popping out?" Alexis asks as she and Mignon drop down in a pair of chairs across from us.

"Josh's when he sees her in the dress she's designing for Winter Formal," I answer.

Mignon laughs. "That means Josh would have to actually get up the courage to ask Reagan out first."

Reagan slumps back in her chair. "See? Seriously, that boy is killing me."

"What's the holdup? I mean, every chance he gets, he's by your side," Alexis says.

"He's scared she's going to shoot him down," I say. "I've been watching him and he's terrified."

Mignon laughs and Alexis says, "You friend-zoned him too long."

Reagan rolls her eyes. "Well, we *were* friends first. I don't know what else I can do to let him know I'm into him. Maybe I'll just have to ask him out."

"Show me the dress," Mignon says.

Reagan holds up her sketchbook and they both gush over her drawing, but my eyes are drawn back to the counter.

Or rather, to who is at the counter. There are two girls placing their order, and one of them is the girl who walked off the field with Grant after the Battle of the Paddle game. The girl his arm was around. The girl that should have been me.

"Who are you staring at?" Reagan asks.

Mignon and Alexis turn around to look, then Mignon jumps up and runs to the counter.

"Does she know them?" I ask, hoping to keep the horror I'm feeling out of my voice.

"Looks like it," Alexis says.

Before I can form another sentence, she's dragging them back to our area. Oh God, they're going to sit with us.

"Everyone, this is Rebecca Meyers and her friend Lindsey. Rebecca and I played travel soccer together when we were younger," Mignon says, and then points to each of us, introducing us by name.

Both girls say hi and sit on the couch next to me. Lindsey, the girl who was with Grant, is only inches away and I'm finding it hard to breathe.

Rebecca leans forward, looking at Reagan's sketchbook that's sitting on the coffee table. "This is hot!" She looks up and asks, "Did one of y'all draw this?"

Reagan gives a small little wave. "I did. It's a design I'm working on."

Lindsey takes a peek at the drawing. "Do you just design or do you make them, too?"

"She's an all-around badass," Mignon says. "From idea to finished product."

Rebecca sits back. "That's pretty cool. Do you sell any of your clothes?"

Reagan shakes her head. "I wish. That would be a thousand times better than working at the courthouse."

"Please," Alexis says. "I would take your job over watching the Bradford triplets after school every day. Those parents are lucky their little monsters are still alive by six o'clock."

Mignon pats her leg. "Think of it as a good form of birth control."

We all laugh and the tension of sitting next to Lindsey lessens a little.

"You work at the courthouse?" Rebecca asks Reagan. "That sounds cool."

"The part I work in sucks. All I do is file all day. Kate's got a little more action where she is. She works for the prosecutor that got the River Point case."

I cringe and Lindsey chokes on her coffee. Reagan has no idea Grant was hanging out with Lindsey at the game the night before he was shot. Lindsey's face gets red, either from swallowing her coffee the wrong way or from the talk of Grant's case. She turns slightly away from me, refusing to look my way.

"Oh, God," Rebecca says, leaning forward so she can see me on the other side of Lindsey. "Can you tell us what's going on? That's all anyone at St. Bart's can talk about right now."

Lindsey ducks her head and crosses her arms in front of her. She's as uncomfortable talking about him as I am.

I shrug and answer, "Not really. We're just working through everything right now. There's not a lot to go on."

Lindsey chews on her lip and drags in a deep, long breath before letting it out in a rush. Rebecca looks at her, sending her some sort of silent message, and Lindsey shakes her head slowly back and forth.

I seem to be the only one who notices how weird they're acting.

"It's so sad. His friends must feel terrible," Alexis says. "I can't imagine if I accidentally hurt one of y'all."

"I know, right?" Rebecca says. "They were all so close. It's got to be tearing them apart."

Lindsey pops up from the couch. "I'll be right back. I need to go to the restroom." And then she darts into the side hall.

"Is she okay?" Mignon asks.

Rebecca tilts her head to the side and shrugs one shoulder. "Yeah, she's fine. We were good friends with all of them. It's been hard on our entire school."

They were good friends. What if I totally got it wrong when I saw them together? What if it wasn't what I thought it was?

What if I missed my last opportunity to be with Grant over unfounded jealousy?

Even though I didn't think it was possible to feel worse than I already do, I was wrong.

• • •

I'm still feeling down almost a day later. And stupid. I'm feeling sad and stupid. We're in the break room, eating a quick lunch before our shifts officially start, when Camille pops her head in. By the expression on her face, I can tell she's got some good gossip.

Reagan kicks out the seat across from us with her foot and says, "Sit. And spill it."

"You two owe me info," Camille says, plopping down in the chair. "I'm not sharing until I hear something good from y'all."

Reagan and I share a look.

"Fine," Reagan says. "Grant's dad showed up at Morrison's office yesterday afternoon. He's hired his own investigative team. Thinks we're a bunch of morons and doesn't trust any of us. He was asking for a copy of everything, plus he wants his guys to examine the evidence."

I'm sure my mouth is hanging open. "Really?" I ask, then nudge her in the side. "And I'm just now hearing this."

She shrugs. "I would have told you, but you've been sneaking out of here before me every night this week. Want to tell me where you've been going?" Reagan gives me a pointed look.

Touché.

Camille waves her hands in front of us, drawing our focus back to her. "So what did Morrison say?"

"She doesn't know what to say. We've never had a case like this, ever, so we're all making it up as we go. She's told him to give her a few days and she'll figure it out."

This case really should have been sent to the attorney general. The reason we could get the grand jury scheduled so quickly is because there's little else going on here. I don't blame Mr. Perkins for bringing in experts from the outside.

"Now it's your turn, Camille. And yours better be good," I say.

Camille sits up a little straighter in the chair. "The River Point dads met with Gaines this morning. All four of them. And then when they were leaving the office, that group of protesters showed up . . . you know the ones who've been picketing in front of the building down the street?"

Reagan and I nod. We have to pass them every day when we leave the courthouse.

"Well, they must have spotted Mr. Forres when he came in, because they were waiting for him when he came out."

"Why?" I ask.

"Because it's his construction company that's doing the work on that building. And they're blaming him for charging the city millions more than he should have and they're blaming Gaines for not doing anything about it."

"So what happened?" Reagan asks.

"Mr. Forres all but ran out of here and Gaines ducked back in his office. Morrison had to boot the protesters out of here."

Even though Gaines is the DA, Morrison is really the one who runs this place. She's the backbone of this entire operation and runs her domain with an iron fist.

I can't help the sigh of disgust that escapes. "That's just like Gaines— let this city go bankrupt before holding one of his friends accountable."

Reagan shifts uncomfortably. "Well, we don't really know the whole story."

Reagan is in the tricky position of being related to Gaines through marriage. She sees what happens up here, but she's loyal to her family, so she never outright criticizes him. I usually keep my mouth shut about him around her, but he's gotten so bad I can't help it.

I crumple up my brown bag and stuff it in the trash.

"I'm heading up," I say. Camille waves 'bye, but Reagan just gives me a nod.

I trudge up the stairs, exhausted from my restless sleep last night. I dreamed about Grant and his blond wavy hair and devilish smile. He was walking off that field, his arm wrapped around Lindsey, but instead of the football jersey he was wearing that night, he was dressed in camo just like the boys were in the video interviews. And then he staggered back, the bullet tearing through his jacket and ripping his chest open. Lindsey was kneeling on the ground next to him, crying.

A shudder runs through me and I shake my head quickly to rid myself of the images.

I relieve Mom so she can go get lunch, and I head into Mr. Stone's office.

He's eating a chicken salad sandwich at his desk with his headphones on. I wonder if he's listening to the recordings Mom makes when she reads stuff for him or if he's listening to the ones I've been making of the interrogation tapes.

He pulls off the headphones when I move closer to his desk and presses stop on the player.

"I'm here. Need me to do anything?" I ask.

Before he can answer, there's a knock on the door. A short, balding man sticks his head inside Mr. Stone's office.

"Yes?" Mr. Stone says.

The man holds up a thick file folder. "Here's the coroner's report on the River Point case."

Mr. Stone nods for him to put in on his desk and thanks him before he leaves. I can't help but think this is why the River Point dads were in Gaines's office this morning. I bet they already have their own copy.

He shoves the report into a messenger-style bag and throws the rest of his sandwich away. "Damn. I was hoping to get this before I left for River Point. I'll try to read the summary on the way while your mother drives."

"Why are you going to River Point?"

"I scheduled a visit to the scene. I need to get a feel for what happened that morning."

He can barely see across the room. What's he going to be able to see in the woods?

Mr. Stone seems to be looking for something on his desk and not doing a very good job.

"I know what you're thinking, but your mother will be there to help me," he says.

I can't believe I'm about to offer this, because it's the last thing on earth I want to do, the last place I want to be.

"Would you like me to come? I can bring my camera, take pics of everything."

He stops and turns his head to the side so he can look at me.

"This is a crime scene. A boy you know was killed there. Are you sure you're up for that?" he asks.

I swallow hard and say, "Yes."

We remain there in tense silence for what seems like forever until he finally asks, "Do you have your camera with you?"

"Always."

"Grab your bag."

I gather my things and send a quick text to Reagan while Stone tells Mom about the change in plans.

I'm going to River Point with Stone.
And I'm freaking out.

Freaking out is actually an understatement, because I'm not sure I can handle seeing where Grant died, even though I just promised I could.

REAGAN: You're going there? You're
going to see where he died?

ME: YES!!!!!!!!!!!!! I'm not sure I can do this

REAGAN: Just try not to puke or faint or
anything like that. Call me when you're done.

I drop my phone in my bag and take a few deep breaths before I follow Stone to the employee parking lot.

I crank the car once he hands me the keys.

"Do you know how to get there?" he asks.

I nod. "Yes, sir. I think so." There have been maps of River Point on the news attached to almost every story they do. Everyone knows how to get there now.

He settles back in his seat, pulling out the report that was just delivered to him. From the first glance, I can see the type is small and there's no way he can read it on his own. Just before I'm about to put the car in reverse, he hands the report to me.

"Before we go, read me the top summary page, please."

I hate how sad his voice sounds.

"Okay," I answer.

There's a lot of technical jargon, words I can't pronounce, but by the time I finish there's a smile starting to form on his face.

"Okay, you're going to have to translate what I just read to you because I have no idea what I just said."

Mr. Stone punches his fists in the air at a rapid pace. I don't know if I've ever witnessed this sort of excitement from him. "I can do better than tell you—I can show you when we get there."

We're quiet for the rest of the drive and I'm thankful his eyes are closed. My hands are shaking and a thin layer of sweat pops out on my forehead. I want to help Stone any way I can, but I don't know how I'm going to make it through the afternoon. And whatever was in that report had him almost giddy. I'm trying really hard not to get my hopes up, but for the first time since we got this case, I'm feeling somewhat hopeful.

I don't know what I expected, but I'm surprised by all of the cars when we pull through the gate at River Point.

"Who are all of these people?" I ask.

I park off to the side and wait while Mr. Stone gathers his stuff. "That's the thing," he says. "We can be here, but so can everyone else. When I scheduled this visit, I was informed Mr. and Mrs. Forres insisted on being here, since it's their property. I believe the Carlisles will be here as well as Mr. Moore and Mr. McCullar; even the boys were checked out of school to be here. Also, the defense's legal team is here, making sure they are aware of whatever we may discover. Grant Perkins's father requested to be here, so I also made sure there was a deputy on duty in case there is a problem. Also, Detective Pierce will be here to assist us and show us around the property."

The River Point Boys are here. Maybe volunteering to come along wasn't that great of an idea. I swallow hard when I step out of the car. "I didn't realize the police would let them all be here like this."

Mr. Stone lets out a grunt. "This isn't a closed crime scene anymore. All the forensic evidence has been taken, so it's not like they can mess anything up."

We walk slowly up the driveway toward the cabin. Although it's not a cabin. It's a mansion-cabin. The place is made from rough-cut wood and is at least two stories tall, with huge glass windows on every side. Off to the left is a detached garage where most of the bays are open, showing everything from all-terrain vehicles to jacked-up trucks to ski boats. This is definitely a sportsman's paradise.

A crowd of men are gathered on the back porch, waiting for us. I hold my camera up in front of me like it's some sort of shield. And then I spot the group just inside the house. Four of them, watching us from the big windows.

The River Point Boys.

I take a slow breath in and then let it out.

Mr. Stone puts a hand on my arm, stopping me. "This is going to be difficult for me, as you know. Take pictures of everything. Notice everything. It's probably for the best that you came with me instead of your mother. I'm counting on you."

He's counting on me.

I stand up straighter and pull my camera closer. I can do this.

"They're all staring at us," I whisper to Mr. Stone.

"Forres and the others will try to intimidate us, make us rush, make us feel bad for being here, but we're going to ignore them. We have every right within the law to be here. We can stay as long as we need. We can look anywhere we want, take pictures, take measurements, whatever," he answers with a wink.

When we reach the back patio, everyone introduces themselves, and it's not hard to notice the divide: Mr. Perkins and his team on one side, and the four River Point dads and the defense lawyers on the other. And to think these five men were close friends before this happened.

Mr. Stone puts his briefcase on a stone table and pulls out some papers. "All right, we'd first like to see the spot where Grant was found."

My eyes cut to Mr. Perkins and he winces, the pain still fresh on his face. The deputy motions for us to follow him, and we move off of the flagstone patio into the woods. Everyone else follows close behind us, but thankfully the boys stay inside.

I lift the camera to my face and start taking pictures. It's absolutely beautiful here. Giant trees dot the landscape, but with the limbs bare, sun filters in through the space. The ground is covered with leaves that crunch with every step we take. Most are dead, but some still cling to their bright orange and yellow colors.

I'm surprised by how close to the house we are when we finally stop. There are little orange flags stuck in the ground in the rough shape of a body, and I know we've made it to the spot where Grant died.

My jaw feels tight and it's tough to swallow. Blinking back the tears, I drag in a deep breath, hoping to get myself under control. I can keep it together. For Grant.

And what makes it worse is seeing Mr. Perkins. He's started crying and has to lean against a nearby tree for support. In this moment I really want nothing more than to stand with him, hug him, and cry as openly as he is. The others are quiet and keep their distance, uncomfortable with Mr. Perkins's display of emotions.

"Kate, please start taking your photographs. I want pictures of the ground there," he says and points to the flags. "And a shot from every direction."

Mr. Stone turns around to the crowd. "If you please, when my assistant turns in your direction, move out of her shot."

They nod and I get to work. Hopefully, focusing on the task at hand will help me block out the total despair radiating from Mr. Perkins.

"There are no wildlife cameras in this area?" Mr. Stone asks.

The River Point dads all look at each other and then to their lawyers. One of the lawyers answers for them. "I believe you have all of the pictures from any wildlife cameras."

"I understand that. What I'm asking is if there is a wildlife camera in this area."

The lawyer just stares at Mr. Stone, clearly not giving him anything to work with or use against his clients later. Finally, Mr. Stone turns around and opens a file folder but goes to great lengths to hide what he's reading. I move around in a tight circle, still snapping away.

"Kate," Mr. Stone says quietly. "Please take a look at this."

I move next to him and peek inside the file folder. It's a color image of Grant, dead on the ground. My throat gets tight, and there's that funny feeling in my mouth that comes right before you puke.

Turning away from the photo, I stare at the trees in the distance and try to push the sick feeling away. Deep breaths in. Deep breaths out.

"I'm sorry you have to see this, but I need your help orienting me to the direction he was facing when he fell," he whispers in my ear.

I skim across the small type under the image, trying desperately not to look at Grant.

"The report says he was facing northwest."

Mr. Stone nods, closes the folder and repeats the direction to the officer, asking him to find that direction.

It takes a few seconds for the officer to point us the right way.

"Officer, the coroner's report states that, based on ballistics, the shooter was twenty-five to thirty yards away." Stone hands him a tape measure from his pocket. "Please measure thirty yards from this spot in that direction."

I spin around to Mr. Stone and see that same smile he had in the car.

"That's pretty close," I whisper.

He gives me a quick nod.

The officer does as he's asked, and the only sounds are of the birds flying through the trees above us. I notice the investigators Mr. Perkins hired are taking their own pictures and scribbling in notebooks. The other group waits off to the side, but it's easy to see how tense they are.

Once the officer is in place, I'm shocked. I could probably throw a rock and hit him from here.

Even though Stone knew the shooter was close from the officers on the scene, it's different seeing just how close he really was. "Kate, stand next to me and take a picture in the direction of Officer Jones. Then go stand by Officer Jones and take a picture in my direction."

I do as I'm told, trying to forget about all of the eyes on me right now.

My mind spins out of control when I focus in on the officer. There are no bushes or trees blocking the view. I can see him clearly.

Wouldn't that mean the shooter saw Grant?

We stay in that small part of the woods for over an hour, and by the time we head back to the cabin, I've taken nearly five hundred pictures.

The others walk ahead, but Mr. Perkins waits for us.

"My wife and I have been searching for Grant's watch and class ring. They're not at home, and the Forreses say they're not here. We were given a list of Grant's things that were . . . on him, but the watch and ring weren't listed. Have you seen any mention of those items anywhere?"

Mr. Stone puts a hand on Mr. Perkins's shoulder. "I'm sorry, no. I haven't come across that, but I will keep an eye out for it. You should fill out a report, though. At least you could file it on your insurance."

Mr. Perkins nods and says, "It's not the money I'm worried about. We just wanted his things back."

Mr. Perkins walks away and Mr. Stone and I let him get a little ahead of us before we start back.

"I guess I always thought the one who shot Grant mistook him for a deer," I say quietly. "But . . . the shooter had to have seen him."

"Of course he did. These boys were drunk and stupid. They were probably walking out to their stands, screwing around, and someone was clumsy with their gun. They were extremely negligent. That's why they're not giving up the one who pulled the trigger, because there's no way a jury would let them off."

I swallow hard. "So it was an accident?" I ask.

He slows down, increasing the space between us and everyone else. "That's where it gets tricky. Could this have been an accident? Yes. A stupid, senseless accident. Could it have been more than that? It very well may be."

"Do you think he was . . . murdered?" I whisper. I can barely wrap my head around this.

Stone stops. "There's only one thing separating negligent homicide from murder, and that's evidence of intent. We're still trying to figure which one of them pulled the trigger. If we can't discover who did it, there's no way to know if there was intent. We have to take this one step at a time."

We start walking again, and just before we reach the others, Stone says, "I'm really proud of how you handled yourself out there."

I can't help but smile.

Mr. Forres moves toward us, gesturing to where our car is parked down the driveway, and says, "I'm sure you've gotten everything you need."

Mr. Stone shakes his head. "We'd like to inspect the inside."

Oh God.

Mr. Forres consults with his defense team, and there is a quiet argument while Mr. Stone acts like he has all day.

And, just as Mr. Stone called it, Mr. Forres has to let us enter the house.

I follow Mr. Stone inside, and he turns to the boys, who are standing near the kitchen area.

I keep my eyes down because I'm scared to death to look at any of them right now. The disgust roiling around inside of me when I think about how they're protecting each other makes me sick.

"Maybe you boys want to wait outside while we're in here," Stone says to them.

I hear them shuffle out, but I don't move until it's quiet.

"Kate, do your thing."

And I get to work. Mr. Stone and I move through every room while I take detailed pictures of every inch. Mr. Perkins and his investigators follow every step I take.

I pass through a small den and recognize the couch where Shep was questioned, then the office where Logan sat near the desk. Moving through the house, there's the room where Henry sat nervously on his barstool. Toward the end of the tour, I see the bedroom where John Michael was questioned.

When we circle back to the main room, the sun has dropped farther down in the sky and the light has turned a fuzzy orange color. I zoom in close to a wooden board with a map stretched across it. There are nails sticking out in different areas across the map, and small, circular metal tags hanging from the nails. On each disk, there are names engraved . . . GRANT, HENRY, JOHN MICHAEL, LOGAN, and SHEP. I take several pictures of the board before moving on.

"We're done, Kate. You can head to the car while I say our good-byes."

I can't get out of there fast enough. I exit through the front door while Mr. Stone goes to the back porch, where everyone else is waiting. I'm just out of the door when I hear a voice.

"Kate, can I talk to you?"

And there is Shep, standing on the porch, watching me.

"No," I say, my voice full of disgust.

I move down the front steps and hear him following behind.

"I had no idea you would be here. I know how hard this is . . . for you. But I need to talk to you."

I stop and throw a glance at the house, checking to see if Stone is witnessing this, but we're all alone out here.

"There is absolutely nothing you need to say to me unless it is admitting to killing Grant or telling me who did."

His clenched fists hang by his side.

I spin around, and just before I stomp off to Mr. Stone's car, he says, "I didn't shoot him."

A deep breath shudders out of me, but I don't turn around or move until I hear him walk away.

The second all the lawyers and that prosecutor and the girl with the camera left, they sit us down and start chewing our asses out.

They'd known the one who shot Grant was near him, but no one was prepared for how damning it looked when the officer measured off the distance.

"It's time to stop all this bullshit and tell us which one of you pulled the trigger," one of the dads says.

"We'll stand by you. We'll use every resource available to make sure you don't go to jail," another one of the dads adds.

"My son wouldn't have done this," one of the moms says.

The woman next to her spins around. "And mine would?"

They're turning on each other.

"Maybe we should just get our own lawyers," one dad asks. "Maybe we're better off individually."

"Oh, so you can make a deal on the side? Have your boy go in alone and rat the others out?"

"The lawyers told us we're better off if we stick together. If the police can't pin this on one of them, it's not likely they can pin it on any of them," another dad says.

The four of us sit on the couch, side by side, as a united front.

These are the same arguments we made to each other in the parking lot of that abandoned store. These are the same things we fight about. It didn't change anything then and it doesn't now.

We have no choice.

We made a pact in those woods.

Either we all get out of this or none of us does.

We all know the consequences.

It's as simple as that.

8

GRANT: Battle of the Paddle starts at 5.

I can pick you up at 4

KATE: oh no! I totally forgot! I have to take pics at the science bowl. I signed up for it weeks ago. Can I meet you at the party when I'm done?

GRANT: Yeah that's fine

KATE: Sorry I won't see you play

GRANT: It's cool

Thank God for Fridays during football season. Once the pep rally is over, Reagan and I will only have about two hours before we leave for work. It's a joke, really.

Reagan and Mignon sit on the bench against one wall of the gym while I plop down next to Alexis on the floor in front of them. Reagan nudges me with her knee, and when I look back at her, she asks me in a quiet voice if I'm okay. She's asked me this four times already this morning. Yesterday was hard on me and I can't exactly hide my bloodshot eyes or the dark circles under them, but I nod, giving her a tight smile.

We're off to the side, ready to document, photograph, and basically ensure full coverage of the pep rally for the newspaper, website, and yearbook. The other two photographers are stationed on the other side of the room.

I check my camera settings while we wait. Our football team is good. Maybe even great. We make the playoffs every year and most times win state. Our cheerleaders perform in Orlando on ESPN, and they had to build a new glass case for the trophies the dance line wins. So every pep rally is a show, especially this one since it falls on Halloween.

But I can't get into it this morning.

Mignon leans closer and says, "So Alexis and I want to do a piece for the newspaper on the River Point Boys, and we need some pics of them to go with it. Maybe after the pep rally we can pull them aside and you can take them?"

"I'm not supposed to talk to them," I say. And I'm not sure I could if I wanted to. I'm having a hard time getting over the crime scene visit.

Her face scrunches up. "So don't talk. Just take a few pics."

Reagan leans in close. "What are you going to ask them?"

"I just have a few 'get to know you' kind of questions," Mignon says.

Reagan leans back. "Boring. Ask them who pulled the trigger."

"Have you even asked them for the interview?" I ask.

Alexis smiles. "No. We're going for the ambush approach. That's why we need you ready."

This is a bad idea on so many levels, but I find myself warming to the idea of witnessing this confrontation. What if she did ask them who pulled the trigger? If they were caught off guard, would their facial expressions give something away?

As soon as that thought enters my head, the four of them appear in front of me, shoulder to shoulder, as they search for a place to sit. Minus the mandatory blazers with the crest on the pocket, they are still dressed as they would be for St. Bart's. And despite how they seemed to be falling apart in the parking lot next to Pat's, they are a united front here at school. If I hadn't witnessed them fighting, I would've never known there was a problem between them.

Just like on the first day they arrived and the crowd parted for them in the hall, a space opens up on the bleachers, front and center. But the difference is, people aren't making room in an attempt to avoid them. In the week they've been here, they've become something close to living legends. The horror of what they are accused of has morphed into this crazy fascination with them.

"I'll come with you on the ambush, but there's no way they're going to talk to you," I say to Mignon.

Alexis leans forward. "They will. We *always* get our story."

The gym goes dark for a few seconds, and screams and cheers echo through the cavernous space. I can feel Alexis move past me as she gets up to film the dance line's opening. A black light pops on overhead and there are thirty girls dressed in all black, with glow-in-the-dark stripes outlining their bodies, bent at odd angles. The blast of music makes us all jump, and within moments they start their routine. In keeping with the Halloween theme, they look more like skeletons than girls, and it's amazing to see their kicks and flips in perfect synchronization in the dark gym. Girls are flying through the air and tumbling across the room, and you can't help but be in awe of these performances. I turn away from the show and try to make out the four boys in the front row. They are easy to spot, since their white dress shirts are glowing in the black light, illuminating each of their faces.

Shep and John Michael are spellbound by the show, but Henry and Logan have their heads bent in deep conversation. I analyze their every movement, look, and gesture just like I do when watching their videos.

I feel like I know them. Sitting at that desk at work, their voices coming through the headphones with everything else blocked away, I get sucked into their world.

So now, here in the gym, I can tell Logan is saying something Henry doesn't like, because Henry's knee is bouncing, just like it did in the video.

It's easy to see what no one else does.

Studying them, I try to think about which one of them stood thirty yards away from Grant early that Sunday morning. Was the safety off? Did his finger slip and hit the trigger? Was he so drunk that he was waving his gun around in the air, being stupid? Or was it more than that?

The routine ends to massive applause, and now that the overhead lights are on, I move through the gym, taking random candids of students while Julianna, the cheer captain, introduces the football team. When my camera lands on Shep, he's staring right at me. I'm zoomed in so close, I actually jump back, startled by the directness of his stare. I pull the camera away from my face and study him without the camera between us. He doesn't look away, even though this is extremely awkward. Instead, he nods his head toward the far side of the gym. I glance back in that general direction, trying to figure out what he's gesturing to, but all that's back there is a door that leads to the hallway.

I peek back at Shep and he nods in that direction again, then points to his watch and holds up both hands with his fingers spread wide.

What does that mean? Does he want me to meet him there? In ten minutes? At ten o'clock?

What could he possibly have to say to me?

As much as I want to blow him off like I did yesterday, that's the one thing that's been driving me nuts—wondering what he wanted to talk about.

I turn away and sit down with my friends, trying hard not to panic. This could go spectacularly wrong . . . but what if I find out something that helps Grant's case?

I have to risk it.

Julianna jogs up to my side. "We're ready." And then she looks at me closer. "Are you okay? You look pale."

A hand flies to my cheek as if I could actually feel the change in color. "I'm fine." I follow her to the center of the gym, where the captain of the football team is standing with Coach Ford, who retired a few years ago. They are presenting him with a plaque for all his years of service to our school. I was so distracted by Shep I completely forgot I was supposed to grab this picture. I rush up and snap a few shots.

As soon as the pep rally is over, Mignon and Alexis make a beeline for the River Point Boys. Alexis glances back at me, urging me to follow them.

By the time I reach them, Alexis has a small handheld recorder thrust in front of them, and Mignon is asking them questions. All four boys stare at them for a few seconds, then slowly turn in my direction. All of them except Shep glare at my camera before looking at my face. It's hard not to flinch.

Henry shakes his head, like he's disgusted by all three of us, before turning to walk away. Logan follows right behind him, then John Michael. Shep is the last to leave.

My friends chase them halfway across the gym before finally giving up.

Everyone files out of the gym, headed back to their homerooms, the River Point Boys no exception. I track their progress across the room, and just before they leave, Shep looks back at me. His eyes flicker to the same door he motioned to earlier, then he moves out of sight.

TRANSCRIPT OF THE OCTOBER 5 INTERROGATION OF HENRY CARLISLE BY DETECTIVE MILLER, WITH BODY LANGUAGE COMMENTARY BY KATE MARINO

DET. MILLER: Seems like you've been able to get out of trouble easily in the past, but today is going to be different.

HENRY: There's no trouble for me to get out of. I didn't do anything, Officer.

KATE: Henry is on the stool, leaning back against the counter. He would look relaxed if it weren't for that leg that keeps bouncing.

DET. MILLER: It's Detective.

HENRY: So sorry . . . Detective.

DET. MILLER: So what's going to happen if Daddy can't get you out of trouble this time?

HENRY: Like I said, I didn't do anything wrong.

KATE: Henry runs his hand through his hair. It's sticking up all over the place.

DET. MILLER: Something else interesting happened last night. A girl was brought into the ER just after midnight. She was unconscious. Took something, but her friends didn't know what it was. They said she got it from you. That was one helluva party. Did John Michael hook you up with something? I hear he's got everything you need out there.

KATE: Henry shrugs, knee still bouncing.

DET. MILLER: What did you give her?

HENRY: I have no idea what you're talking about.

KATE: He's trying to come off cocky, but it falls flat.

DET. MILLER: I can arrest you for that alone and screw up your entire future. I bet you'd lose that shit-eating grin then.

HENRY: I guess you can try.

KATE: Henry is sweating. If I can see it, the detective must see it.

DET. MILLER: I spoke to the girl's friend who brought her in. She was very eager to tell me about the party. Said there was fighting. Lots of fighting. She said your little group is falling apart. What do you think she means by that?

HENRY: I think it means she was drunk and doesn't know what in the hell she's talking about.

KATE: Henry runs his hands over his forehead, then across his mouth.

DET. MILLER: So is that what you have to do to get girls? Get them high? Does it make it easier for you that way?

KATE: Henry shakes his head. Then rolls his eyes.

HENRY: No. I get plenty of girls on my own.

KATE: Henry's hands are clenched around the edge of the counter. His face is red and a vein in his forehead is throbbing.

DET. MILLER: Maybe you were high this morning? Maybe when you're out of your gourd like that, poor Grant looks like a beautiful ten-point buck? Were you the one using the Remington?

KATE: Henry tucks his lips between his teeth and shakes his head back and forth.

DET. MILLER: Or are you covering for one of them? When friends turn into secret-keepers, they don't stay friends long.

UNKNOWN VOICE: Interview is over. Parents want a lawyer present.

KATE: Henry pops up from the stool and disappears from the screen.

9

OCTOBER 3, 11:17 P.M.

KATE: Is it crazy that I'm kind of nervous
about seeing you tomorrow?

GRANT: Is it crazy that I'm considering going
to that science bowl so I can see you sooner?

It's been fifty minutes since Shep signaled me in the gym. We're both in English class, listening to Mr. Stevens drone on and on about the importance of MLA format, and Shep hasn't looked at me once. I'm starting to believe I imagined the entire thing.

A shrill ping that always precedes an announcement from the office pierces through the room and we all cringe.

"Mr. Stevens, please send Shepherd Moore to the office."

It's ten minutes to ten.

Shep started getting his books together before his name was announced, like he knew they were calling for him. Mr. Stevens motions for Shep to leave and he heads to the door. Just before he exits the room, he throws a quick glance in my direction.

My breath catches in my throat.

He wants me to meet him at ten o'clock. I didn't imagine it.

The second hand of the clock above the whiteboard moves along at a swift pace while I try to decide what to do. I know Mr. Stone will be so disappointed in me if I meet Shep, with good reason, but my curiosity is winning out.

With a minute to go, I slowly raise my hand.

"Yes, Miss Marino?" Mr. Stevens asks.

"May I be excused? I forgot I'm supposed to take pictures for the debate team." And now I'm lying. The debate team is taking pictures, but Miranda is handling it, since she's got study hall this hour.

Mr. Stevens lets out a deep huff. "You know I don't like you missing class for stuff like this."

I nod. "I know. It won't happen again. I'm sorry."

I can't believe I'm doing this. I'm lying to my teacher. I'm going to meet one of the suspects in a case my boss is prosecuting. I'm going to be in a huge pile of trouble if I get caught.

I head to the gym, texting Reagan while I walk.

FYI—I'm meeting Shep Moore in the back
hallway behind the gym.

At least someone will know where I am and who I'm with.

God, I'm acting like he's going to kill me and dump my body in some remote location.

My footsteps echo across the empty room, and my pulse starts to race the closer I get to the back door.

I can't believe I'm doing this.

With my hand on the door's bar, I take a deep breath before I push my way through.

Shep is waiting there, exactly like I knew he would be. We watch each other a moment, the silence heavy between us.

His forehead scrunches as he stares at me; then he lifts his phone, tapping the screen. My paranoid brain rushes to the first possibility—he's taking a video. I start to back away. I can't get caught here with him, like this. I can't be on some recording that will be produced later and get me in a world of trouble.

And then my phone buzzes in my back pocket, scaring me to death and making me jump. It's probably Reagan texting me back. I pull it out and my heart drops. The notification on the front screen reads:

Grant Perkins now
iMessage
Slide to reply

Words I've prayed to see but never thought were possible flash in front of me. How is this happening? This can't have come from Grant's phone. Grant's phone is locked up in Stone's desk at work. I've seen it. I've been trying to get my hands on it for two days. My hand shakes when I swipe the message open.

This is Shep. You've been talking to me
this entire time, not Grant.

I look at Shep. This can't be possible. There's no way this is possible.

My eyes drop back to my phone. I read the message again before my eyes move to the previous message above it: *I'm sorry. Please give me a chance to explain.* Grant's last message to me.

Not Grant.

Shep.

My eyes go to his once more and the truth is there.

No.

This is all wrong.

This is not happening.

I turn back to the door, pulling it open so roughly it bangs against the wall. I feel gutted. For a second, I thought it was possible Grant wasn't really gone. There had been some big mistake. He was somewhere texting me. Somewhere alive.

The tears roll down my face as I sprint through the gym, away from Shep.

I can't even process what he just told me. How could I have been talking to him this whole time and not have known? Everything in my brain rejects this. I reject this.

I think back to when I first met Grant. I was at the library studying. Shep was with him. They were sitting down the table from me, being loud, disturbing everyone around us.

I asked them to be quiet. Neither one of them would have noticed me if I hadn't spoken to them first. Grant scooted down until he was right in front of me, and Shep followed along. We all talked for a while, more quietly than before. I knew who they were, had heard their names, but I'd never seen them in person or spoken to any of the boys from St. Bart's.

Grant carried the conversation that day at the library, and just like everyone has said—he was utterly charming to be around. Funny and sarcastic and telling stories that had me blushing, Shep was quieter, listening and watching more than talking. When I was just about to leave, Grant grabbed my phone, and I remember my heart was racing when he added his number to my contacts. He even looked at Shep and laughed, saying, "I guess I'll give her yours, too." He sent a text to both of their phones, from mine, to make sure they had my number, too.

They left shortly after and I was giddy. Flying.

When Grant texted me later that night, I was beyond excited. Shep texted me a few days later, but it was clear he was just looking for a hookup.

I hear footsteps behind me. "Wait, Kate! Please. Let me explain." I ignore him and keep running. I make it to the far side of the gym before Shep catches up with me. I whirl around and hold out my hand. He stops.

His gaze is soft . . . hopeful, even.

I look at him. Really look at him.

This can't be true. This is a trick. This isn't real.

Twisting back around, I race through the door.

Everywhere we go, we are asked questions.

Our parents ask us questions.

The lawyers ask us questions.

Who used the Remington?

Where were you hunting?

Why do you have to be such a fuckup?

None of us talk about what will happen after. After the grand jury. After everyone stops asking us these ridiculous questions.

Maybe they'll never stop asking us.

Standing together like we are to protect each other should make us stronger. It should make us closer. But it doesn't.

Our silence is ripping us apart.

There will be time to put things back together once this is over. We will be closer than ever. We will be like brothers again.

We will not always be the River Point Boys.

10

SEPTEMBER 19, 8:57 P.M.

~~GRANT~~ SHEP: Im at a party at river point.
The guys are pissed at me

KATE: Why are they pissed

~~GRANT~~ SHEP: Because I'd rather be
sitting in the back room texting you than
hanging out with them

I don't go back to class. I don't go to the media arts room. And I certainly don't go to work. I need time alone. To think. To sort all of this out in my brain. But every time I think about Shep, I remember those disgusting texts he sent and my stomach turns.

But that wasn't him, I remind myself. It was Grant.

My mind is about to explode.

Since Mom and Mr. Stone have been spending most waking hours at work, she's relieved his normal driver and taken over that duty herself, leaving me with her Honda. I've never been so happy to have a car in the parking lot as I am this morning. I'm only ditching one class, and that shouldn't throw up too many red flags, especially with everything going on today. My teachers just assume when any of us are missing, we're off doing stuff for the media arts department.

My phone buzzes again and I'm scared it's Shep. I glance at it as I slide into Mom's car.

It's Reagan.

Just seeing this. What in the hell are you doing?
Do I need to come rescue you?????

I reply, *I'm fine. Leaving school early. I'll c u at work later.*
It only takes a few seconds for her to reply:

Is this code for something? I'm not sure if you're
really asking for help.

I can't help but laugh. I text her I'm fine and throw my phone across the seat. I drive around aimlessly, trying to let my mind go. I roll the windows down and crank up the radio, hoping that if I can't hear myself think, my brain will shut off.

It helps for a little while.

Without consciously being aware of where I was going, I find myself at Columbia Park. My go-to place for downtime. I've taken some of my best pictures here.

It's empty this time of the day, since the bigger kids are in school and the younger ones are probably inside having an early lunch right now.

I drop down on one of the benches under the big oak tree near the swing set and pull out my phone, scrolling through my messages until I find Grant's name.

But it's not Grant. It's Shep.

I try to reread the messages I thought were from Grant and picture Shep's face in my mind, but it's hard to do. I don't get too far back before I have to stop. It's too painful.

Dropping my phone, I bury my head in my hands and cry. It's like finding out Grant's dead all over again, but this time it's the Grant that I was falling for—the one in my heart and in my mind.

I hear heavy footsteps behind me and I spin around quickly, almost falling off the bench.

It's Shep.

"Did you follow me here?" I ask wildly. I drove around for at least twenty minutes before winding my way back.

He shakes his head. "No. I just figured you were here."

I can't stop the eye roll. "You just thought I would be at this tiny little park in a part of town you've probably never been to before."

He moves a little closer. "You've talked about this park. A lot. Talked about this oak tree. Described the pictures you took here."

My breath catches.

This isn't real. This can't be happening. Shep wouldn't know about this park. He couldn't know. I told Grant about this place.

But it wasn't Grant.

I feel sick.

He moves even closer, just steps away from the bench.

"Please give me a chance to explain," he says in a quiet voice. The same exact words Grant said in his last text to me.

No. Shep.

"I don't understand," I say, then drop my head against the back of the bench. I think back to that first time I met them, trying to make sense of everything. "Grant put y'all's numbers in my phone. Did he switch them? Why would he switch them?"

Shep lets out a deep breath and sits on the ground, his arms resting on his pulled-up knees. "When you got up to go to return that book, I told Grant I thought you were cute. Told him I was going to ask for your number. He beat me to it, but I was glad he at least gave you my number, too. But he switched them and put my number under his name and his number under mine. It was his idea of a joke. I swear I didn't know." He leans his head back. "He was always doing stupid shit like that."

I didn't think I could feel any worse, but I do. I'm humiliated. And confused. And heartbroken. And furious.

"At some point you must have figured it out," I say through gritted teeth.

He nods. "The day of the Battle of the Paddle. You sent that picture of Grant and Lindsey, and you were so mad at me and I couldn't figure out why. Why would you send that pic to me? So I asked Grant and he almost pissed himself he was laughing so hard. He had no idea we had been texting for those few weeks. That's when I found out what he'd done. I sent you that last text, hoping you would let me explain."

I jump up from the bench and start pacing around. "So for weeks, I was talking to you, not Grant."

It's not really a question, but Shep answers it anyway, "Yes. It was always me."

It's like I'm being split in two. The half of me that fell for Grant over late-night conversations and has mourned his death every day battles with the other half, who is looking at this stranger, who may also be a killer, and realizing he's not a stranger at all.

"I just don't know how it's possible that I didn't know it was you instead of Grant. That *you* didn't know I didn't know. I can't . . . believe this."

He stands up and moves toward me. "I've thought about it for a while. I've read back through all of our texts. It's not like I signed my messages 'From Shep.' We were strangers. We got to know each other through those messages. You had no reason to think I wasn't Grant. I had no reason to think you didn't know it was me." He inches closer. "And everything I said to you, I meant. I still do."

I push away from him. My brain is in overload, trying to reconcile what I've learned. And what I already know. "Then why have you waited so long to tell me?" I scream at him. "You knew I thought I was talking to Grant. And he died. I've been out of my mind, regretting that last text—regretting that he died believing I was mad at him."

The tears race down my cheeks and his hand brushes them away before I can stop him.

"Kate, I've—I've been in a pretty bad place." His voice is raw. "One of my best friends is dead. Killed by one of my *other* best friends. I'm being questioned, we're all being questioned. I may go to *jail* for this. My parents are furious and scared, and basically, my life is a nightmare right now. I just thought—I don't know, I just thought it would be better to let you go. You didn't need to be a part of any of this."

I step closer to him, pained by the expression on his face and the hurt in his voice.

"So why tell me now?" I ask.

He swallows. "I missed . . . I miss talking to you, Kate. There are . . . so few people I can talk to right now. I didn't know how hard it would be, seeing you every day. I feel like I know you, like there was something between us, but when you look at me, I'm a stranger to you. It kills me."

His head lowers. We are just inches apart. My eyes scan his face, memorizing it so I can try to match what I was feeling in those conversations to the person in front of me. Grant's name screams through my head, but it's not the same Grant I knew five minutes ago. It's all so fuzzy.

"So the texts I got that I thought were from you were actually from him?" I ask.

He nods, his jaw clenching. Just like it does in his interrogation videos.

"Why am I in his phone under the initials *FWS*? Do you know?"

His head cocks to the side, like he's trying to figure out a puzzle. I can tell the instant he gets it. I can also tell he doesn't want to tell me what it stands for.

"Tell me. Please," I beg.

Finally, he says, "It stands for 'Fuck With Shep.' That's what he said when I asked him about you. He said, *'Operation Fuck With Shep worked out after all.'* It was all a game to him."

I drop back down on the bench. It was a game. "I can't. I can't do this. Not with you. Not right now," I whisper.

He kneels in front of me. "I know you. And deep down, you know me, too. You just know me by the wrong name."

I hug my arms tight around my body as if I can stop myself from shattering into a million pieces. "When I see you, I remember those messages I thought were from you. They were . . . disgusting. Why would Grant say those things?"

Shep visibly cringes. "Can I read them? His messages?"

Squeezing my phone tightly, I try to think of any reason not to hand it over, but I've got nothing. I scroll to his messages and give my phone to Shep.

He must read through them more than once, because it takes a while for him to hand it back.

"Please switch our names. I hate seeing those messages with my name at the top of the screen."

I do as he asks. "Why did he do this?" I ask again.

"Grant's sense of humor was twisted. He knew I was going to text you. He knew . . . I was interested. And he knew, at least at first, you would think I was him. And then if you got some shitty messages you thought were from me, well, that would make it even better. He was always screwing with people like that."

"But people loved him. Everyone I've talked to loved him. This doesn't make sense."

"People were amused by him. He was fun and entertaining until you found yourself on the wrong side of his jokes."

Shep sits down on the other end of the bench, keeping a safe distance between us. "I'm so sorry, Kate. You have no idea how sorry I am that you've had to go through this."

He reaches out for me, but I shrug away. The sadness on his face shatters me. Everything about this shatters me.

"I work for the prosecutor who's handling your case." I scoot even farther away to put some distance between us. "I'm glad you told me, but it doesn't change anything. I can't talk to you. Or be seen with you."

His head drops. "I know. I probably shouldn't have told you. I thought maybe if you knew the truth, you wouldn't be sad anymore."

I jump up from the bench, white-hot anger suffocating me from out of nowhere. "Seriously? I've been mourning Grant for *weeks* now. It's not like a switch I can flip on and off." I spin around and move toward the swings, shoving one so it sways violently back and forth. "And then there's you. You're sitting there telling me you know me. Expecting me to be okay with this . . ."

Shep moves behind me; his hands are gentle on my shoulders. My heart is pounding. There is a desperate part of me that wants to step back into him. This stranger who is not a stranger.

But I can't.

I step away from him and his hands fall away.

Without turning around, I ask, "Were you the one who shot Grant?"

His breath lets out in a loud rush. "No. I told you the truth yesterday. I've never lied to you—not when we were texting and not now. I swear I didn't shoot him. If there's only one thing you will believe, please believe that." His voice cracks and I can't help but turn around. I look at him like I've never looked at him before.

I study his face; his brown eyes that are begging me to see him for who he really is, and his tense expression that shows me that this is as hard for him as it is for me.

"But you're covering for the person who did! That's almost as bad!" I cry. My hands are shaking.

He shakes his head. "No. I'm not," he says in a quiet voice. "I don't know who did it. We all stood over his body, and no one would admit to shooting him. No one would admit to using that gun. But I swear to you, it wasn't me. Please believe me."

It's hard to swallow for the lump in my throat. I search his face, seeking some sign he's lying. I know him, but I don't. I know the person on the other end of those messages. That person I would believe. But is that the same person in front of me right now?

"I'm sorry. I can't do this. I can't be here."

"Kate?" Shep says, but I shake my head and turn away. When I get in my car and pull out of the parking lot, he's still there, sitting on my favorite bench under the big oak tree.

• • •

I'm only a few minutes late to work. Mom's in the office with Mr. Stone, so I drop down in her chair, giving myself a few more minutes to come to grips with what I've learned.

As I scan the mess on top of her desk, a half-buried piece of paper catches my eye when I see a number circled in red ink. I pull it out of the pile, making sure I don't disturb anything else, and written next to the number is a date—October 5—and the name Lindsey Wells.

The girl Grant was with the night before at the Battle of the Paddle game.

The same girl who acted really weird at Rhino Coffee the other night when we started talking about the River Point Boys.

October 5. This is the call he deleted from his phone the morning he died.

"Kate, you're here," she says, and her eyes go to the paper I'm holding.

"Looks like you figured out who Booty Call 3 is," I say, keeping my voice even.

"Yes, but she wasn't any help. Said she had been with Grant the night before, but they had gotten in a fight. Apparently, he called her that morning, trying to make up with her, and she blew him off. Probably why he deleted the call. Poor dear was so upset. Couldn't stop crying."

I get up from her seat while she puts the papers back in a folder. "And don't go running off and telling Reagan what I just told you. You know how that girl loves to gossip."

I nod, not even trying to defend Reagan, since it wouldn't do any good.

Mom's face is full of concern when she finally looks at me. "You look like you've been crying. Are you okay?"

I rub a hand across my face. "I'm fine."

She stares at me a moment but doesn't push it. "Okay, well, I'm going to step out for some lunch. Mr. Stone is on a conference call right now but should be done shortly." Mom points to the area off to the side of her desk. "He's got an interview cued up, ready for you. Do you want me to bring you back anything?"

I shake my head, unable to answer, because at my little corner desk, Shep's face is frozen on the screen, waiting for me.

"Okay, I'll see you in a few," she says, just before stepping out of the door.

She leaves the office and I slowly make my way to the table. All I can focus on is Shep's face. He looks different on the screen than he did a few minutes ago in the park. Here, his face is set in stone, no trace of any emotion. Not like at the park, when he was a breath away from falling apart.

I sit at the table and put the headphones on. This is going to be the hardest one I've done, now that I know who he really is. I take a deep breath and brace myself.

Then I press play.

**TRANSCRIPT OF THE OCTOBER 5 INTERROGATION
OF SHEPHERD MOORE BY DETECTIVE ARCHER, WITH
BODY LANGUAGE COMMENTARY BY KATE MARINO**

DET. ARCHER: So let's go back for a minute. How long have you been friends with these boys?

SHEP: I met them when my family moved here three years ago—midway through our freshman year.

DET. ARCHER: And you moved here from Texas?

KATE: Shep rolls his eyes. Collapses back in his chair. Looks frustrated.

SHEP: You know I did. You know my dad. Why are you asking me stupid questions?

DET. ARCHER: Don't get smart with me. I'll throw your ass in that squad car outside and we can move this discussion to a jail cell if that's what it takes. How many times have you been to River Point?

KATE: He doesn't move. Looks at the detective with mild disinterest.

SHEP: A lot. Too many to count. During hunting season, we spend almost every weekend here. We're here in the spring because the fishing on this part of the river is better than anywhere else. We're here in the summer because John Michael has ski boats and Jet Skis we can use. We're here all the time.

DET. ARCHER: Damn, son, pretty lucky for you to hook up with some rich friends like that.

SHEP: Yeah, I'm super lucky.

KATE: His posture matches the sarcastic answer.

DET. ARCHER: Henry, Logan, and John Michael have known each other since they were attached to their mamas' breasts, and John Michael and Grant's dads do a lot of business together. You didn't come into the group until a few years ago. Ever feel like the odd man out?

KATE: He shrugs. His eyes flick around the room. He's looking everywhere but at the detective.

SHEP: It's not like you're trying to make it sound.

DET. ARCHER: How am I trying to make it sound? I'm just trying to get some idea of the dynamics.

SHEP: We're all close. There're no problems in the group.

DET. ARCHER: Okay, okay . . . let's talk about last night. So y'all got plenty of booze for a huge crowd. Whose idea was the party?

SHEP: John Michael always has a party here after the Battle of the Paddle game.

DET. ARCHER: Yeah, the big game. We had a lot of calls the last several weeks about pranks getting out of hand. You know anything about that?

KATE: He fidgets around in his chair. Studies his hands.

SHEP: Nope.

DET. ARCHER: Nope? That's funny. There was a man in here a couple of weeks ago. Wanted to press charges for some damage to his daughter's car. And then there was something about a smoke bomb going off in the junior hall. They all claim a group of seniors were behind the pranks. Some are even saying that picture of those three girls had something to do with the prank war. Know anything about any of those events?

KATE: He leans forward, elbows resting on his knees.

SHEP: No. And what does any of this have to do with what happened to Grant this morning?

DET. ARCHER: Let's move on. What time did other people start arriving at River Point?

KATE: He leans back and shrugs his shoulders.

SHEP: I guess around seven. People were pretty much coming and going all night long.

DET. ARCHER: How many people were here, would you say? Were they all seniors?

SHEP: I don't know. Maybe fifty. Maybe seventy-five. It was a mix of people from all grades.

DET. ARCHER: Anybody fight? Any trouble?

KATE: Shep shakes his head. Doesn't look at him.

DET. ARCHER: That's funny. Grant had some marks on his face that didn't have anything to do with the gunshot wound. Looks like someone beat the hell out of him a few hours before y'all went hunting. And, looking at your knuckles, it seems like you might have been the one to deliver those punches.

KATE: Shep clenches his fists, in and out.

DET. ARCHER: What were you fighting about?

KATE: Shep's eyes go straight to the detective. He looks like he doesn't want to answer.

DET. ARCHER: Shep, don't make it worse than it has to be. You've got marks on your knuckles and he has marks on his face. When we ask other people at the party, what are they going to tell us? It'll look a whole lot better if you explain it to me first.

KATE: Shep shuffles around in his seat. He grips the armrest of the couch.

SHEP: We had a disagreement.

DET. ARCHER: What kind of disagreement? Was he messing around with your girl?

SHEP: You could say that.

DET. ARCHER: I did say that. Would you say that?

SHEP: Yeah, I would.

DET. ARCHER: Help yourself out, Shep. Tell me why y'all were fighting about your girlfriend.

SHEP: She isn't my girlfriend. Just a girl I really like. There was some . . . confusion. Our numbers got mixed up and she thought she was talking to him instead of me. When I asked him about it, he laughed. Said now that I had primed her up, he'd happily step in and close the deal for me. So I punched him.

DET. ARCHER: Hell, I'd punch him, too. So what's her name?

KATE: Shep shakes his head, looks down at the floor.

SHEP: Just a girl. It's over. It doesn't matter who she was.

UNKNOWN VOICE: Parents are here. No more questions without a lawyer.

DET. ARCHER: Come on, Shep. You can answer one more before you run off to Daddy. Maybe the fight had you so upset, you weren't paying close enough attention this morning when you went out hunting. Maybe you were distracted and saw some movement in the woods. Maybe you thought Grant was the buck you were hunting. Is that what happened?

SHEP: I want a lawyer.

11

OCTOBER 4, 8:15 A.M.

KATE: I'm nervous about going to River
Point. I won't know anyone there.

~~GRANT~~ SHEP: You know me

Reagan texts me she's on the way over with our costumes, but I'm having trouble getting off the couch. Where I've been since I got home from work. I've replayed the conversation with Shep in the park a thousand times in my head. I've thought about his interrogation video almost as much.

He and Grant got in a fight that night. Over me. Those are the marks across his knuckles I saw the other night. Marks he got when he hit Grant. Because of me.

But why didn't he tell me that they fought when we were at the park? It seemed like he was telling me everything else, so why leave that part out? What else is he leaving out?

I hear a loud honk outside our duplex, so Reagan must be here. I rush outside to help her get everything out of the car before she has a chance to lay on the horn again.

"Mr. Wiggins is going to leave another nasty note on the door," I say when I meet her at the back of her trunk. Reagan knows it drives my neighbor crazy when she honks the horn.

Reagan rolls her eyes. "Screw Mr. Wiggins."

My eyes get big when I get a good look at what's in the trunk. "What are we wearing?"

"Oh, just you wait and see," she says as she pulls several bundles of fabric out of the trunk.

She hands them off to me, then pulls out a few more bags before we head back inside. Once we're in my room, she starts laying everything out on my bed.

Reagan holds one of the outfits up. "This one is mine." It's two pieces. The top is long sleeved and looks like it will fit her like a second skin. The dark blue fabric is sheer except for the swirling black and deep purple beaded sections that will cover her chest. The short skirt is made of jagged strips of silky fabric that seem to change colors from dark blue to black as she moves it back and forth.

"Reagan, that is gorgeous. You're going to look stunning." And she will. "But what are you?" I ask.

She drops her outfit on the bed and grabs the one closest to me. "Just wait. Look at yours."

She holds up the other outfit. It's identical to hers, but where hers is dark, mine is light. The sheer top is the color of honey, with gold and bronze beading while the skirt changes from pale yellow to a light orange when she shakes it.

"We're Day and Night," she says, with a huge smile across her face. "Or really, the goddess Nyx and the goddess Eos. But no one is going to get that, so we're just going to say Day and Night."

I'm stunned by her creativity. And her abilities. "You have to put these in your portfolio." I reach out and touch the fabric. "They belong on a runway."

Reagan blushes and shakes my compliment off. "Let's get this on you and hope to God it fits."

When we're both dressed, we spin around in front of the mirror that's attached to my closet door, and the strips that make up the skirts twirl with us.

"I'm glad there's a built-in bra. Not gonna lie, I was a little worried when you held this top up," I say.

Reagan winks and spins around again. She's wearing black tights and tall black boots, while I'm wearing cream tights and a pair of her tall, light tan boots. I'm so lucky we are the same size, because there is no way I could ever afford shoes like this.

Even though my skin is covered from head to toe, I feel sexier than I would if I was in one of those awful sexy nurse or sexy pirate or sexy . . . anything costumes the stores sell.

"We look badass," I say.

"I told you, we're going out with a bang. Now it's time for hair and makeup."

I sit down on the chair in front of my dressing table while Reagan opens up her tackle box of cosmetics and starts working her magic.

She's drawing some swirly design in gold paint starting at the corner of my eye and moving toward my temple. I'm mesmerized by her steady hand.

"So I think you need to make a move on Josh tonight," I say. "Send him a clear message that he's no longer in the friend zone. And this is the perfect outfit to do it in."

"Quit talking or I'll end up smearing this down your face."

I'm quiet while she finishes my makeup, but when she moves to my hair, she asks, "So what was that about today, with Shep?"

Truthfully, I'm surprised she waited this long to ask me. I kept expecting her to show up at Stone's office all afternoon.

I can't lie to Reagan. She's my best friend.

So I tell her everything. I tell her just how hard I fell for Grant . . . then about finding out it wasn't Grant, just a sick prank.

It's a while before she says anything.

She curls the last long piece of my hair and pins it up with the rest. "Oh, Kate . . . why didn't you tell me earlier how you felt about Grant, I mean, when you thought it was Grant? I knew you were upset, but I didn't know how bad it was for you."

"I don't know. This has really messed me up. I mean, I've been mourning Grant for weeks. And then I find out it wasn't him. But when I look at Shep, he's still a stranger to me. I'm so seriously screwed up right now."

I take a deep breath. "And now I can't quit thinking about how different things could have been. What if I hadn't seen Grant at the game with that girl? I would have met up with Shep, thinking I was going to meet up with Grant. Would I have been mad? Or would we have laughed over Grant's prank? Or what if Grant had never switched the numbers? What if I'd known it was Shep all along? The what-ifs are killing me. Not to mention, Shep is one of four boys who could have killed Grant. This whole thing is a nightmare."

Reagan leans down, hugging me from behind, and it's like a weight has been lifted off my chest now that I've said the words aloud. I should have talked to her about this before now.

When she pulls away, she asks, "So what are you going to do about Shep?"

I shake my head. "I can't do anything about him. I can't even think about him without my head spinning. I asked him if he did it. You know, shot Grant. He told me no."

Reagan's forehead scrunches up. "Do you believe him?"

I shrug. "I would have believed the boy who texted me in a second. I don't know if I believe Shep."

Reagan cocks her head, not having to point out that it's the same person.

Rolling my eyes, I say, "I know. I told you I'm screwed up right now."

Reagan puts her hands on my shoulders and looks at me in the mirror. "Be careful. No one knows for sure what went on in the woods that morning."

So true. Even after all this time, we know next to nothing about what happened. And for some reason this makes me think of Lindsey and how she acted so weird when I said basically the same thing at Rhino. She talked to him just before he was shot. Is it possible she knows something?

· · ·

I grab my camera out of my bag as soon as I get out of Reagan's car.

Reagan shakes her head. "For now, put the camera away and let it all go. You've been too stressed-out lately. And it totally clashes with your outfit. Let's have fun, okay? Plenty of time to take pics later."

I drop the camera back in my bag and nod. "You're right."

We head for the far side of the parking lot, where most of the student body is tailgating before the game. There are burgers cooking on grills and music blasting and booze hidden in Styrofoam Sonic cups. This is what I need.

And most everyone is dressed up in costume. We find our group of friends, who are dressed like Minions, and Reagan and I strike a pose in front of them.

"Whoa," Mignon says. "Don't know what y'all are supposed to be, but damn."

"You two are the only ones who show up in couture Halloween costumes!" Alexis squeals. "I love it!"

"I'm Night and she's Day," Reagan says as we twirl around like we practiced in the mirror.

Josh and his group of friends notice us and move a little closer.

Even though our costumes are identical except for the colors, Josh only has eyes for Reagan.

I give her a nudge and she moves toward him. "What do you think?" she asks.

"I think nighttime is my favorite time," he says, his mouth turned up in a cute smirk.

They sit down side by side and I want to do a little cheer.

"They just need to hook up already," Josh's friend Mark says, as he takes the empty seat next to me.

I laugh. "So it's that obvious to y'all, too?"

"You could say that."

We hang out a while, talking to people that pass by our little spot, laughing at some of the costumes. Mark flirts with me and it's nice to feel like a normal girl instead of obsessing about Shep, like I have for most of the day, or Grant, like I have for the past few weeks.

"Y'all coming to the party at my house after?" Max Oliver asks as he drops down on the ground next to Reagan. We've known him forever, and parties at his place are always a good time.

"Yeah, we'll be there," Reagan says.

Mignon and Alexis quickly start talking about who will be there, while I just sit back and listen, taking it all in.

By the time we make our way to the stands, it's dark. As my friends fight their way through the crowd to the student section, I stow my gear bag behind the table where they sell T-shirts and other school-spirit paraphernalia, taking only my camera with me down the steps to the field.

I hate shooting the games. I'd much rather be in the stands with my friends than stalking the players as they move on and off the field. It's chilly out, and the wind blows straight through the sheer material of my top. I get the first group of shots I need from the players, bouncing around, trying to keep warm, then turn my attention to the cheerleaders.

They're wearing their regular uniforms, but their hair and makeup make them look like zombies. Julianna notices me and gathers the girls into a quick formation so I can grab a couple of images of them before moving to the student section to capture all of the costumes.

Scanning the crowd through my viewfinder, I snap a pic of Taylor, a girl in my English class, who wears a cow-print vest, pigtails, and exaggerated freckles. Maybe she's that cowgirl from *Toy Story*. Oh, yeah, there's "Woody" right next to her. A few spaces down is a group of girls wearing gray T-shirts, each with a different day of the week printed on it, and a shark hat. What the heck are they supposed to be . . . ohhh . . . they're Shark Week. Now that's clever. I take several shots of them, and they pose for me once I'm spotted.

Moving on, I see a few superheroes, a group of what I'm guessing are sexy kittens, and some zombies that look way scarier than the cheerleaders' version.

And then I spot Shep. He's sitting with the other River Point Boys toward the top of the bleachers. They weren't tailgating earlier, but then again, I'm not sure they even know that's what we do here.

They've kept to themselves all week, and now they're here at the game. Why?

Shep watches me and I watch him.

Click, click, click. I fire off a few quick shots, then study him through my zoom lens. It's different looking at him now that I know the truth. His features are softer somehow, or maybe that's because I'm trying to see him in a different light. He gives me a hesitant smile, and his hand goes up, like he's going to signal me again; maybe he wants to talk, but then his face changes. His forehead scrunches up and he stands, staring at something behind me. I drop my camera and notice that whatever it is has a lot of people turned that way.

I spin around and know instantly what's got everyone's attention.

There's someone in a mask with a blond wig. He's wearing the uniform from St. Bart's, except there is a huge red stain across the chest.

He's dressed up as Grant Perkins.

I glance back at Shep and see all four of the River Point Boys moving down the row, trying to get to the bleacher steps. They look pissed.

The guy in the costume is close to where I'm standing, and I can feel the anger building inside of me. He's stumbling around, grabbing his chest, and people in the stands are both horrified and fascinated. It's like a tennis match, with everyone's eyes moving back and forth between him and the River Point Boys.

I grab his arm and it takes everything in me to pull him in the opposite direction, down a set of steps that lead away from the bleachers and out of sight. I'm not sure why I'm intervening, except somewhere deep in my heart and mind, Grant lingers, and it kills me to see this person mocking him.

I yank off the mask and it's Mark.

"What in the hell are you doing?" I say. Pulling the blazer off of him, I take all the pieces that make him "Grant" and shove them in a nearby trash can.

"What?" he says in an annoyed voice. "It was a bet. Couldn't pass it up. And it's just a joke. Lighten up."

I push him in the chest and he almost falls over backward. "Well, it's a horrible joke. You're making fun of someone who's dead!"

"Why do you even care?"

I don't know how to answer that, so I don't. Mark rolls his eyes and walks away, shaking his head. I drop down to the ground, the adrenaline leaving me as fast as it came.

A minute late, the River Point Boys bound down the other stairs and skid to a stop when they see me.

"Where is he?" Henry growls.

Logan scans the area while he chews on his bottom lip. Shep is quiet, standing toward the back of the group, his eyes never leaving mine.

"He's gone," I answer.

"Who was it?" John Michael demands, his hands balled at his sides.

I shrug and we have a standoff of sorts. Finally, they turn away and go back the way they came; Shep is the last one to leave.

When I finally feel like my nerves are under control, I head back to the stadium. Scanning the crowd, I search for any sign of the River Point Boys, but they're gone.

The rest of the game drags on, and by the time we get to the party at Max Oliver's house, I'm exhausted.

Thankfully, there's a fire pit in the backyard, so Reagan and I dash to get a seat up close.

"So maybe I should have made us some jackets to go with these outfits," she says.

I hold my hands out, trying to soak up as much warmth as I can. "You think?"

The rest of our group pulls up chairs, and it doesn't take long until I'm toasty.

Mignon holds up both hands. "I can't believe I forgot to tell y'all! Guess who got her placement letter today? Looks like I'm heading to Costa Rica!"

Mignon is taking a gap year before college through some program that places you in a Latin American country where you are totally immersed in the language and culture of the area while also doing community service projects.

Alexis throws a chip at her. "I can't believe you're moving so far away," she says.

"I'll only be gone a year—it's not like it's forever," Mignon says. "We'll all be back here for summer break next year."

This seems to catch Reagan's attention, and she leans forward to look across me to Mignon. "You're going to meet some ridiculously gorgeous guy, fall in love, and we'll never see you again. You know I'm right."

Mignon smirks at Reagan. "It wouldn't be the worst thing that ever happened to me."

We all laugh, except Alexis.

And Reagan is right; Mignon has always had a wanderer's soul, so it wouldn't surprise me if she just keeps going. Reagan and I will hopefully be relocating to New York next fall. We both applied to the New School, and there's nothing I want more than that acceptance letter. Reagan's parents started a college fund for her when she was little, so her tuition is covered, but I've been saving every penny since I started working for this and applied for scholarships and tuition assistance. So now we're just waiting to hear if we got accepted. Alexis got early acceptance to Northwestern, where she wants to major in journalism. But we all promised to meet back here next summer.

Alexis says, "See! This is how it starts! We'll never be together like this again."

"Y'all are going off to college. Not dying. Quit being so dramatic," Josh says, laughing. Reagan nudges him but laughs too.

Mignon jumps up and grabs my and Alexis's hands. "Let's go dance and leave these lovebirds alone."

Both Reagan and Josh look embarrassed, but they both stay at the fire. It shouldn't be long before Josh is completely out of the friend zone.

When we finally leave the party, it's close to midnight and we're all starving. I forfeit my usual spot so Josh can sit in the front seat next to Reagan. Mark ditched him at the party without a ride home. I didn't tell anyone he was the one in the mask. In the backseat, I fight for every possible inch of space with Alexis and Mignon and Josh's other friend, Parson. Reagan pulls into the drive-through at Whataburger and it seems like we aren't the only ones wanting a midnight snack. The line of cars is almost to the road.

"Do we want to go in?" Reagan asks.

We all pivot and look inside. There's a crowd at the counter, and it seems every seat in the dining area is already taken. This is why it sucks to only have one fast-food restaurant open this late.

"Drive-through will be faster. And since y'all are all staying at my house, we can eat when we get there," Mignon says.

"Awww, thanks for the invite. Can I borrow some PJs?" Parson says.

"I'm only staying if we can have a pillow fight," Josh adds.

Reagan playfully hits him on the arm and her cheeks flush.

Parson shifts around, leaning over Alexis to roll down the window. "Mark Roberts, you suck!" he yells out the window.

We all look out of the side window and see Mark in the parking lot. He's turned in our direction, trying to figure out where that shout came from.

"Thanks for ditching us!" Josh shouts from the front seat.

Mark is standing next to the driver's-side door of a black Tahoe. Logan McCullar's black Tahoe.

Mark laughs and flips us off, then turns back to the car. Josh rolls up the window, shaking his head. "What an ass."

"Who's he talking to?" Mignon asks.

"No telling," Parson says.

The others forget Mark as fast as they saw him, now trying to decide what they're going to order, but I keep watching him out of the window.

Why is Mark talking to Logan? Does Logan know he's the one who was dressed up like Grant at the game?

"Earth to Kate!" Reagan says, startling me. "What do you want to eat?"

"Chocolate milk shake. And fries," I say, still staring at the Tahoe.

"Ooh! That sounds good. I want that too," Alexis adds.

A fistful of cash appears out of the driver's window and Mark takes it, quickly stuffing it in his pocket, then moves away to his car. I watch both vehicles until they pull away from the lot. I never get a good look inside Logan's car, but I know it's his.

Mark said someone bet him to dress up like Grant. Was it Logan?

Images of the person dressed up like dead Grant Perkins are all over social media.

Some posts say it was the funniest thing they had ever seen, while others called it disgusting and cruel.

The funny thing about this is Grant would have loved it.

He lived for a good prank. The nastier, the more people affected, the better.

The media has made him out to be a saint. He is now the poor boy whose life was cut short, gunned down by a friend.

Would they change their tune if they knew what he was really like?

It was easy to find someone to dress up like Grant. Hell, that guy was busting a nut to pull a stunt like that.

The others are pissed.

They want revenge.

I go along with them, but they don't understand. What happened tonight needed to happen.

We needed something to bind us together. We are all outraged over someone mocking Grant. Making him into a joke online. Making *us* into a joke.

We're moving back in the right direction. We are finding our way home.

The girl surprised me, though. I didn't expect that. Not at all. It won't hurt to keep an eye on her. The last thing we need is someone poking their nose in where it doesn't belong.

TRANSCRIPT OF THE OCTOBER 8 INTERVIEW AT ST. BARTHOLOMEW HIGH SCHOOL OF REBECCA MEYERS BY DETECTIVE PIERCE, WITH BODY LANGUAGE COMMENTARY BY KATE MARINO

DET. PIERCE: Rebecca, looks like from some posts on your Twitter account, you were at River Point last Saturday night. Is that right?

REBECCA: Yes, sir. I was there.

KATE: She looks really sad.

DET. PIERCE: Want to tell me what was going on out there that night?

KATE: She shrugs. Looks a little confused.

REBECCA: Just the same ol' party that happens almost every weekend there.

DET. PIERCE: We've had some reports that there were some fights, lots of drinking and drugs. Was that normal?

KATE: She's chewing on her bottom lip.

REBECCA: It was. Well, a year or so ago that wouldn't have been normal, but it's normal now. It didn't used to be like that out there. They didn't used to be like that.

DET. PIERCE: What did they used to be like?

KATE: She sighs and then smiles. She still looks a little sad, kind of wistful.

REBECCA: I've known them since elementary school. Except Shep, but he and I have been friends since freshman year. They always made me laugh even back when we were kids. I mean, they were a little wild but not in a bad way. They were fun.

DET. PIERCE: You're using the past tense, so I'm gathering something changed.

REBECCA: Things did change. Or really, Grant changed. He was still as wild as ever, but there seemed to be a mean side to him that wasn't there before. Some of the jokes he made or pranks he pulled weren't funny anymore . . . they were cruel. And he was always pushing things. Drinking too much. Partying too much. Driving too fast.

DET. PIERCE: What about the other boys? Did they change too?

REBECCA: I guess in a way. They tried to keep Grant in check most times, you know. Tried to slow him down. Sometimes it worked, sometimes it didn't. And then they were all partying more. The vibe around them was definitely different.

KATE: She's back to gnawing on her lip. I can tell she's really torn about telling the detective all of this. It's all over her face.

DET. PIERCE: When you said "mean side" earlier, what do you mean by that?

KATE: Her head dips back and she closes her eyes like she's trying to think of an example.

REBECCA: Well . . . like with my friend, Lindsey. They've been seeing each other on and off since sophomore year. One minute he's all into her, and another he acts like she doesn't exist. He was playing some shitty mind games with her . . . like seriously screwing with her head. And it changed her. She's not the same girl she used to be.

KATE: She squeezes her eyes shut, then runs her hands over her face.

REBECCA: I can't believe he's gone and I'm sitting here talking about him like this. And talking about Lindsey like this. God, what is *wrong* with me?

DET. PIERCE: You're helping us get a clear picture of what was going on with him, and hopefully we can use that to find out what really happened that morning.

KATE: She nods, seems to take a deep breath. She sits up a bit straighter.

DET. PIERCE: So, back to the party. How late were you there?

REBECCA: We left close to midnight. My friend I was just telling you about, Lindsey . . . well, she and Grant got into a huge fight. I'm not even sure what it was about this time, but she wanted to leave, so I took her home. I didn't even care. I was so ready to leave by then.

DET. PIERCE: Do you know if Grant contacted Lindsey again? Either that night or the next morning before he died?

KATE: She shrugs.

REBECCA: I don't know. I know she's devastated he's gone. She's got so much to worry about right now. Her little sister is sick, really sick. She's been at St. Jude's, but she's home right now. Probably not for long, though. I think she goes back in a few weeks for another round of chemo. I'm really worried about Lindsey, but part of me is glad Grant can't screw around with her anymore.

12

SEPTEMBER 25, 5:12 P.M.

~~GRANT~~ SHEP: Apparently, it's not a good idea
to microwave food on a plate that has a metal
rim around the edge

KATE: oh no. how bad was it??

~~GRANT~~ SHEP: There was fire. Lots of fire.

The cross-country meet I was shooting ended a few minutes ago, and while I'm stowing all my gear in the back of Mom's car, I notice Logan stopped at a red light.

I'm not sure what makes me do it, but I jump in the car, and just as the light turns green, I'm on his tail. I'm telling myself it's okay, since Stone all but gave me the green light to spy on them, but I know there's more to it than that. I can't get past the fact that I was duped about Grant and Shep, and now I'm second-guessing everything I thought was true. Why were he and Mark talking in the parking lot last night?

I follow him for miles and it's clear he's heading back to Pat's. Is it time for another meet-up? But instead of stopping in the parking lot, he turns the corner and disappears behind the building.

I glance quickly at the cooking trailer, but thankfully it's close to noon and the line for fish is so long Pat doesn't notice me.

How can I drive back there without Logan seeing me? I circle back around and turn down the street on the other side. There is a break in the trees, and if I angle just right, I can see Logan's Tahoe.

If I thought the fronts of these abandoned stores looked bad, the back is even worse. The wooded area is littered with trash and debris and old furniture and God knows what else. From this distance, the only way I'll know what Logan is up to is through my zoom lens.

I start snapping even before he gets out. He wanders around the area, kicking things in his path, and I take pictures with every step he takes.

He stands in the middle of the garbage, staring at the ground, until something seems to startle him and he turns back toward his car.

I turn the lens so I can view a wider area, and flinch when I spot a couple of guys getting out of a white truck and approaching Logan. One of them is tall and dressed in jeans and a long-sleeved camo shirt. The other is about the same height as Logan. He looks preppy, dressed in a light blue button-down shirt with the sleeves rolled up.

Logan's posture changes immediately. His shoulders are back, and when I zoom in, I can almost see the muscles bulging in his neck. This doesn't seem like a friendly meeting. Logan seems to hand the preppy guy something, but I can't see what it is.

I take pictures of Logan, of the two guys, of everything. Why would he meet them out here unless he was up to no good?

Preppy Guy looks down, I guess checking out whatever Logan gave him. I hate this angle! I can't see anything. Preppy Guy finally turns and walks back to the truck. Tall Guy is still standing there with Logan. I stare at them through the lens, wondering what kind of standoff they're having. And then Tall Guy rears back and punches Logan so hard in the stomach that Logan falls to the ground.

"Oh my God," I say, out loud, then snap another picture.

I missed it. It happened so fast and then it was over. I have a shot of them standing there, and then I take one of Logan crouched over but not the hit.

With my finger poised over the button, I wait for anything else that may happen, but Tall Guy just stands there and watches Logan stagger back to his Tahoe.

Logan crawls into the driver's seat and peels out of the area, leaving the same way he came. Tall Guy is still standing there, watching. He turns around, scanning the area, then stops. He crouches down and cocks his head to the side. He's looking right at me through the gap in the trees.

"Shit!"

Throwing the car in reverse, I back out of the space. My hands are shaking as I turn back on the main road, and my eyes stay on the rearview mirror longer than they stay on the road ahead.

My phone rings and it scares me so bad I nearly swerve off the road. It's Reagan.

"Hello?"

"I thought you were meeting us for lunch at Sake Sushi. Are you coming?" Reagan asks.

My heart is still pounding in my chest. "Yeah. I'm coming. I'll be there in a few minutes."

I hang up and take several deep breaths, hoping to calm myself down. What will my images show? Not much. Logan standing around with a couple of guys, then Logan crouched on the ground. He could say he dropped his keys and was looking for them.

I really suck at spying.

. . .

When I finally get home, I decide to try cyberstalking instead of spying. It doesn't take long to find every one of the River Point Boys' social media accounts. Grant's accounts follow a ton of people, but he never actually posted anything; I had already looked him up when we first started texting.

When I thought I was texting Grant.

I guess Grant was more of a lurker. But the other boys seem more normal; they definitely don't post as much as the girls I follow, but there is at least something there to look at.

There are a lot of group shots of them on Henry's account. I study one of them from last summer. All five of them are sitting on the back bench of a ski boat. I look at them in this image and think about how different they are at school. There are the little things I've picked up on. Shep tries to come off like he doesn't care about anything, but I can see through his act. He watches everyone—me, his friends, other students, the teachers. His eyes take in everything around him.

And Shep is a doodler. There's always a pencil in his hand, and during class, it never stops scratching along the edge of his paper. I almost fell out of my seat one day in English trying to get a look at what he was drawing. Even at lunch, he twirls the pencil through his fingers as if it were an extension of his body.

Henry can flirt with a girl without even talking to her. It's the way he looks at her—just long enough to get her attention, but not so long that he comes off like a weirdo. With perfectly timed glances, he's got the girl falling for him, and he hasn't even opened his mouth.

Logan is the loud one in the group. His voice is loud. His laugh is loud. And somehow, even his mannerisms come off . . . loud. He's the kind of guy that can't sit still. When they are walking anywhere, he circles the group, always bouncing around from one person to the next, never walking in a straight line next to them. He must be exhausted by the end of the day.

Scrolling down, I see a picture of Logan, with several tall stacks of poker chips and a huge grin on his face. The gambler of the group. The bookie. Did he bet Mark to dress up as Grant?

John Michael is in the picture with him, with only three chips in front of him, but he's smiling just as big. John Michael is the hardest to read. He's laid-back, not just in personality but in posture, too. His straight brown hair is always messy and there's always one part of his button-down shirt that isn't tucked in. Out of all of them, he's the one most likely to speak to someone outside of their little group. He's in no hurry to get where he's going and comes across as bored in almost every situation I see him in. But then he'll lean over to one of the others—it's always just one, not all—and he says something that only the two of them can hear, and the other person laughs as if it's the funniest thing ever.

I switch to Shep's account. Scrolling through the posts, I study the images, read and reread the captions. In almost all the pictures, it's Shep with the other River Point Boys. The most recent ones show them hunting and fishing as well as partying. In one, Grant and Henry are passed out on some flowery-patterned, oversize papasan chair–looking thing. I can tell the shot was taken at River Point, because I can make out the back porch of the cabin behind them. Both boys are in nothing but their underwear, and the caption reads, *Lightweights*.

I can't help but laugh.

It's weird scrolling back and seeing them get younger. By the time I get to some pics from freshman year, they look like babies. I study one of the first images where all five of them are together. There are three muddy four-wheelers lined up, and the boys are piled on top. They're just as dirty as the machines, and the only clean body parts are their eyes and lips. And they are all smiling bigger than I've ever seen anyone smile. The caption reads, *Mud Nationals. Best day ever.*

It does look like they've had a good day. A dirty one, but good. I scroll down and accidentally "like" the image.

Oh crap.

I'm *four years* deep in his account and I "liked" his picture. Will he get an instant notification? Should I hit it again to "unlike" it?

Yes. I hit it again and the red heart goes away. Did I undo it in time? And then I see I have a new notification.

Shep Moore is following you

I could die. I suck at stalking more than at spying.
And then there's another notification.

One new private message from Shep Moore

Oh. God.
I click on the message.

If you're curious about me, I'll tell
you anything you want to know

I close out the app. Then power down my phone and bury my head in my pillow.

TRANSCRIPT OF THE OCTOBER 8 INTERVIEW AT ST. BARTHOLOMEW HIGH SCHOOL OF DANIEL HARDY BY DETECTIVE PIERCE, WITH BODY LANGUAGE COMMENTARY BY KATE MARINO

DET. PIERCE: Daniel, you were at the party at River Point the night before Grant Perkins died, is that right?

DANIEL: Yeah. That party was sick. I mean, all their parties are crazy, but that one was the best. Sucks there won't be any more out there now.

KATE: He's smiling. Bouncing in his seat.

DET. PIERCE: No, I can't imagine there are going to be any more parties out there now. Tell me about it.

DANIEL: Sure, what do you want to know? And hey, can you tell me which one of them shot Grant?

DET. PIERCE: No. You posted a video online of a fight with the caption "Shit just got real at River Point." We're going to view it together and I want you to tell me what was happening.

KATE: The detective moves a laptop next to Daniel so Daniel can see it, but it's also in view of the camera. Oh, I guess you can probably see that. Sorry. Well, anyway ... okay ... the video is starting. I'm going to tell you what's happening while they watch it, just in case you haven't seen it.

The video starts with Daniel panning the camera across the patio. People are standing around, lots of red cups. Then the camera moves to the left. There's a girl. Her hair is long, probably brown or black ... It's hard to tell in the dark.

DANIEL: Oh yeah. This girl came out of nowhere. I mean, literally from the damn woods. She was screaming at Grant.

DET. PIERCE: Do you know who the girl is? From your angle, it's hard to see her face.

DANIEL: Man, I don't know who she was. Like I said, she came out of nowhere.

DET. PIERCE: What was she saying? The audio isn't clear.

KATE: Daniel leans in close to the laptop and pops his knuckles. He's got a weird smile on his face. I think he's enjoying this. His enthusiasm is grossing me out. Okay, the girl in the video is making a beeline for Grant. He doesn't even see her coming. She jumps on his back and is pounding on him. They both fall to the ground.

DANIEL: I don't know what she was saying, I wasn't that close. Damn, you ever seen a chick riled up like that? It was hot. I mean, seriously hot. You see those leggings she was wearing? I wouldn't have minded having her all over me like that if I was Grant. Not at all.

KATE: Daniel is disgusting. Sorry, I know you don't want personal commentary, but he's disgusting.

DET. PIERCE: Why do you think the girl was upset with Grant?

KATE: Daniel shrugs. And then in the video, Henry is there. He pulls the girl off of Grant . . . pulls her off to the side, farther away from the camp. His hands frame her face. He's talking to her. Their heads are close. She leans forward until her forehead rests against his. His hands slide back into her hair while her hands come to his shoulders. Oh wait, now she's pushing him away and running back the way she came. She's gone. Henry watches her go, then turns back toward Grant.

DANIEL: I walked a little closer so, you know, I could hear what they were saying. Henry got right up in Grant's face. They argued for a few minutes, pushing each other.

KATE: The video ends.

DET. PIERCE: What were they arguing about?

DANIEL: Henry was yelling at Grant. Said something like, "You better hope you didn't do what I think you did."

DET. PIERCE: So what did Henry mean by that?

DANIEL: Man, I don't know.

DET. PIERCE: What happened next?

DANIEL: Henry went chasing after the hot girl and Grant went back to the party.

13

SEPTEMBER 23, 9:13 P.M.

~~GRANT~~ SHEP: Where are you applying
to college?

KATE: The New School

~~GRANT~~ SHEP: What new school

KATE: haha no, The New School

~~GRANT~~ SHEP: Where is that? Next to The
Old School? I think you're messing me.

By the time I get to the field, all of the cheerleaders are there, dressed and ready. I pull Julianna off to the side. "Y'all go through some of your regular stunts and routines and I'll just stand off to the side and snap some pics."

"Okay," she says, then turns to the other girls, giving them instructions.

It really is amazing to watch them in action. Girls are flying through the air and flipping around, and they make it look so easy. When I feel like I've got what I need, I signal Julianna again.

"I'm going to upload these now. Want to come to media arts with me and look at them?" I ask her.

"Oh yeah! I'd love to see them. I might get you to send a few of them to me, if that's okay," Julianna says.

"Of course."

The other girls walk off the field toward the locker rooms while Julianna and I turn in the opposite direction to head to media arts.

"I met a girl the other night at Rhino who goes to St. Bart's. Rebecca Meyers? Do you know her?"

Julianna smiles. "Yeah! We played soccer when we were younger."

I'm about to ask her if she knows Lindsey too, when we run into the River Point Boys, who are just leaving the cafeteria. Since all of them, except Shep, went to elementary and middle school with her at St. Bart's, they stop.

Henry moves in first, stopping just a few feet in front of her. "Man, it's good to see a friendly face around here." His eyes are on her, and I take a step back, trying to separate myself from the group.

"How are y'all holding up?" she asks.

Henry shrugs, and then Logan and John Michael move in a little closer. Shep keeps his distance, but his eyes move over everyone.

"We'll be back at St. Bart's soon enough," Logan says. "They'll look like idiots once this is all over."

Julianna pivots toward me and says, "Y'all, this is K—"

Before Julianna has a chance to introduce them to me, Henry interrupts her. "We know who she is."

"Oh, okay," Julianna says weakly.

Logan looks at my camera, then at me. "You might want to rethink who you're hanging out with, Ju."

Julianna is clearly confused by the hostility in their voices. Shep is the only one who isn't staring at me with daggers in his eyes.

Henry moves away, saying, "We'll catch up with you later. Wouldn't want to give *her* anything to report back."

I try not to cringe at his words. Shep looks like he's about to say or do something, but then he just turns around, following Logan and Henry at a distance.

But John Michael lingers. He leans close to Julianna and nods toward me. "She's playing for the other side is all, and we're in enough shit as it is." He winks at her before turning away. Julianna looks at me funny.

I give her a weak smile and a shrug. "I work for the prosecutor assigned to Grant's case. So I guess you can say they aren't my biggest fans."

Julianna gives me a slow nod, looking between me and the retreating River Point Boys. "I guess not. Don't let them bother you. They can be jerks."

When they're finally out of sight, I ask, "Do you think any of them will ever admit what really happened out there that morning?" I ask.

Julianna's forehead scrunches up. "No. I don't. They may be different now from when we were kids, but some things never change. I think they'll cover for each other forever."

We head to the media arts room and Julianna pulls a chair up next to my desk. We scroll through the images, picking the best ones, and then she bounces out of the room just before the bell rings.

I'm gathering my things so I can head to work when Miranda, one of the other photographers, pops in and moves to the giant dry-erase board that lists everyone's assignments.

She scribbles out: *Downtown, 5 p.m.—Key Club donation.*

"What's going on downtown?" I ask, as I balance my backpack on one shoulder and my camera bag on the other.

"Mrs. Deason just stopped me in the hall. There's a barbecue cook-off fund-raiser for St. Jude's. Friends and families of patients are putting it on. Ten bucks to sample the food with all the money going to the hospital. The Key Club is presenting some money they raised."

The second she says "St. Jude," I think about Rebecca and her interview, where she mentions Lindsey's sister is a patient there.

"You looking for someone to cover it?" I ask.

"You want it?" she asks.

"Sure, I'll already be down there, so it shouldn't be a problem."

Miranda marks my name by the assignment and we leave the room together. "Perfect. They're presenting the money right after the winners are announced," Miranda says. We part ways at the end of the hall, with her heading to fifth period, me to work.

. . .

I pull into the employee parking lot and it looks like the cookout will be happening on the front lawn of the courthouse. People are already getting ready for the event. There's a band setting up off to one side and rows and rows of grills lined up along the sidewalk.

The afternoon flies by, and before I know it, most of the people who work at the courthouse are filing out onto the lawn, chasing the smells that have been teasing us all day.

"I'm going to eat so much barbecue that you're going to have to roll me home," Reagan says. "Every time the main door opened, we got a whiff of whatever they're cooking. I don't think I've ever been this hungry in my life."

We pay our ten dollars, and one of the volunteers gives us wristbands. There are people everywhere. On the raised platform, there are several judges eating barbecue, including the district attorney. I smirk when I catch a glimpse of Gaines's face covered in sauce.

The group from my school is off to the side, holding one of those ridiculous oversize checks, made out to St. Jude's for five thousand dollars.

"You do your thing. I'll catch up with you later," Reagan says, then heads toward the food.

"Leave some for me," I call back. I stop in front of the Key Club group. "When do y'all present it?" I ask.

"Right after they announce the winner. They're about halfway through the judging process right now."

I motion for them to get together behind the check so I can take a couple pictures of them.

When I'm done, I wander off, checking out the scene. There are families spread out on blankets and kids running around everywhere. The air is rich with sweet and tangy aromas, and the smoke pouring out of the grills hovers just below the tree canopies.

Reagan is halfway down the line and has somehow talked herself behind one of the grills and is flipping barbecued chicken.

Even though I'm only here to take pics of the Key Club donation, I can't help but grab a few candids of scenes that catch my eye. I move around the edge of the crowd, taking in everything. There's a little boy toddling around, holding a turkey leg that looks bigger than his head, and a girl sitting next to a tree, crying, while she rubs a napkin over a stain on her dress. Through the lens, I sweep across the lawn and spot Henry and John Michael across the street. John Michael is still, his head resting against the old brick wall of an abandoned building, while Henry is pacing around in a small circle.

I fire off a few shots of them. John Michael says something to Henry that has Henry cracking a smile, but he doesn't stop pacing.

Moving to the nearest tree, I step behind it just enough to conceal most of my body. Henry stops pacing the second a girl comes out of the coffee shop next door. She's wearing a T-shirt with the coffee shop's logo, so I'm guessing she's just getting off work. She's looking at the ground, her long hair covering a portion of her face, so it's hard to see what she looks like. Henry calls out, startling her.

John Michael is still leaning against the building, but Henry takes a few steps until he's right in front of where she stopped, in the center of the sidewalk. She pushes her hair out of her face and I'm able to get an unobstructed shot of her. Henry inches even closer, his hands framing her face, then sliding back in her hair. She tips her head toward his.

Wait. I've seen this before.

The girl in the video the perv witness took. Henry handled her the same way. Wrapped his hands in the same long, dark hair while she leaned into him.

I didn't get a good look at her, but this is too familiar to ignore. It's got to be the same girl. But who is she?

They stand this way for a few seconds until the girl starts shaking her head. Henry's hands slip away, but he doesn't move.

They watch each other a moment, then the girl sprints across the street, toward the courthouse. Henry turns to John Michael, who has been waiting patiently off to the side, absorbed in his phone. John Michael shoos him off, and Henry follows after the girl. I lose sight of them once they mix with the crowd. When I turn back around, John Michael is still just standing there, hasn't moved an inch. Then an older-model car pulls up to the curb. John Michael doesn't hesitate. He pushes away from the building and gets in the backseat. The car pulls away and I take a quick pic of the license plate.

Weird.

I move away from the tree and walk down the sidewalk in front of the contestants, eager to get a taste of what they're cooking, but I almost lose my breath when I notice the posters hanging from each table, show-ing the child they are honoring while they cook.

"You want to try some brisket?" a man in a KISS THE COOK apron asks.

"Sure, thanks," I answer, and take the small sample plate. My gaze is drawn to the image of a bald-headed little girl on the booth's sign as I take a bite of the food.

He sees me looking. "That's Mazie, my granddaughter. She's at St. Jude's right now, so we're down here cooking for her."

Oh, wow. This is so sad. "Is she going to be okay?" I ask.

"We're hopeful," he says, with a small smile.

"Your brisket is delicious. I hope you win."

Moving down the line away from the judges' table, I stop at every station. Reagan serves me an extra-large helping when I get to the booth she's in.

"What are you doing?" I ask.

She shrugs. "They were shorthanded. I offered to help. I get all the chopped-beef sandwiches I want," she says with a huge smile.

I sample everything while I read each detail about the children represented here. My chest is tight by the time I get to the end of the line.

I stop at the next to last table, looking at the picture there.

"Want to try some ribs?"

My eyes pop up and I'm looking at Lindsey.

I've been so engrossed with the posters that I almost forgot I came here on the off chance I would see her.

"Sure. Thanks," I say, and take the sample plate she's offering.

"I met you the other night, didn't I?" she asks. I can tell by her expression that she knows exactly who I am.

I nod. "Yeah, at Rhino Coffee."

"You're the one who works for the guy who has Grant's case," she says. It's not a question.

"Yes, I am."

She glances back at the man working the grill, probably her dad, and then leans closer so no one else hears her. "You said y'all don't have much on his case. Is that still true?"

I was right. She knows something.

"I'm afraid that's still true." I wait a second before adding, "He called you that morning, didn't he?"

Her shoulders go back and she glances over her shoulder again. Then, in a quiet voice, she says, "I'm pretty sure I already answered that question. Some woman called me about this a few days ago."

I nod. "I just thought there might be more you could tell us. Right now, we have . . . so little to go on. Even if it was an accident, I think the one who did it should answer for it, don't you?"

Lindsey bites her bottom lip but doesn't say anything else.

Okay. I can see this is going nowhere. I hold my sample plate up and give her a small smile. "This smells wonderful. I'm sorry about your sister."

I turn away, prepared to stop at the last booth, when I see Henry instead. He's with the girl; they're sitting on a bench. His arm is around her, and her head is on his shoulder while he's saying something in her ear. The pose is so sweet that my fingers itch for my camera.

I turn to set my plate down to free my hands and I notice Lindsey is watching them, too. Her eyes narrow, and she's still chewing on her bottom lip. Then she spins around and heads to the back of her booth. I grab a quick shot of them and then study them through the lens.

Henry is really protective of this girl. And whatever happened to her has something to do with Grant, but what? How does she fit into this puzzle?

It's dangerous to be back here. We've all been instructed not to come back to River Point without supervision.

But I'm not going to find what I'm looking for if my parents won't let me out of their sight.

I wander around the property, around to the back patio and out into the woods.

How did Grant do it?

I walk back to the patio and take in every inch. All those nights spent out here and we never knew what he was really up to.

But how?

It's not the first time I've been here trying to figure it out, and it won't be the last.

Grant held his secrets close, but secrets can't stay hidden forever.

14

OCTOBER 1, 11:49 P.M.

KATE: Reagan is making me watch old
Halloween movies for inspiration for our
costumes and we watched Children of the Corn
and I'm pretty sure I'll never sleep again.

GRANT SHEP: Malachai!!

KATE: That's so wrong

I've been to Pat's every night for three nights in a row with no luck. I'm not sure why I keep coming back.

Tonight, I'm early. There's a chance they've moved their regular meeting time, and the only person who would know that is Pat.

Once I park my car behind the bushes, I make my way over to his cooking trailer. He's busy, just like he is every other time I've been here. He sees me coming and raises the hand that's holding a spatula in a wave.

I wave back and step up onto the back of the trailer.

"How's it cooking?" I ask.

He smiles and says, "Can't complain. You and your mama want some dinner?"

"It's just me tonight. She's working late and Mr. Stone had some food delivered."

He grabs a Styrofoam to-go box but I stop him. "If I'm not in the way, I'll eat here. Better than eating at home alone."

He nods. "I'm happy for the company." Pat loads up a paper plate with fish and fries and hands it to me. "There's some bottled water in the ice chest over there."

I grab the water and wedge myself in a corner of the trailer, hoping to stay out of his way.

Pat turns to the line of customers.

"Two large orders to go, please," a man says. Pat takes the money, then starts filling the order.

I watch him work as I drag a piece of fried fish through his special sauce. He glances at me, just as I take a bite, and says, "Why don't you tell me why you're really here?"

I swallow hard and choke slightly on my food. When I finally stop coughing, I say, "Am I that obvious?"

He gives me a look like, *Do you think I'm that stupid?*

I nod to the other side of the parking lot. "Checking to see if those boys are still meeting here."

Pat stops what he's doing and turns to face me. "You got no business being out here with the likes of them."

"Mr. Stone has the River Point case. He's okay with me watching them."

He cocks one eyebrow up. "Is your mama okay with that?"

I nod and hope to God he doesn't call my bluff. He watches me for a few seconds, then turns back to the fryer. "Are they still meeting out here?" I ask, completely ignoring what he just said.

Pat glances over to their usual place, then goes back to work. "Yeah, not as much though. That redhead must like it out here, 'cause he's been back a few times, but he's tending to a different sort of business."

I drop the rest of the uneaten fish on the plate. "What sort of business?"

Pat lets out a deep laugh and shakes his head. "Not the good kind."

Last time I saw any of them here, it was Logan and those two guys behind these buildings. I think back to his interview and the mention of gambling. "He's a bookie, right? Is that what he's doing out here?"

This surprises Pat, and he glances at me quickly before handing off the order to the man in line and taking another order from the woman behind him.

He's about to answer me, but his attention focuses on something else. "Well, it looks like you're in luck," he says in a dry voice.

I pivot around just as Logan's Tahoe pulls into the parking lot.

"I do need a to-go box," I say, grabbing one off the counter and dumping the rest of my food inside. "Thanks, Pat!" I say, then turn to leave, but his hand on my arm stops me.

"If that one is meeting with his other friends, not the rich ones, you need to stay right here."

His hand drops away and I stay where I am, practically vibrating with the need to leave. No matter who Logan meets with, I want a picture of it, but I left my camera in the car.

Pat goes back to work, but I know he's watching me. I'm anxious, waiting to see who will pull up next—the other River Point Boys or the two guys I saw Logan with last week.

When John Michael's BMW pulls in, I let out a sigh of relief.

"I'll be fine, Pat. Really, I promise," I say, then jump down from the trailer before he can stop me a second time. I wind my way around to where my car is hidden. Once inside, I pull my camera out of the bag and get ready.

I take a few pics of the two of them. Their vehicles are close enough that John Michael can hand Logan something across the short distance. It's a big Ziploc bag. I zoom in close and see an assortment of pills and rolled joints inside. Logan sees the contents and smiles.

Within a few more minutes, the other two boys arrive.

And it doesn't take long before there's trouble. Henry says something and Shep is on him. Shep hits Henry squarely on the face, knocking him to the ground. Logan pushes Shep, but John Michael pulls Logan off of him. And then Henry's up, but it's not long before they collide and fall to ground in a huge clump of bodies. I snap away, although I can't tell who is hitting who anymore.

I widen the angle and almost drop my camera when I see Pat running at them, spatula still in his hand.

Pat hits Henry on the back of the head with the spatula, then starts pulling the boys apart, yelling at them and pointing toward their cars. He stands over them, and the boys are right to look scared. Pat can be very intimidating when he wants to be.

One by one they skulk off to their vehicles. The boys pull out of the parking lot, Shep last in line, but just before he turns onto the street, he spots me.

Oh crap.

It's easy to see his every move since his Jeep is wide open. He hesitates for a second or so, seemingly looking back at Pat, but then drives away.

I drop my head back against the seat. Pat's in the lot, pointing for me to go, too. I nod, giving him a thumbs-up, and he walks out of view, back to his cooking trailer and the customers he abandoned.

I crank Mom's car. Or try to.

But nothing happens.

Oh God, no.

I try several more times before deciding I'm going to have to ask Pat for help. Now I feel really terrible. I can't see his trailer from here, but I can see the line of customers that is almost to the street.

A knock on the window has me jumping in my seat.

I scream as my hands fly to my chest.

Shep's there next to my car.

"You scared me to death!" I say loud enough for him to hear me with my window raised.

"Sorry," he says. "Sounds like your battery is dead."

I open the door and step out. I look behind my car and see his Jeep not far away. He pulled in the same way I do when I want to make sure Pat doesn't see me.

It's weird seeing him here, right in front of me, rather than watching him through my lens.

"Why did you come back?" I ask.

"I wanted to talk to you." He runs a hand through his hair. "Really, I wanted to find out what you're doing out here." He nods to my camera. "Taking pictures of us?"

I suddenly feel like the biggest creeper.

"I . . . was . . . uh . . ."

Shep shakes his head and moves in a tight circle, then stops abruptly. "Did you get what you wanted? Will your boss like the shot of me punching Henry?"

My mouth opens, but no words come out. I'm completely speechless. I can feel the blood rushing to my face.

Shep watches me a few more seconds, then turns back toward his

Jeep. I think he's leaving, until he pulls around and stops with his bumper just a few inches away from mine.

He pops his hood and then brushes past me to open my door so he can do the same for my car. Then he fishes out a set of jumper cables from the back of his Jeep. Once everything is hooked up, he sits in the driver's seat of my car. It takes a few minutes until he's able to get it cranked.

"Let it run a few minutes," he says when he gets out of my car.

"Thank you," I mumble. I feel awful.

He stops just inches from me and his hand wraps around mine. "It was real, wasn't it? What we had. We both felt it, didn't we?"

My breath shudders out of me. I stand there, concentrating on that single point where we are connected and think about how closely his thoughts echo my own.

"I thought so," I answer.

"The only thing that's different is my name," he says. His hand squeezes mine gently.

I swallow hard and find it difficult to look at him.

Then his hand drops mine. "But it's more than that for you, isn't it?"

I don't answer, just kick a few rocks on the ground between us.

"Do you think I shot Grant?"

Gnawing on my bottom lip, I finally look at him and say, "You said you didn't."

"That's not an answer," he says.

I push away from him and pace next to my car. "I don't know what to believe. All of you are saying you didn't do it, but one of you is lying." I stop, and he's watching me, his eyes glued to mine. "Do you think it was an accident?" I say.

His face changes instantly. He's pissed. "Of course it was an accident.

You think one of my friends killed Grant on purpose?" He takes a few quick strides closer and I instinctively shrink back. "Do you think I killed him on purpose?"

His face is hard and his shoulders tense. I don't want to believe that the boy I texted could do something like that. But I'm not sure who Shep is. I'm not sure of anything anymore.

Shep must see this struggle on my face, because his shoulders droop and he squeezes his eyes shut. He spins away from me, removes the jumper cables from both cars, and puts them back in his Jeep. He slams the hood of my car shut, then his. But instead of leaving, he moves closer to me again. This time I lock my knees and hold my ground.

"You can't trust me because you got played by Grant. And now all you want is justice for Grant . . . even if that means thinking the worst about me . . . that I would kill one of my best friends. Why?" He steps forward, closing the distance between us, and brings my hand to his chest, holding it there. I can feel his heart pounding against my palm. His head dips toward mine. "You didn't know Grant. He wasn't the one you talked to all night long for weeks. That was me. He wasn't the one waiting to see you that night. That was me."

He inches closer.

"He wasn't the one who texted you every night just before he went to sleep. That was me."

Another small step.

"He wasn't the one who texted you when he first woke up. That was me."

I feel shaky. And confused. "I know," I whisper.

"Do you?"

We're so close. I swallow hard and search his face, my eyes landing on his lips. My heart is beating as fast as his. I can't answer. I can barely think.

"I didn't shoot him," he whispers. "By accident or on purpose. I don't know who did. If I knew, I'd be first in line to tell your boss. We want the same thing, Kate. Me and you—we're on the same side."

He walks away quickly, hops in his Jeep, and is gone within seconds. I crumple against the side of my car, trying to process everything that just happened.

That was not the same Shep I've seen at school or in that police interview. That felt like the boy I talked to in those texts.

The boy I fell for.

The boy I would believe.

The girl with the camera is going to be a problem.

15

SEPTEMBER 29, 4:29 P.M.

KATE: We had lots of parents in today
complaining about the seniors at your school.
Apparently, all the cars in the juniors' parking lot
had all the air let out of their tires.

~~GRANT~~ SHEP: Uh, I have no comment.

KATE: Y'all are terrible

~~GRANT~~ SHEP: ☺

The next day at school, I feel the River Point Boys' eyes on me. I'm not surprised or unnerved by Shep's gaze, because he has sought me out in every crowd since he got here, but I'm on the other boys' radar even more than before and it's making me tense.

I knew walking into English that it would be the hardest class to get through. Something shifted between Shep and me last night, and I don't know what it is, or what to do about it.

I wait until the bell is about to ring before I slip into class. John Michael and Henry throw a glance my way, but Shep tracks me from the second I pass through the door. Henry's left cheek seems a little redder than the right one, and John Michael's bottom lip looks a bit puffy, but Shep escaped yesterday's brawl unmarked.

Just as Mr. Stevens is about to start his lecture, the fire alarm shrieks through the room and we all wince at the loud, shrill sound.

"Okay, class. Quickly, but orderly, let's make our way outside."

We've done this drill before, so there is no rush among the students to get outside. The hallways are packed, the entire student body moving in a single force toward the nearest exit, backpacks and purses bouncing between bodies like pinballs. We are all pressed together, so I hardly notice the hand that brushes against me. It's only when it lingers, there on the small of my back, that it catches my attention. It's got to be Shep's.

But then my heart drops when I spot him several people away, in front of me. He glances back at me, giving me a searching look before disappearing in the crowd.

I spin around quickly, colliding with everyone around me. Faces I know surround me; girls and guys I've been in school with for years all look at me with some confusion.

By the time I get outside to the front lawn of the school, I've convinced myself I imagined it.

It's cold outside, and general mumbles of annoyance ripple through the crowd until the piercing wail of the sirens drowns everyone out. Fire trucks don't usually show up for drills, so confusion replaces the irritation.

The principal meets the group of firemen and points them in a certain direction; they rush into the school. The crowd is quiet as truck after truck arrives. I try to find Reagan in the crowd, or Mignon or Alexis or really any of my friends, but I don't see them. They were all probably in the media arts room on the other side of campus when the alarm went off.

We all get restless as we wait. If there is a fire, will they just release us for the day? As it is, I only have one more class until I leave for work, and it's almost time for it to start.

I scan the crowd until I find Shep in a group with the other River Point Boys off to the side. Anyone watching them now wouldn't know anything was wrong. They stand almost shoulder to shoulder in a circle, heads bent in quiet conversation.

I shiver from the cold, or maybe from the memory of Shep's quiet words in the parking lot last night, and shove my hands into the pockets of my jacket.

My fingers slide against something there, wrap around it, my mind trying to identify what it is, to remember what I put there.

I pull it out and the ground tilts. I stumble into the girl next to me, who grabs my arm to steady me.

"Are you okay?" she asks.

I nod and turn away from her. I move through the crowd, away from the school, with the single purpose of finding somewhere to sit down, or collapse, or just freak the hell out.

Once I get to the edge of the crowd, I lean against a tree and slide down until I'm sitting on the ground. I pull my hand back out of my pocket and stare at the picture.

It's Shep and me, last night in the parking lot across from Pat's. We're standing just inches apart in front of our cars with my hand on his chest. The photo is grainy, like it was taken from far away with a shitty zoom lens, but there is no mistaking who is in the image.

But the worst part is what is written in red at the bottom:

Can we all hope for special
treatment from the DA's office?

I stand quickly, shoving the picture back in my pocket.

Shep wasn't the only one who spotted me last night. And he wasn't the only one who came back to check on what I was doing there. One of the other River Point Boys took this picture of us.

Shep glances my way and it must be obvious I'm freaked-out. He takes a step in my direction, but I shake my head, hard. He stops, worry all over his face.

We stare at each other across the distance, me trying to tell him to go back, get away from me, and him searching for what's got me panicked.

The announcement from the PA jars us both, drawing our attention back to the school.

"False alarm. Please make your way in an orderly fashion back to the class you were in before the alarm. You can gather your things, then proceed to your next class."

I can't go back to English. Not yet. Before Shep turns his attention back to me, I slip into the crowd, finding Mr. Stevens.

"I've already got my things. Can I go to the media arts room from here?"

He waves me off and I sprint away from Shep and the other River Point Boys.

TRANSCRIPT OF THE OCTOBER 8 INTERVIEW AT ST. BARTHOLOMEW HIGH SCHOOL OF PHOEBE CAGE BY DETECTIVE PIERCE, WITH BODY LANGUAGE COMMENTARY BY KATE MARINO

DET. PIERCE: Phoebe, were you at the party at River Point the night before Grant Perkins died?

PHOEBE: Maybe.

KATE: Her arms are crossed tightly over her chest and there is a scowl on her face. She really looks like she doesn't want to be here.

DET. PIERCE: Well, I've got about a dozen pics of you there that night. I called your parents, asked them if I could talk to you. They gave me their permission. Maybe I need to show them the pictures I found of you there, too. Do you think they'll like to see the image of you sitting on that boy's lap with his hands—

PHOEBE: Okay, okay. What do you want to know?

DET. PIERCE: I want to hear about any fights or anything strange going on. Did you witness the altercation between Henry and Grant?

KATE: She looks confused. Head tilts slightly, brow scrunches together.

PHOEBE: No, you mean between Logan and Grant and those other guys.

DET. PIERCE: What other guys?

PHOEBE: I don't know who they were. They showed up late. Really late. Most everyone else was gone. They pulled up in a white truck. There were two of them. They looked older, like they were in college or something. They asked where Logan and Grant were and we told them they were outside on the back porch.

DET. PIERCE: What happened next?

KATE: *She's chewing on her thumbnail. She doesn't want to talk. Doesn't want to tell him anything.*

DET. PIERCE: I will call your parents and let them know you aren't cooperating, Phoebe. Don't push me on this.

PHOEBE: Fine, we all went to the window. One guy pulled Logan up out of his chair, while the other guy got up in his face. He pulled a knife, held it against Logan's neck. Logan was terrified. My friend and I cracked the side door so we could hear what was going on. The guy with the knife was really pissed. He kept yelling, "Where's the money?"

DET. PIERCE: Why do you think they were there looking for money? From the pictures we found, you were a regular out there. Don't act like you don't know what was going on.

PHOEBE: Logan placed bets for anyone wanting to put some money on a game. Didn't matter if it was football, baseball, or water polo. My guess is that it had something to do with that.

DET. PIERCE: So Logan placed the bets through these guys?

KATE: *She shrugs.*

DET. PIERCE: What happened after those guys left?

KATE: *She's chewing on her bottom lip. Her hands are tapping nervously on the table.*

DET. PIERCE: Phoebe . . .

PHOEBE: Logan pulled Grant off to the side and they argued. Logan said, "You were supposed to deliver it two days ago! Where is it?"

DET. PIERCE: What was "it"? The money?

PHOEBE: I guess. Grant said it was gone. Then he walked away. Logan grabbed the whiskey off the table and the bottle was shaking when he took a drink. He was seriously freaked-out. I'm not sure I've ever seen him as scared as that.

16

NOVEMBER 7, 5:23 P.M.

PRIVATE NUMBER: It's me. I'd rather not say my name if you know what I mean. I need to see you. Very important.

SHEP: OK. Tell me when and where

PRIVATE NUMBER: My backyard. Midnight. Can you figure out where that is without me saying my address?

SHEP: Yes. I'll be there.

Just before midnight, I change quickly into some black yoga pants and a black sweater, hoping Shep is taking the same precautions about not being seen. I stopped at Walmart after work and bought one of those prepaid cell phones so I could text him without it showing up on my phone records.

Tiptoeing through the kitchen, I pause at the back door, listening for sounds of Mom. The soft hum of her snoring floats across the room and I turn the knob slowly, trying for stealth.

The old wooden ladder to the tree house is half-rotten, and each step has me terrified the entire thing will tumble to the ground. It's been years since I've been up here.

When I was four, the Hernandez family moved into the other side of our duplex and they had a daughter my age and a son a couple of years older. Their dad worked construction jobs and he built this tree house for us on the weekends. The three of us spent hours up here. They only lived here a couple of years before moving to Texas when Mr. Hernandez got a better job. I came up here a few times after they left, but it was never the same.

When I finally get inside, it's so much smaller than I remember. But it's just like we left it. There's the small table in one corner with a dust- and cobweb-covered tea set and a few wooden swords and shields scattered around the floor.

I can't believe Shep is coming over here. I can't believe I'm going to talk to him. To see him. I unfold the picture that was left in my pocket and put it down next to me.

All evening and into the night, I've been thinking which one of them left it for me and what it could possibly mean. One thing I'm certain about now: Shep is telling the truth about not knowing who shot Grant. There's no way this didn't come from whoever pulled the trigger.

It doesn't take long before I hear the creak of Shep coming up the steps. My heart is pounding and I scoot across the small space, wedging myself in one of the empty corners.

When Shep pops up through the hole in the floor, it feels like I've lost the ability to breathe. He climbs inside and the interior of the tree house shrinks even more. Once he's sitting on the floor, he has to duck his head slightly. We are close without even trying and it's like we're in our own little cocoon, just Shep and me.

"I thought you'd be up here when I didn't see you in the yard," he says.

I give him a small shrug. "I couldn't think of anywhere else we could meet."

He shifts around, hits his head on a branch that has grown through the side wall of the tree house, and lets out a low growl. "Clearly, this establishment was built with someone much smaller in mind," he says, one corner of his mouth lifting up in a smile.

I laugh quietly.

"Ah, so you find amusement in my pain," he says.

"I'm laughing because I haven't been up here in years. I always thought it was so big. When I was six, I thought I could live here once I grew up so I could still be close to my mom." I duck my head, embarrassed to share such a personal memory with him.

We both get quiet and just watch each other. Finally, I pick up the picture and hand it to him.

"What's this?" he asks, confusion all over his face.

"It was shoved into my coat pocket during the fire drill," I answer.

He studies the image and then looks at me. "This is why you looked freaked-out at school when we were waiting to go back inside."

I nod, and his attention goes back to the picture. His expression gets more intense the longer he stares at it. He moves toward the steps. "I've got to go," he says.

Grabbing his arm, I stop him. "Where are you going?"

"I'm going to talk to *Henry*," he grinds out.

"Henry?" I shake my head. "No. Let's think this through. If you go to him all mad and ready to fight, things will only get worse. And there's a chance it was John Michael or Logan."

"They can't do this—threaten you—and expect me not to do anything about it," he says.

"I agree. But hauling off and calling them out isn't the best way to go. You told me last night that we're on the same side. Is that true?"

He nods and scoots closer to me. "Yes."

"Then we find out who shot Grant. It's probably the same one who gave me this picture. That's the only way to end this."

"I'm not sure I can be around them and not say anything about this," Shep says, waving the picture back and forth.

"Did the other three know you were texting me before . . . Grant died?"

He shakes his head. "They knew I was into someone, but they didn't know who. I wouldn't tell them who you were."

Pulling back slightly, I can't help but feel hurt. Was he embarrassed about me?

Shep sees my reaction and says, "No, it's not like that. You don't understand how it was with them. Nothing was off-limits. If they knew I liked you and I was talking to you, they would have gotten involved with it somehow. Made a joke of it and tried to humiliate me. I didn't want that. I liked having you to myself. It's why Grant didn't know we were texting until I confronted him that night."

"Oh." It's all I can think to say, and I'm hoping it's too dark out here for him to see me blush.

I tuck a loose strand of hair behind my ear. "I've had most of the day to think about this. Maybe they're testing to see what's between us. If they didn't know we were texting before, maybe they think you're approaching me now because I'm on the case. Maybe they want to see what I'll do, see if I'll tell Mr. Stone or you about the photo. Or maybe they want to see what you will do if I do tell you. So what if nothing happens? Really, the picture was taken when you helped fix my car. We weren't doing anything wrong. I mean, my hand *is* on your chest, but I could say I was pushing you away." I can feel my cheeks get warm again.

He nods. "Okay, okay. So we ignore it."

"So why do you think it was Henry who left me that picture?"

He cocks his head to the side. "I've been pulling away and he's noticed. He's always asking where I've been or where I'm going. I feel like he's been watching me."

"You two always seem to be fighting," I say.

"Yeah. Well, he always manages to say something that pisses me off. We meet in that parking lot after we leave the lawyer's office. We keep our mouths closed when we're in front of everyone but let it all out once we're alone. Henry's been taking a lot of jabs at me lately. But hell, it could be John Michael. I wouldn't put anything past him. He's always disappearing and then turning back up but never says a word about where he's been."

I think about him jumping in that car the day of the St. Jude's barbecue. I logged onto Mr. Stone's computer and ran the plate. I wasn't surprised to see it belonged to a guy he'd prosecuted for distribution a few years ago.

"And then there's Logan. He's a hothead. I can see him reacting like this if he saw me with you. Plus, John Michael and Logan have side businesses that could get them in a ton of trouble, and Grant was screwing around with both of them."

"Yeah, I saw John Michael give Logan a huge bag of rolled joints and pills."

Shep lets out a sharp laugh. "They would be considered each other's best clients."

"I know who was in the Grant costume at the football game on Halloween."

He jerks his head toward me. "Who?"

"A guy who goes to Marshall. He said someone bet him to do it. And then I saw him later that night standing next to Logan's Tahoe."

He looks up at the ceiling of the tree house, disgust on his face. I can tell he's trying not to get angry.

"It looks like it's you and John Michael against Logan and Henry. Has it always been like that?"

His eyes are back on me. "No. That's a new thing. We're not all agreeing how we should handle this."

"What do you mean?"

He rubs his hands across his face. "They're okay never knowing who shot Grant. They don't say it, but they feel like he got what he deserved. Grant could really be an asshole. They just want all of this to go away. We're the only ones who seem to give a shit about finding out what happened that morning."

"Do you think Henry shot Grant, or do you think it was one of the others?"

He shrugs. "I don't know. I've been racking my brain since this happened, trying to remember anything about that morning that would help. And it's hard to look at my friends, to hang around them, and know one of them is being a coward and not owning up to the accident."

My head falls to the side. "So you're sure it was an accident."

Shep takes a deep breath. "I am. I really, really am. I know these guys. I can't see any of them killing Grant on purpose. I mean, I can't even wrap my head around it."

I think about the photo I took at River Point, how close Grant and his shooter were, and don't feel nearly as sure but don't push it. I feel bad for Shep, that he's stuck in this impossible situation.

He twists his fingers in mine and chills race up my arm. "So . . . you don't think it was me anymore?" he says softly. "Was it because of this picture?"

"No, I don't think it was you. I thought about what you said last night, and you're right. I didn't know Grant. But I do know you."

A small smile appears on his face.

"The picture didn't hurt," I add, and he lets out a soft laugh.

Maybe it's because his face is partially hidden in the shadows and we're tucked away from the world in this small space, but right now, I could say anything to him. "I wish we could have met that night, like we planned."

Pain slashes across his face and he closes his eyes, taking a deep breath before he says, "I wish we could have met that day, too." He opens his eyes slowly, pinning me with his stare. He moves just an inch or so closer, and the moonlight filtering in through one of the rough-cut windows bathes his face in light. "Don't get me wrong, I love them like brothers and we always had fun, but it was getting old hanging out at River Point every weekend. The drinking. The partying. And then the heavier stuff. I kept thinking that whole day . . . the day of the Battle of the Paddle . . . that once you got there, we would leave and go somewhere else. We would go eat or see a movie, anything other than stay at that party. Things were out of control that night, and all I wanted was to be with you."

His words wrap around me, easing some of the lingering doubt away. I don't have to ask if he was one of those into the heavier stuff. I've already read the toxicology report on all of them, and I know he and Logan were the only ones who tested positive for alcohol but negative for drugs.

And for the first time, I hate how much I know about his case. He has no idea I've studied his interrogation tapes or read the coroner's report.

I relax the grip around my knees, changing positions until I'm sitting cross-legged.

He's silent a moment; then, trying to lighten the mood, he says, "If I had it to do over again, I'd ask you out, right there in the library. I'd blow Grant off, ask you to dinner. That's what I wish I'd done."

"Oh," I say, and feel lame.

"When this is over, we're going on a real date. In public. We'll go to that fancy new restaurant where they make that dessert next to your table with all the fire. And then we'll go to a movie. Or to get ice cream. Or hell, just walk down the damn street holding hands."

I can't stop the smile. "I like it. That'll be our first date."

And then Shep and I talk. Not by text message but face-to-face. We talk about music and movies, family vacations and crazy relatives, and everything else in between, avoiding anything to do with the last couple of weeks. He has shifted around until he's lounged against the wall of the tree house, legs stretched out in front of him. I've moved closer too. I know the exact points along my body that are making contact with his. The toes of my right foot against his. My left knee against his outer thigh. My hand near his upper arm.

I yawn and he checks his watch for the first time.

"Damn, it's late." He's sitting up, likes he's getting ready to leave.

I glance quickly at my own watch. Two thirty in the morning. I had no idea we'd been out here this long.

I sit up straighter. My eyes have long since adjusted to the darkness, so it's easy to make out every detail of his face.

We watch each other for a long moment. And then he moves in closer and I meet him halfway. His lips press against mine, his hands are in my hair, my hands pull at his shoulders.

Every reason why I shouldn't be here with him melts away and all I can think about is kissing him. Without breaking contact, he lifts me up, moving me into his lap, my legs draped over his.

We kiss until my lips are swollen. When we finally pull apart, we're both breathing hard and I bury my head against his neck, embarrassed to face him. His hand runs up and down my back in a slow, rhythmic motion.

"Yeah, we should have done that weeks ago," he says, laughing quietly.

I nod, still hiding from him.

He pulls me back, hands cupping my face. "We're on the same team, right?"

"Yes, we're on the same team." I lean in and kiss him softly once more on the lips.

We're close, his forehead against mine, his arms around my back, my arms around his neck. "Can I see you tomorrow?" he asks.

"I don't know," I answer softly. "We need to be really careful. Seem to be a lot of eyes on us right now."

It's a while before he says anything else. "Yeah, you're probably right. I better go."

He kisses me once more; then I move off his lap, back into the corner I was in when he first climbed up here.

He slips through the hole in the floor, down the ladder, but stops just before he's completely out of sight.

"It's going to be hard to be near you at school and not talk to you," he says.

I can't stop the smile that breaks out across my face. "We'll figure something out."

With one last glance, he ducks out of the tree house. I wait until he's down the ladder, then out of the yard. When I finally head back inside, I'm startled to find Mom up.

She's standing at the sink, peering out the dark window that leads to the backyard. Oh, God, did she see us? Did she see Shep? My heart is thudding so loud I feel like it's echoing off the kitchen walls.

Mom gives me a small smile and I let out my breath.

"What's wrong? Are you okay?" I ask.

"Nothing, sweetie, just couldn't sleep." She nods to the back door I just came through. "Should I be worried about who you were out with or what you were doing at this time of the morning?"

Since it's almost always just been the two of us, we're more like a team than mother-daughter. I have very few rules, but then again, I've never really stepped out of line.

I shake my head, instantly guilty. "No. No reason to worry. I was hanging out with a friend who needed to talk." She would be so disappointed if she knew I just spent the last several hours talking to Shep, *kissing* Shep, and my happiness washes away.

"I trust you, Kate. Don't make me regret that," she says.

Hugging her quickly, I tell her good night, then head back to my room. Once I'm in bed, I can't sleep. This isn't the first time I've stayed up most of the night talking to him, but before, it was always by texts on the phone. And this was the first time that I knew exactly who I was talking to.

Shep.

Questions tumble one after another when I replay the conversation with Shep in my head. Why didn't we talk like that weeks ago? Why did we hide behind all those text messages?

I thought I knew him before, but now I realize we were just scratching the surface.

**TRANSCRIPT OF THE OCTOBER 8 INTERVIEW AT
ST. BARTHOLOMEW HIGH SCHOOL OF JENNA
RICHARDS BY DETECTIVE PIERCE, WITH BODY
LANGUAGE COMMENTARY BY KATE MARINO**

DET. PIERCE: Jenna, according to your post, you were at a party at River Point the night before Grant Perkins died, is that correct?

JENNA: Are you going to tell my parents?

KATE: She's very nervous. Fidgety. Keeps playing with the bracelets on her arm.

DET. PIERCE: We had to ask your parents' permission to speak with you today, so they already know you were there.

KATE: She flings herself back in the chair.

JENNA: That's just great. My dad's going to kill me when I get home. That's the one place I'm forbidden to go.

DET. PIERCE: Why was it forbidden?

KATE: She leans in close.

JENNA: Because it's wild out there. He knows it. Everyone knows it. If you want a guaranteed good time, you go to River Point.

DET. PIERCE: Tell me about that night. Were there a lot of people . . . ? Was anyone fighting . . . ? Were there any problems?

KATE: Jenna shrugs, tosses her hair around.

JENNA: The usual. Some fighting. Some girl puked in the bushes. Everyone was drunk.

KATE: She sits up quickly. Tucks her hair behind her ear.

JENNA: But not me. Or my friends.

DET. PIERCE: Of course you weren't. Who was fighting?

JENNA: I don't know. It was a crazy night. Just before we were leaving . . . We couldn't stay long because my dad is a total tyrant. I mean, who has a curfew of ten thirty on a weekend? It's so ridiculous. I mean, it's embarrassing. None of my friends were ready to go, but I drove, so . . .

KATE: Her hands are flying around and she's probably rolled her eyes ten times in the last minute and a half. Lots of drama with this one.

DET. PIERCE: Jenna, back to the party, please.

JENNA: Oh yeah. Anyway, just before we were leaving, Grant was standing on the counter in the kitchen. He had filled up a couple of water guns with vodka, and he lined some girls up—each a little farther away from the next—and was trying to squirt shots in their mouths. Then he started spraying everyone. And it was going all over the floor and the furniture. John Michael and Grant had been arguing earlier, but now John Michael was really pissed. He told Grant to stop and clean up the mess, but Grant said, "Don't forget, I've got the trump card." Anyway . . . John Michael stopped and just looked at him. It was weird.

DET. PIERCE: Why was it weird? I'd be mad if people were destroying my house.

KATE: She puts both hands on the table, looks directly at the detective.

JENNA: John Michael usually doesn't care about that kind of stuff. I mean, he's so totally cool with whatever is going on out there. Whatever you want—he has. Or he can get.

DET. PIERCE: You mean, like alcohol and drugs. That's the sort of stuff he can get if you need it?

KATE: Okay, Jenna's eyes get huge. She is legit freaking out right now.

JENNA: No! Never. I don't do drugs. I never said that. Please don't tell my dad any of this.

DET. PIERCE: What do you think Grant meant by "trump card"?

JENNA: Who knows?

KATE: She's checking her watch. Looking at the door.

JENNA: I think I should go back to class now. I have a test this period I shouldn't miss.

DET. PIERCE: One last question . . . What were John Michael and Grant arguing about earlier that night?

KATE: Jenna tosses her hair around again.

JENNA: I don't know. I swear, I don't know. Can I please go now?

17

SHEP: Can't sleep

PRIVATE NUMBER: Me either

The next week crawls by and I'm just going through the motions at school and at work. By looking at us, no one would guess that Shep and I even know each other. It stings when he doesn't search for me in the crowd, but it seems like the other three River Point Boys have lost some of their interest in me, too.

I've been watching the other boys closer than ever. I see what Shep means when he says Henry is watching him. He does. Shep can't walk across the room without Henry's eyes on him at every step. But I think it's a mistake to discount Logan or John Michael.

At least Shep and I are back to being able to communicate by phone. And then there's the notes he leaves me.

Three days after we met at the tree house, he sent me a text early in the morning telling me to check inside the last volume of the untouched encyclopedias on a shelf in the back of the library.

I raced over there the second I got on campus and pulled out a folded piece of paper in the shape of a triangle. There were words written on one side:

One of my favorite things

I smile now, just thinking about it. In the tree house, I had asked him to tell me something no one else knew. Something that would surprise me.

And he told me he loved to draw. He was embarrassed to talk about it when I started asking questions. But before he left that night, I asked him to draw something for me, draw one of his favorite things.

He drew a picture of me, lying on my side, one hand propped up under my head. My long hair is loose and falls over my shoulder. It was the exact position I was in that night in the tree house while we were talking—me lying on my side looking at him, and him lying on his side looking at me.

Somehow, he was able to capture every detail, like the small scar on my forehead from when I tripped over a rug when I was four and split my head open on the corner of the coffee table.

I left a picture for him that day, too. The close-up I'd taken of him at the football game last Friday night. With the stadium lights and the people behind him out of focus, Shep is framed by a blur of color and light. I wrote across the bottom of the image, *One of my favorite things.*

I bury the one he left for me this morning in the bottom of my bag, just as Reagan pops her head into the media arts room.

"Hey, what are you doing after work?" she asks. "Any plans?"

"You have that look. I get a little twitchy when you get that look," I say.

"I'm headed to Breathe Yoga for Power Hour. Want to come? And then we can go eat after. I think Josh may meet us, too."

"Josh is going to yoga?"

Reagan lets out a sharp laugh. "No. Dinner, but now I may have to talk him into trying yoga, too!"

"How's it going with him?" I ask as I pop open the back compartment of my main camera.

"I think he got the message on Halloween. We're going out this weekend."

She's giddy, and I'm just about to tell her I'm glad he finally got a clue but stop. I look down to where my fingers had been groping in the back of my camera. The memory card is missing.

I start digging around in my backpack, pulling out the contents and balancing them haphazardly on the desk.

"What's wrong?" Reagan asks.

I push away from my desk and head to the computers and check the card slots of each one. "I can't find my card."

"The one you use in your camera?" she asks.

"Yes."

I turn the room upside down but it's nowhere to be found.

"It's gone," I say as I sink into the closest chair.

Reagan looks over the same area I just did. "Are you sure you checked everywhere? What was on the card?"

My mind clicks through the recent images I've taken. "Some shots I took during the last pep rally, and the headshots for the class officers were on there, and . . ."

Oh God. The pictures I took the last time I saw the River Point Boys at Pat's.

"So the headshots will be a pain to redo, but I wouldn't worry about the pep rally ones. I think Alexis got some great video, and we can use some stills from that," Reagan says.

I nod but don't say anything else. Where was my bag? Could someone have taken the card out of my camera?

I mentally retrace my steps from the morning. I'd left my bag in the hall when I went outside to take the group shot of the class officers. That was the only time it was out of my sight.

"Kate!" Reagan says, and I jump. "Are you all right?"

"Yeah, sorry. Just trying to figure out where I lost it."

"Maybe it will show up. But right now, we need to go or we're going to be late for work."

. . .

I'm almost done with work when I feel the now-familiar buzz from the burner phone in my coat pocket.

SHEP: Hey

PRIVATE NUMBER: Hey! What's up?

SHEP: Need to talk to you but not here.

PRIVATE NUMBER: Ok

I'm expecting him to text back, so I'm surprised when he calls instead. I duck into the hall so there's no chance Stone can overhear me.

"I really need to see you. Any chance I can come back to the tree house tonight?" he asks when I answer.

"Okay. Midnight? Is everything okay?"

"No. But I can't talk about it right now. I'll see you tonight." And then he's gone. Something's wrong.

I kill time until midnight searching through all of the images I've taken—the ones at River Point, the ones of the boys, the ones from the barbecue of Henry and his mystery girl. My eyes are blurry and tired from searching every frame, praying for some little detail that would shed any light on the case, but it's like playing a rigged game of Where's Waldo. There's less than a week until the grand jury hearing, and we're running out of time.

When midnight finally approaches, I push my laptop aside. My hands are shaking as I shove pillows under my comforter in the vague shape of a sleeping body, then crawl out through my window. I don't want to run into Mom in the kitchen again.

When my head pops through the floor of the tree house, my heart drops at the sight of Shep inside. He's wearing a dark sweater and jeans, sitting in the corner of my childhood playhouse, looking devastatingly handsome with only the moonlight illuminating his face.

It only takes one second for me to see he looks just as tense as he sounded on the phone. "What happened?" I ask.

He hands me something instead of answering. It's two pictures— the first is a copy of the image I found in my coat pocket, minus the threat at the bottom, of Shep and me after he fixed my car. When I glance at the second one, I suck in a stunned breath. It's an image I recognize. Because I took it.

The picture shows that perfect frozen moment when Shep's fist connected with Henry's face, and was one of the shots on my memory card that turned up missing this morning. On the bottom of the image, written in the same handwriting as the message on the fire drill photo is:

Make her stop

"Oh, God," I say and look up at him. He looks tired. And worried.

Shep runs a hand across his face. "We had to go back to River Point. Our lawyers wanted us to walk them through what happened that morning. I didn't want to go, but I had no choice. We went back into the woods. Walked through our steps that morning. Ran to the spot where we found Grant. Then they showed us where the shooter was. It was so close. I didn't know it was so close. And I stood there and had to look at my friends and wonder which one of them did it and if it was really an accident. And I can tell they're looking at me and thinking the same thing. I left as soon as they let us. It wasn't until I was halfway home that I saw an envelope wedged between my seat and the center console."

"You don't know which one of them gave this to you?" I ask. He shakes his head. "No. And it would suck if this got out—me beating up on Henry. Me looking like the violent one. And then it would come out that you took these, and then there's this one of us together. How'd they get this picture?"

I lean against the side of the tree house and hug my legs in front of me. Guilt swamps me. What if something I've done makes things worse for Shep? "I noticed the memory card was missing out of one of my cameras this morning. My bag was out of my sight for a few minutes while I was taking pictures for the yearbook."

"What time was that?" he asks.

Staring off into space, I try to pinpoint exactly when that was. "We started during the break between first and second period and finished just a few minutes after the bell rang."

Shep says, "I don't have any classes with them then. It could have been any one of them."

"I should have cleared that card." I drop my forehead onto my knees. "That was stupid of me to leave them on it. I just never thought anyone else would see them."

Shep pulls me closer to him, hugging me close. "This is on him. Not you. We just need this to be over, because whoever is doing this isn't going to go away. He didn't get a reaction from the picture he left for you so he's making a point by sending one to me."

I look up at him. "Do you still think it was an accident?"

"I do," he says. "But I also know the evidence makes it look like it's not. Truthfully, I don't know what the hell to believe anymore."

I lean against him. "Tell me what happened. Show me why you think it could have been an accident."

His fingertips skim up and down my back. "We never really went to sleep that night. After Grant and I got in the fight, I started drinking. I hadn't had one until then, hoping you would be there any minute. I thought it would be pretty shitty to be drunk on our first date."

He pulls back and I turn to look up at him. "What?"

"Now that I think about it, that was a pretty dick move—asking you to meet me at a party for our first date. I'm surprised you said yes."

Laughing, I say, "If you remember, I was supposed to be taking pictures until late, so I'm the one who offered to meet you there."

He settles back on the wall of the tree house. "Whatever. I should have done better."

I nudge him in the side and he squirms around. "Just finish the story. If we can get through this, you'll have plenty of opportunities to make it up to me."

He squeezes his arm around me. "I will make it up to you."

"I know."

"So, like I was saying, I started drinking. A lot. I was pissed. Pissed at Grant. Pissed I was there. I wanted to leave, but I couldn't drive home. Grant was on everyone's shit list that night. He had it out with Logan and then with Henry. Hell, he even fought with John Michael."

"But all of you stayed that night anyway?"

"Yeah, John Michael didn't have a choice since it was his place, and I don't think the rest of us really wanted to be there anymore, but none of us was in any condition to go home. Usually, there were always other people staying the night there, not just us. People passed out in bedrooms and on couches, but Grant ran them off. He said it needed to be just us. Said we needed to make things right between us."

"Why would he say that?" I ask.

"Because our group was imploding. We were always fighting about something, and it was getting harder and harder to make things as easy as they had been."

Shep shifts around until we're facing each other again. "So when everyone else cleared out, we grabbed some beer and sat around the fire pit on the back porch. Grant loved hanging out on the back porch, always wanted to party out there. They passed a joint around, but I didn't take a hit. I was already drunk enough. And we just sat there, staring at the fire. For hours."

"Y'all didn't talk?"

"No, not really. Maybe someone would say something every now and then, but for the most part, we were just there."

Shep is quiet a moment, like he's been sucked back into that night. And for the hundredth time, I wonder how different that night could have been if things hadn't gone so wrong for us.

"And then the sun started to come up. Normally, you should be in the woods, ready to hunt long before there's any light. But we didn't care. It's like we all knew things between us were changing. We were all pulling in different directions and it was never going to be like it was before."

Shep paints the picture and it's like I'm there, watching them sit around a dwindling fire, the early-October-morning light filtering in through the trees.

He's quiet, lost in that memory. "What happened next?" I ask.

"We all got up, staggered inside. We each grabbed a gun and some ammo. There's a big board in the main room that has a map of the property. There are nails stuck in the different sections. Before you go out to hunt, you hang a marker on the spot you're going to so anybody coming in knows where the hunters are."

I remember seeing this and not knowing what it was.

"We all picked a spot. We hunted there so often that we each had our own silver metal tags with our names engraved on them—a gift from John Michael's dad last Christmas."

"So everyone knew where everyone else was going?"

"Yep. I can remember thinking when I dropped my name tag on the nail marking my spot that it would probably be the last time I would ever do that. And then we all went outside through the garage. We could have taken a four-wheeler or a truck, but without even saying anything, we all walked to where we were going. For me, I had no plans to shoot anything. I shouldn't even have had a gun on me. But somewhere deep down, I knew this was probably going to be my last time to hunt here, and I was looking forward to finding a tree to sit against so I could watch the sun come up. I wished I had brought my sketch pad and pencils instead of my shotgun. River Point is a beautiful place."

He runs his hands across his face before continuing. "I found my spot—a wide tree to lean against. Slid down the bark until I was sitting on the ground. It was quiet and a little cold. I remember seeing my breath puffing out in front of me. I was still a little drunk and very much in need of some sleep. My head fell back against the tree and my eyes closed. I was a moment from passing out when I heard the shot. It was so unexpected that it scared me. Made me jump. And just like that, my heart was racing and the adrenaline was pumping. I could tell the direction it came from, knew it had to have been Grant who shot something. So I started running that way. Before I got there, I saw everyone else, tearing in from every other direction. We all saw him at the same time."

He buries his face in his hands. I run my hand up and down his arm. "I didn't shoot him. I know it. I try to visualize that gun cabinet in the house. Who picked up the Remington? But I don't know. I can't see it. And then I think back to everyone running toward Grant. Running toward the sound of the shot. I saw all of them. We were all coming from somewhere else. That's why I think it was an accident."

I pull his hands away from his face and sit in his lap. "But whoever shot him was close. Really close. The shooter wouldn't have had to run to where he was—he would have already been there."

"I know. I've thought about that. What if he was scared? And he panicked? Made it look like he was running in from somewhere else. It could still be an accident."

He knows these boys better than I do, but I think friendship and loyalty are clouding his judgment.

Shep holds my hands in his. "But now that we're getting these pictures, I don't know. I don't know what to believe."

"So what are you going to do about this?" I say, pointing to the images.

"Nothing. Ignore it." And then he says, quietly, "I've been keeping my distance from them, but not anymore. It's time I started watching them as closely as they are watching me."

Scrolling through my phone, I stare at the images of us fighting.

We're falling apart.

We're turning on each other.

It wasn't supposed to be like this. Things were supposed to be better.

I swipe across the screen again and look at the image of Shep and the girl with the camera . . . Kate. What is he really doing with her? What's going on between them? Is he going back on the pact to keep quiet and stick together?

There is something there between them. Something none of us knew about. Secrets are what tore our group apart the first time. Shep has forgotten what's important.

Is he playing his own game, making sure he knows what's going down before we do? Did he tell her where to find us? Did he know she was taking those pictures? At just the right moment, all it would take is for him to "remember" seeing one of us with the rifle that morning.

Is he forgetting we could do the same to him?

Before, I wasn't sure if Shep knew about the picture I slipped in her pocket, but he's seen it now.

Shep is predictable. He won't ask who left those pictures for him, but he'll try to figure it out.

Grant was predictable, too.

Always hunting that same little spot. Always thinking he could do whatever he wanted without any consequences.

I swipe to another picture. One I look at every day. One I keep close to remind me: Grant forgot what was important, too.

18

NOVEMBER 17, 1:45 P.M.

SHEP: We're all nervous.

PRIVATE NUMBER: Have you found
out anything that could help?

SHEP: No. Things are getting weird.
They're all acting weird.

The afternoon before the grand jury, Mr. Stone seems defeated.

The last few weeks, he's been steadily plugging away at the case, but even the new evidence of the shooter being at a closer range than first thought doesn't prove this was anything other than a very unfortunate accident. And without the identity of the shooter, it is very unlikely a grand jury will bring charges against all four of them.

He said early on that if he didn't have the identity of the shooter, there was no way he was going to try to convince twelve random people to look past the absence of evidence and indict all four of them.

I can't stand the idea that the shooter might get away with this. That he could hide behind his privilege and his friends' silence. Grant might not have been who I thought he was, but he still deserves justice. Yet there is a small, selfish part of me that can't help feeling relieved knowing it could all be over soon. If there's no indictment, the shooter will get what he wants and there will be no more threats, no more hiding my relationship with Shep, no more lying to my mom or Reagan or Mr. Stone.

Because the truth is, knowing someone has been following me, taking photos and going through my stuff, really rattled me. I'm jumpy and exhausted. The only thing that keeps me going is Shep's drawings. Every day I go back to that spot in the library and find something new he left me.

I scan the office, making sure no one is around, and pull out the latest one. It's the tree house with a full moon shining down on it. And there I am, in the small cutout window. He drew me looking out into the yard, my long hair in a braid hanging out of the window. And at the bottom he wrote, *My favorite place.*

And I remember what I left for him. A photo of the table in the library where we first met with a message written in book titles on the spines of a stack of books I placed there:

Once We Were
Dreamless
Forever, Now
Awake and Dreaming
Every Day
Until We Meet Again

We're almost done for the day when my regular phone chirps, breaking me out of my thoughts. I slide on Reagan's name to open the message.

Heads up. You got a live one headed your way.

It's that girl we met at Rhino.

I've barely read the message when Lindsey walks into the office.

Mom's away from her desk on a smoke break, so I'm sitting in her chair.

She's nervous. "Hey," she says.

I stand up so quickly, Mom's chair hits the wall behind me. "Hey."

Lindsey shuffles from one foot to the next. "I came to talk to your boss."

Motioning for her to wait a moment, I stick my head into Mr. Stone's office to tell him he has a visitor, but he's leaned back, eyes closed, listening to something over his headphones.

I tap him on the shoulder and he cocks one hazy eye at me. Removing the headphones, he says, "What is it, Kate?"

"There's someone here to see you."

Lindsey didn't wait at Mom's desk; instead she followed me into Stone's office. I should head back out to Mom's desk and leave them alone, but I'm dying to know why she's here, so instead I step behind Mr. Stone's chair.

"Can I help you?" he asks.

She moves farther into the room, her eyes darting from Mr. Stone to me and back again. His eyes are directed right at her, but I know, for him, she's just an unfocused blob of color. More likely, he's got a clear view of the window next to his desk.

I lean down and whisper in Mr. Stone's ear, "It's Lindsey. The girl Grant called the morning he died."

He nods and raises his eyebrows at her.

"I, uh, I need to tell you something. I, ummm, I wasn't sure if I should come in. I don't want to get involved in . . . this, but I can't stand it anymore."

She's wringing her hands and looks on the verge of tears. I start to head back to Mom's desk, thinking she may do better without me there, but Stone catches my arm.

"Kate, why don't you stay? And Lindsey, please have a seat."

Lindsey drops down in the chair in front of Stone's desk and he motions me to take the one next to her. I give her a reassuring smile and she lets out a deep breath.

Mr. Stone leans forward, his voice low and gentle. "Start at the beginning. Tell me why you're here."

The words spill from her mouth like a waterfall. "I was with Grant Perkins the night before he died. I was at River Point. We got in a big fight and I left."

I can feel my heart beating in my ears.

"I was on the phone with him that morning. It was early. I was still pissed, so I was ugly to him. Picked another fight with him." Big tears well up in her eyes, making them an even brighter blue. "I shouldn't have done that."

So I wasn't the only one with regret that morning.

Mr. Stone hands her a tissue and she mops her face, smearing her makeup.

"Keep going," he encourages her.

"Then it got . . . disturbing."

She picks up her phone, flipping it over and over in a nervous rhythm. We all thought this was a dead end, but it seems like there's more to that conversation that morning. Is this why she looked so haunted whenever I saw her?

Mr. Stone leans forward, and says, "Tell me exactly what happened."

"We were talking, arguing, and he was saying, *'Baby, I'm sorry I was an ass last night. Let me make it up to you. You know I can make it up to you . . .'* That same old bullshit he says every time I get mad at him." She runs a finger under her eyes, wiping away the tears. "Then he said, *'What the hell do you think you're doing? You think you're going to point a gun at me and . . .'* and he stopped, midsentence, just like that. And then I heard it."

"Heard what?" Mr. Stone asks.

She takes a deep breath and says, "An explosion so loud it made me drop the phone. When I picked it back up, all I could hear was a scratchy silence."

I've hardly taken a breath since she started talking.

"Did the line go dead? Did you hear anything else?" Mr. Stone asks. He's excited, understandably so, but still trying to come across calm.

"I didn't know what to think at first. I thought maybe one of the other guys shot a deer and he hung up on me. The line went dead. I tried to call him back, but it went straight to voice mail. I should have called the police right then, but I just didn't think he was dead. How was I supposed to know he was dead?"

Bile creeps up the back of my throat and I'm nauseous. Lindsey covers her face with her hands and cries quietly.

Mr. Stone pulls out a small recorder and sets it next to her. "Please start again at the beginning," he says in a tight voice.

This changes everything.

I don't want to listen to it again. Before I can come up with an excuse to leave, she repeats the details from that morning. I get out of my chair and turn away, making myself look busy at his filing cabinet while I try to block out Lindsey's voice. It's no good. Her words seep into me and I know I will never forget a single word of her story.

This was not an accident. One of those boys shot Grant on purpose.

I'd suspected it, but hearing it confirmed is different. I feel numb, paralyzed.

Lindsey is crying loudly now, her makeup running down her face. I should go to her, comfort her in some way, but I can't move.

"For the record, can you tell me your full name?" Mr. Stone asks her.

"Li-Lindsey Wells," she stutters out.

"Lindsey, I want to thank you for bringing this to my attention. This was very brave." Stone turns his chair around and says, "Kate, go grab the list from your mother's desk that has Grant's phone records and contacts."

"Yes, sir."

My hands are shaking as I shuffle papers around on her desk.

I bring the list back to Stone. "This one right here," I say pointing to her number on the list. I see the nickname, Booty Call 3, and my stomach turns.

"Can you verify your number for me?" he asks.

She rambles off seven digits and I whisper to Mr. Stone that it matches.

"And one of your parents works for Simon, Banks, Wells, and Fuller since the phone is registered under that name?" Stone asks Lindsey.

"Yes, sir," she says. "And before you ask, my dad doesn't know I'm here. He is going to kill me when he finds out, but I can't keep this to myself anymore."

"How old are you?" Mr. Stone asks her.

"Eighteen. Why?" Lindsey answers.

"Just making sure we can talk to you without your parents present. If you don't want to tell them you've come forward with this, you don't have to, but they will find out eventually."

She nods and says, "I'll worry about that then."

"I believe my assistant called you about this a couple of weeks ago . . . asked you about your call from Grant that morning. But you told her that you fought and nothing more."

Her head hangs. "Yes, sir. I know. And I'm sorry."

"Can I ask why you're telling us this now? Was it the worry about how your dad would react?" Stone asks her.

Her voice cracks when she answers. "When I heard the news that Grant . . . died . . . and who could have possibly done it—I didn't know what to do. Those guys are my friends. John Michael, Shep, Logan, and Henry . . . we're all friends. And it sounds like it wasn't an accident. I just didn't know what to do. And then your assistant called. My parents were right next to me and I freaked out. I didn't know what to say. I mean, my parents are friends with all of their parents. But then I keep seeing them—Henry, Logan, Shep, and John Michael. Grant's gone, and they're just acting like nothing's changed."

I know she's thinking about that day in front of the courthouse, of Henry and that girl.

But her testimony changes everything. Stone finally has something really strong to go to the grand jury with tomorrow, and I'm not sure that it's going to matter that they don't know who the shooter is.

Lindsey rubs a hand across her face and pulls herself together. "I just kept thinking I needed to turn this over to y'all. I don't want to be the only one who knows what really happened that morning," she says.

She's here because of me. She's here because of what I said to her.

Mr. Stone smiles and says, "Lindsey, I'm going to have to call someone over to log your statement into evidence. We're going to have to keep your phone for a little while. Is that okay?"

She nods and then blows her nose loudly into the disintegrating tissue. I hand her a fresh one and she thanks me.

Mr. Stone throws me a glance over his shoulder and mumbles, "Call Detective Pierce. Ask him to come up."

I leave his office and move to Mom's desk, picking up her phone. After I make the call to Detective Pierce, I slump down in her chair. I shouldn't have deserted Lindsey and Mr. Stone, but I can't bring myself to go back in there.

One of those boys killed their friend in cold blood, and probably the same person is threatening me and Shep.

I don't move when Detective Pierce arrives; instead, I just gesture him to Mr. Stone's office. There's no way I can listen to her story again.

Mom comes back just as Detective Pierce is taking Lindsey's statement. Another copy of the statement is made and logged into the computer, and her phone is bagged and sent down to evidence to be processed in. Detective Pierce leaves while Mom walks Lindsey to her car. She is a mess.

Mr. Stone calls me into his office once they all leave.

"That was hard to hear," he says.

I nod, afraid what my voice will sound like if I try to talk.

"If he was on the phone with her when he was shot, then obviously he wasn't the one who deleted the calls from his phone log."

His words hang in the air. I lean against the door so I don't fall over.

"So whoever shot Grant knows there is a chance someone overheard the whole thing," I say.

He nods. "That seems like a real possibility. The best thing Lindsey has going for her is her contact name was Booty Call 3. Although if they were a known couple, it wouldn't be hard to figure out whom he was talking to. I've told her she needs to keep quiet about this. Detective Pierce is one of the few police in this town I totally trust. We're logging the evidence in under Jane Doe for now. So make sure this information does not leave this office."

I nod and bite down on my lip to stop it from trembling.

"Do you think she's safe?" I ask. "I mean, they wouldn't do anything to her, would they?"

"I don't know what they would do. I know if I go to Gaines with this information, the River Point dads will have every detail within the hour, and then so would the boys. Detective Pierce is going to assign an extra patrol around her neighborhood under the guise of responding to recent break-ins in the area. If it becomes necessary, we can make other arrangements for her."

"So this changes things for tomorrow," I say.

"Absolutely. When the grand jury hears Lindsey's testimony, there should be no problem getting the indictment once we show the shooting was deliberate, and with the other boys' silence, it's clear they are covering for whoever pulled the trigger. It should be a slam-dunk getting all four of them on the hook for this. And there should be no more threat to Lindsey. It wouldn't do any good to hurt her at that point, since her testimony will be well out there. And truthfully, I think once there is an indictment, the others won't waste a second turning on the shooter."

One loose thread is all it takes to unravel everything.

That phone was always going to be Grant's downfall.

It was his tool and his weapon.

That's why he didn't use real names. If someone looked at his phone, he wanted to make it hard for them to understand who he was talking to.

How could I have known he would have been on the phone so early in the morning? When his phone rang as we all stood around him in the woods that day, I knew it was whoever he had been on the phone with, calling him back.

I knew there was a chance that person heard something.

Erasing the calls was stupid, but I panicked. Instead of using those few seconds before the others arrived to alter his call log, I should have tried to figure out what number belonged to Booty Call 3, since that contact name meant nothing to me . . . and *she* probably meant nothing to Grant.

I've been watching and waiting to find out who was on the other end of that phone.

We're downtown, near the courthouse, leaving our lawyer's office when I notice a woman helping Lindsey into her car. Lindsey was at the top of my list, and seeing those red, crying eyes is all I need to convince me she's the one I'm looking for.

I glance at the others, but no one else has a clue about what's going on across the street.

One last thread to tie up.

19

NOVEMBER 17, 4:32 P.M.

SHEP: Just leaving our lawyer's office.
Are you done for the day?

PRIVATE NUMBER: Soon. We
need to talk later. Important.

SHEP: Should I be worried?

Because of Lindsey's testimony, Mr. Stone's entire line of questioning will change. Mom sends me home in the car, telling me she'll be late again, with a heavy sigh.

I feel bad for her. She's not used to these hours, and it's showing all over her face. I offered to get food, but she had already put in an order for delivery.

I need to talk to Shep. I've got to give him some sort of warning about what is going to happen tomorrow.

Suspects don't testify in a grand jury hearing—there isn't a defense attorney out there who wants his client on the stand with the potential of them saying something that could hurt them later—and they can't be in the room, so at least they won't be ambushed with this. Mr. Stone would kill me if he knew I was going to share what we found out today, but he doesn't know we've been getting threats.

Right now, the defense believes there is no way an indictment will come down, because there's little to no evidence. Even all of the talk about fights and bad behavior between the boys the police got from the witness statements would be considered unreliable, since those interviewed were all under the influence when they "witnessed" it.

But everything is different now.

I drop my bags on the floor in the kitchen and burrow down in my bed, still fully clothed, so I can text Shep.

Is it a good time to talk?

My phone rings immediately.

"Tell me something good. Tell me this will be over soon," he says on the other line before I even get a chance to say hello.

My heart breaks. This is so far from over.

I squeeze my eyes shut, forcing the tears to stay trapped inside. Once I tell him about Lindsey, everything will change, and selfishly, I want just a few more seconds before I shatter him.

"What's wrong?" he asks. When I don't say anything: "Kate?"

"A girl came into the office this afternoon," I say.

He's quiet on the other end, so I keep going. "I'm not supposed to tell you this. Oh God, you'll find out soon enough."

"What is it?"

"This girl . . . she was on the phone with Grant . . . when he was shot."

"What . . . what do you mean?"

"She said he started talking to someone else. Asked what the hell he was doing pointing a gun at him. And then . . . and then she heard the shot."

"No. No, no, no. That can't be right. It just can't . . ."

I take a slow breath and listen to him struggle to process this. He never wanted to consider this as an option. Never thought it was possible.

"It was an accident. It was an accident," he says over and over in a quiet voice.

I pull the covers tight around me and hold the phone close to my ear. "I'm so sorry, Shep."

"One of my friends killed Grant on purpose."

We stay on the phone, but neither of us speaks. There's not much else to say, since we both know once the grand jury hears from Lindsey, there's a very good chance all four boys will be taken away in handcuffs.

TRANSCRIPT OF THE OCTOBER 8 INTERVIEW AT ST. BARTHOLOMEW HIGH SCHOOL OF ROMAN BRADLEY BY DETECTIVE PIERCE, WITH BODY LANGUAGE COMMENTARY BY KATE MARINO

DET. PIERCE: Roman, were you at the party at River Point the night before Grant Perkins died?

KATE: He nods.

DET. PIERCE: From what I've heard from some of the other attendees, there was quite a lot going on that night. Grant seemed to be on the outs with most of his friends. I've heard about his fight with Logan, John Michael, and Henry. I know from Shep's own mouth that they got into a fight. Did you see it?

KATE: He nods again.

DET. PIERCE: Listen, man, you're going to have to talk to me. Tell me what happened.

ROMAN: Grant and I were watching the LSU-A&M game. Shep comes up and shoves his phone in Grant's face. Asked him why in the hell would he get some text.

DET. PIERCE: Did you read the text?

KATE: He shakes his head.

DET. PIERCE: Then what?

ROMAN: Grant starts howling laughing. Damn near pisses himself he's laughing so hard. Says something about Operation Fuck With Shep was a success.

DET. PIERCE: What does that mean?

KATE: He shrugs.

ROMAN: Something about a girl, and switching numbers or something. Then Grant tells Shep if he's having trouble prying those legs open, he's happy to step in and help.

DET. PIERCE: Then what?

ROMAN: Shep pulls him out of the chair then starts whaling on him. It took three of us to pull him off.

DET. PIERCE: Was that it?

KATE: He shrugs again.

ROMAN: Shep said if he went anywhere near her, he would bury him. Can't say I blame him, I'd have done the same thing, too, if he said that about my girl.

20

NOVEMBER 18, 7:51 A.M.

SHEP: We're not going to school today.
Our parents want us home in case
things don't go well.

PRIVATE NUMBER: I won't be at school
either. It's going to be a long day.

I don't normally get to miss school for work, but Mom made an exception today. Mr. Stone and I are in his office, making sure he has every piece of evidence he needs to show the grand jury.

Normally, only the prosecutor, the court reporter, and the grand jury are allowed in the room during this proceeding. Even the witnesses are only allowed in while they are testifying, and then they have to leave. The defense team is only allowed to be present if their client is.

But because our parish is small, we're short on court reporters, so usually someone who is employed by the DA's office sits in during the proceedings to work the recorder for the transcript. Lindsey is a total basket case this morning and Mr. Stone is afraid she'll chicken out and run off before he can get her in front of the grand jury, so today Mom is going to sit with her until we need her. That means the lucky person working the recorder is me.

I feel like I could vomit.

Once everything is boxed up, Mr. Stone motions for the deputy by the door to take everything down to the conference room. After watching so many legal shows, I always thought the grand jury would take place in the courtroom and it would be very formal and intense, but that's not how we do it here.

Basically, all twelve jurors will be sitting around the conference table in the large conference room we call the grand jury room. I'll be at one end, working the recorder; Mr. Stone will be at the other. Any witness who testifies will sit at the table with the jurors.

It's not nearly as dramatic as you would think.

Stone wanders around the room in a tight circle, mumbling to himself. I catch enough bits and pieces to know he's practicing his opening statement.

When he finally stops at his desk, he holds a piece of paper out to the side where he can focus on it. "Okay, here's our lineup: We'll show the tapes of each boy when they are asked about the gun. Then we'll bring in the detective who worked the case, then the coroner. We'll end with Lindsey. It's all we've got, so I hope it's going to be enough."

A knock on the door startles us both.

"Come in," Mr. Stone calls out.

Mr. Gaines, the DA, sticks his head inside. "All set, George?"

Mr. Stone nods and there is a brief, tense silence.

"Are we all good here this morning?" Mr. Gaines asks, not even sparing me a glance.

I try to blend in with furniture, the wall, or really anything. This is so awkward.

"I'm going to present what we have and leave it up to the grand jury," Mr. Stone says, then shrugs and extends his hands in a helpless sort of way.

A smile breaks out across Gaines's face. "Good. Good. It'll be best for everyone when this mess is behind us."

I'm sure it will mostly be best for Mr. Gaines when he gets the River Point dads off his back.

He bids us good luck, then leaves the office. Mr. Stone starts gathering his papers, shoving them in his bag, and I can tell he's pissed.

"Let's get moving, Kate. The jury is probably ready for us."

We go down a flight of stairs and turn toward the main hallway, smack-dab into a throng of people.

Being on the grand jury is different than being on a jury for a regular case. When you get picked for grand jury duty, you're on the list for six months, and you're called in to hear any case that pops up in that time period. Most times, the jurors don't even know what case they're hearing until they get here, but *everyone* knows what's going down here today.

"Wonderful," Mr. Stone says under his breath.

"Why are they all here?" I ask. "It's not like they can go in."

Mr. Stone shrugs and we keep moving.

On one side of the hall are Mr. Perkins, his lawyers, and his investigators, and on the other are the River Point dads and their lawyers. Shep and the other boys aren't here.

And in the middle of the hall, headed straight for us, are a few reporters from the local station with their camera crews.

We're blinded by the lights from the cameras the minute they're on us. Microphones are shoved in Mr. Stone's face and questions are flung at him from every angle.

"What are your chances of convincing the grand jury to indict?"

"Do you know which boy pulled the trigger?"

"Do you think you can convince the grand jury to indict all four boys?"

"We have no comment at this time," he answers. Then, with his hand on my arm, he forces our way through the crowd, into the conference room.

The room is long, with a massive table running down the center. The walls are paneled with a dark, shiny wood, and at the end of the room is a large window that overlooks the wooded area behind the courthouse.

The men and women of the jury are already seated at the table. They nod to me and smile as I make my way to the far end and sit down behind the recorder, pressing play.

I pull out my notebook and pen from my bag and jot down notes for Mr. Stone. He's basically instructed me to write down everything, no matter how insignificant.

Jurors: 7 men (3 black, 4 white), 5 women (2 black, 1 white, 2 Hispanic).

One of the women turns to me and says, "There's coffee and soft drinks on the cart over there if you get thirsty."

I smile and nod my thanks without making a sound, so I won't show up on the transcript.

Mr. Stone stands at the other end of the table. "Good morning, ladies and gentlemen. I appreciate your time today." On the table in front of him is the paperwork to be completed and signed by the jurors once they've made a decision.

I've heard his opening statement a number of times by now since he's been practicing it for days. He talks about Grant and how his life was cut short and all that wasted potential, blah, blah, blah. Of course he doesn't mention all the shitty things Grant did.

He also tells the jurors that he's asking them to come back with a true bill for either manslaughter or second-degree murder and explains the differences between those two charges. Personally, I don't think there's any way in hell he'll get second-degree murder, since he doesn't even know who the shooter is. He'll be lucky to get involuntary manslaughter.

Then he moves on to the morning of the shooting.

"These boys, who had been drinking and doing drugs all night, had no business going hunting that morning. But I'm going to show you that it was more than just a drunken accident."

This perks everyone up.

"I'm going to show you that it was unlikely the shooter thought Grant was a deer in the woods. I'm going to show you that Grant saw his killer, spoke to his killer, just before he died."

Mr. Stone wraps up his opening remarks, then rolls out a TV on a stand and pops in the disc with the boys' interrogations regarding the Remington. After all four segments play, the jurors are literally on the edge of their seats.

He moves to a side door, where he calls in Detective Pierce.

Detective Pierce sits at the opposite end of the table but turns his chair toward Mr. Stone, who is at his left side.

"Detective, please describe the scene you came upon on the morning of October fifth at River Point Hunting Club." Stone is passing right over the party the night before, since in those events Grant looks terrible and Stone wants Grant to have the jury's sympathy.

Detective Pierce paints the picture. Grant, dead on the ground, the gaping wound in his chest. The other four boys, some still under the influence, some crying, and the rest falling apart in other ways. He talks about which direction Grant had been facing when he was shot. The impact of the bullet that knocked him out of his boots. The fact that all five boys shot the gun during target practice, so all of their fingerprints were found on the gun and all tested positive for residue.

Stone pulls out some blown-up pictures of the crime scene, along with the shots I took with Officer Jones, thirty yards away.

"And was there a phone at the scene? Grant's phone?" Stone asks Detective Pierce.

He's setting up Lindsey's testimony. Planting that seed.

"Yes. His phone was on the ground beside him," Det. Pierce answers.

"Did you examine the phone? Determine whether there were any calls or texts placed or received that morning? Were there any fingerprints?"

"Yes. We checked. According to the log on his phone, there were no calls or texts made or received that morning. Only the victim's finger-prints were found on the phone."

Mr. Stone fumbles around with the papers in front of him and I know he's struggling to find the one he's looking for. Finally, he turns his head to the side, and within seconds, he locates what he needs.

"Detective Pierce, please read from this log from Grant's cell phone provider and tell me what you see on the morning of October fifth."

He hands the paper to Pierce and Pierce takes his time reading it.

"It says there was one outgoing call that morning around seven fifteen that lasted for six minutes. Then there were three more calls coming in from that same number at seven twenty-three, seven twenty-four, and seven thirty-two."

"Can you please tell me from what number those calls came?"

With each number Detective Pierce calls out, Mr. Stone writes it in marker on a piece of paper and holds it up to the jurors. Then he turns toward them and asks, "But you said there was no record of these calls on Grant's phone."

"That's correct."

"What would be the explanation for that?" Stone asks.

Detective Pierce shrugs. "Our assumption was that someone deleted the calls from his phone prior to our arrival."

"But I thought you said the victim's fingerprints were the only ones found on the phone?" Stone asks.

"It was cold out and all the boys were wearing gloves."

Gaines completely underestimated Mr. Stone. I completely underestimated Mr. Stone. Several of the jurors look shocked and I can't imagine what they're going to do when they hear from Lindsey.

Stone wraps it up with the detective and dismisses him with the reminder that his testimony today is confidential and cannot be repeated outside of this room.

Detective Pierce leaves through the doors we came in through, and he's immediately assaulted by cameras and reporters. He shuts the door quickly and the room gets quiet again.

The coroner is brought in next, and his testimony is so technical that several of the jurors begin to lose interest.

Mr. Stone tries to hammer home how close the shooter was to Grant, but it's dry and sort of washes over everyone.

Stone wraps it up quickly and moves on to Lindsey.

When Lindsey comes in through the side door, she looks worse than she did last night. Her eyes are swollen like she's been crying most of the night, and she's shaky. Lindsey sits in the chair and clasps her hands tightly together on the table.

Mr. Stone pulls up a chair from the side of the room and moves it closer to her.

"Lindsey, please describe to the jurors your relationship to Grant Perkins."

She gnaws on her bottom lip. "We were seeing each other. Dating a little bit. You know . . ."

Mr. Stone nods. "Can you verify your phone number for me?"

She rattles off seven digits, and the jurors watch Mr. Stone write them underneath the number Detective Pierce called out from the phone logs, matching them number for number.

"Okay, now tell me what happened the morning of October fifth."

Lindsey takes a deep breath and her bottom lip quivers. She's about to fall apart.

"Grant called me. We . . . we . . . we had gotten into a fight the night before. He called to ask me to forgive . . . to forgive him."

"And then what happened?" he asks, then passes her a tissue.

"Grant said, *'What the hell? What are you doing here? You think you're going to point a gun at me, Shep . . .'"*

My head pops up and the jurors glance at each other.

Did she just say Shep's name?

Mr. Stone looks startled too. For the first time this morning, he's speechless.

"Could you repeat that, Lindsey?"

She repeats the same words, including Shep's name. She just said that Grant called out Shep by name.

Oh my God. What is happening? She never mentioned Shep by name last night.

Mr. Stone recovers somewhat and continues his line of questioning, but I'm reeling. Why did she say his name? Is she making it up? She has to be making it up.

Why would she make this up?

Stone isn't going to push her on it, because this totally works for him. With her testimony, he's more likely than ever to get an indictment . . . against Shep.

I barely listen to the rest of what she says. My mind goes to Shep and last night on the phone. He was shocked by the news that Grant was on the phone and that someone heard the shot. I might have wondered if he was lying once, but too much has happened between us. I would have been able to tell if he was hiding this. But why would Lindsey lie like this? Why would she say this, knowing it all but guarantees Shep will be charged with Grant's murder? Not his death but his murder.

Stone finishes with Lindsey and the damage is done. I'll be surprised if it takes these jurors an hour to come back with a true bill and even more surprised if it's not for second-degree murder.

It was easy enough to mention to Dad what I saw in the courthouse parking lot. He told me to head home while he made a few calls to find out exactly what she was doing there.

I decided to follow her instead.

Dad called moments later with the news of "Jane Doe's" last-minute confession that was conveniently logged in at the same time Lindsey paid a visit. We decided to keep this bit of info to ourselves, but he was worried what this would mean for all of us tomorrow.

I wasn't willing to risk it.

It was easy to "bump" into Lindsey last night. When she pulled into the parking lot of that coffee shop—I knew it was my chance.

I waited on one of the benches outside, knowing she would have to pass me on the way to her car.

Just as she was exiting the store, coffee in hand, I held my phone to my ear and started talking.

"We have to tell them who did it! It's not right."

I know the second she heard me and my words registered. She was frozen just a few feet away. I kept talking as if I didn't know she was there.

"Grant deserves better than this!"

I acted like I ended my call and dropped my head in my hands. She stepped closer to me and I acted startled when I noticed her.

She stood rigid a few feet away, but her panic melted away after she saw my tears.

Lindsey sat down at the other end of the bench, leaving plenty of space between us.

"Are you okay?" she asked.

I held up my phone and said, "I guess you heard?"

She nodded but didn't say anything. I knew from her statement that she didn't know who Grant was talking to that morning.

That would tear our group apart—it wouldn't take long before we were all turning on each other.

I couldn't let that happen.

Lindsey and I have always been good friends. And when I asked her if she wanted to smoke with me, she was practically drooling.

We sat in her car, passing a joint back and forth, and talked about Grant. About how much we both missed him. About how unfair it was that he was gone.

I told her that I was scared, that I had seen who killed Grant but didn't think I could go to the police. That I couldn't convince my friends to go to the police.

Her eyes got big.

I told her I saw it happen. That I saw Grant on the phone talking to someone when the shot ripped through his chest.

She didn't say anything, but I could tell she wanted to. She was practically shaking in the seat next to me.

I took a long drag and decided how to handle this. I reached for the pills in my pocket but stopped myself before I offered them to her when she asked me. "Please tell me who killed him?"

Maybe I could make this problem work to my benefit.

So I told her. "Shep. Shep did it. And Grant saw him. His last words were, *'You think you're going to point a gun at me, Shep . . .'* And then Shep shot him."

I could see her absorb my words, matching them to hers. It doesn't take much to plant a seed, especially when the soil is so fertile.

A part of me hated turning on him like that, but I felt like he didn't leave me any other choice. He's digging deep, trying to find out what happened that morning.

Her brow furrowed in thought, and she took another long drag.

"Shep," she said slowly. "He said Shep's name."

"Yeah, that was the last word he said."

She nodded slowly, lost in her own memory.

I kept the pills in my pocket. They can wait a few days until after she testifies.

21

NOVEMBER 18, 11:22 A.M.

SHEP: How long will it take? The
wait is killing me

Mr. Stone and I leave the conference room out of the back door so the jurors can deliberate and head to the small waiting room.

"Where's Lindsey?" I ask Mom.

She holds up her hands. "She left. Tore right out the second she was done in there."

I turn on Mr. Stone. "Why did she add the part about Shep? She never mentioned him last night."

He sits down next to Mom. "I don't know. Maybe she remembered more from the call once she got home."

Pacing the small room, I try to get my panic under control.

"Do you believe she's telling the truth?" I ask.

Mr. Stone tilts his head and his forehead crinkles. "Why would she lie about something as serious as this?"

I want to scream, *Because there's no way Shep did this! There's no way Grant said his name on the phone that morning!*

Mr. Stone rests his head against the back of the chair and closes his eyes. He did a really good job out there making it seem like his vision is normal, but Mom and I know the toll it takes on him. Mom busies herself organizing the papers he brought with him, and I continue to pace the room.

We're prepared to sit here all day, waiting for the decision from the grand jury, but it doesn't take long at all.

The jury foreman sticks his head into the small waiting room. "We've made a decision," he says, then goes back to the conference room.

This is not good. It was too fast.

Mr. Stone and I follow the juror back into the conference room and I take my spot at the far end of the table, restarting the recorder.

Mr. Stone asks, "Mr. Foreman, has the jury reached a decision?"

The man stands and says, "Yes, we have. We return a true bill of accessory to commit murder on Henry Carlisle, Logan McCullar, and John Michael Forres. And we also return a true bill of second-degree murder on Shepherd Moore."

Each word is like a punch in my gut. Shep is getting charged with Grant's murder.

Mr. Stone rubs his hands together, clearly excited about this outcome. Once the verdict has been returned, I stop the recorder. Mr. Stone says, "Kate, please ask your mother to inform Mrs. Morrison we need to file an indictment with the court."

He's going to enter the true bill today. Now. He's got time to do this . . . It doesn't have to be done today, but I bet he thinks if Gaines has time to bury this somehow, he will.

I duck out of the room and relay the message to Mom. She clenches her hands and leaves the room through the side door.

Sliding into the chair Mom just vacated, I wait for her to return. It only takes a few minutes for her to pop back into the room. I follow her into the conference room, where Mr. Stone is waiting alone, since the jurors have been dismissed.

"Morrison said Judge Ballard is available in courtroom number three," she says, and Mr. Stone nods to her, then motions for us to follow him out of the grand jury room.

I'm not sure how my legs even work right now, but somehow, we're walking down the hall through the sea of cameras and reporters.

Questions are fired at Stone, but he ignores them. I'm not sure he's ever walked so tall, as we make our way down the hall to courtroom three. He feels justice has been served today.

Because this is not a closed hearing, everyone in the hall follows us in and takes a seat in the gallery, including the River Point dads and Mr. Perkins and his group, which I'm sure is exactly what Mr. Stone wanted. Once the public hears what the grand jury decided, there's nothing Gaines will be able to do about it. A bailiff alerts Judge Ballard to our presence, and within minutes, we're in open court.

"Your honor," Mr. Stone says from behind the prosecutor's table. "The grand jury has returned a true bill for accessory to commit murder on John Michael Forres, Henry Carlisle, and Logan McCullar, and for second-degree murder on Shepherd Moore." He hands the signed paperwork to the bailiff, who hands it to the judge.

The crowd behind us roars with angry shouts from the River Point parents and defense lawyers and loud sobs from Mrs. Perkins. Mr. Perkins stands, his arms crossed in front of him, and stares ahead. I sink down in my seat next to Mr. Stone, wishing I was anywhere but here.

The judge bangs the gavel until everyone quiets down.

The defense team has already taken up the table on their side of the room, ready to go into battle for their clients.

The judge turns to the defense and says, "I'll give you one hour to have your clients surrender. One hour or I send officers to arrest them."

One of the lawyers nods, then speaks quickly to another lawyer next to him, gives him instructions to go get the boys and bring them back here. The other lawyer sprints from the room.

"Your honor, the boys will be here within the hour," the lawyer says. "At this time, we request you set bail for my clients."

"For the accessory charges, bail is set at $200,000. For the second-degree murder charges, bail is set at $750,000."

There are gasps behind us. I know these families are wealthy, but I have no idea if they will be able to come up with that much.

The defense lawyer makes a note of the amount on his pad, and just like that . . . it's over.

The defense team and the River Point dads scurry out of the room, and Stone leaves with more pep in his step than I've ever seen. I can't get up from this chair. I stare at the empty courtroom for what feels like forever. A deep, unbearable sadness settles over me while my mind ticks through what this means. Shep is going to be arrested for murder. He's going on trial for murder. Second-degree murder means life in prison.

I pull my phone out and call Reagan, who should already be at work. She answers on the first ring.

"Kate, oh my God. It's crazy down here. Where are you? Morrison is freaking out. The River Point Boys will be surrendering in less than an hour. Gaines is about to lose his shit," she whispers in the phone.

"I need to get out of here," I say. "Can you take me home?"

"Where are you?"

"Still in the courtroom."

"I'm on my way," Reagan says; then the line goes dead.

She bursts into the room minutes later and settles in the chair next to me.

"Kate, what's wrong? I know something has been going on with you. What is it?"

She scoots closer and opens her arms. I fall into her hug, my head on her shoulder, and let the tears flow.

"It's so bad. So bad." My words come out mumbled and Reagan squeezes me tight.

"Shep didn't do this. I know he didn't. I've talked to him . . ."

Reagan looks around the empty courtroom. "Kate, watch what you say here. We'll talk about this later." She pulls me to my feet and adds, "And you know this is just the beginning. Once those defense lawyers get involved, you know that will change things."

I nod, but the part that I can't tell her is what's gnawing at me. Lindsey lied. I know she did. If Grant had said Shep's name on the phone, she would have told us that last night. And now that she's pointed the finger at him, the others will do the same. The charges filed against them will all but disappear if they turn on Shep.

"Can we go?"

I do not want to be here when the boys come in.

Reagan pulls her keys out of her pocket. "I can't leave. It's a madhouse right now and only going to get worse. But take my car. I'll catch a ride to your house as soon as I can get off. We'll eat pizza and ice cream and you can tell me what's going on with you and Shep."

I run my hand across my face. "Okay."

Reagan links her arm through mine. We make it to the end of the hall without running into anyone. But as we turn the corner to head outside, we're met with a wall of people.

There is twice the number of reporters that were here this morning, but they're not looking at us. They're zoned in on the group walking up the steps and headed inside.

All four boys walk shoulder to shoulder, dressed in suits and ties. They look amazing. Their heads are held high and, on the outside at least, they are fearless.

But I've spent hours scrutinizing these boys, watched them in their lowest moments, and it's easy to pick out the cracks in their façade.

John Michael's lower lip trembles slightly and I know he's a hairsbreadth from crying. Henry taps his fingers against his leg as he walks inside. I bet if he were sitting, that knee would bounce him across the room. And Logan . . . his face has gone pale, making his red hair seem redder.

But what completely crushes me is looking at Shep. He's on the edge of the group with distance between him and the others as if he is already somehow separate. On his own.

His eyes dart around, scanning faces in the crowd, but stop when he finds me. I see the release of his breath from here and then his eyes take in the details of my face. I'm sure he can tell I've been crying. He flattens his lips and gives me a small nod.

Cameras are in their faces and flashes pop from all directions. The boys walk with purpose into the courthouse, their parents and defense team close behind.

Reagan and I push ourselves against the wall so we stay out of the crowd. Shep gives me one last glance as he passes. I would give anything to be able to touch him right now. Squeeze his hand or kiss his face, something to let him know I'm with him. I support him.

Once the boys leave through the door that will take them to booking, the reporters quiet down. Just as we're about to try to ease out of the building, another group catches the reporters' attention.

Mr. Perkins and his group of investigators are coming from the other end of the hall.

They stop just inside the door, not far from us.

"I want a transcript of what happened in the grand jury hearing," Mr. Perkins says.

One of the investigators shakes his head. "I'm not sure I can pull that off."

Mr. Perkins jabs his finger in the man's chest. "Make it happen. The defense is going to use everything they have to pull this case apart, and we need to be ready for that."

I think about Lindsey and wonder how she'll hold up with both sides tearing into her story. Maybe her lie won't stand up to questioning.

"I've got to get back. Morrison is texting me. I'll see you later."

I nod numbly to Reagan but stay rooted in my spot as I watch Mr. Perkins and his men head toward DA Gaines's office.

Finding a spot off to the side, I drop down on a bench and wait. I thought I couldn't stay here and watch this, but now I know I can't leave until Shep does.

DET. PIERCE: Mrs. Flynn, you are the vice principal of St. Bartholomew High School, is that correct?

MRS. FLYNN: Yes. I've held this position for the last fifteen years.

KATE: Mrs. Flynn is sitting ramrod straight. She looks . . . stern.

DET. PIERCE: So how well would you say you know the boys associated with the River Point case, including the victim, Grant Perkins?

KATE: Her face cracks a bit.

MRS. FLYNN: Very well. St. Bart's isn't a big school and I know most every student here, especially by the time they make it to their senior year.

DET. PIERCE: I have to tell you, I've been surprised by the stories I've been hearing about what goes on over the weekends. You've got a wild bunch here.

KATE: Her eyes narrow. She's pissed. Didn't like hearing that.

MRS. FLYNN: I certainly hope you're not implying that St. Bartholomew students are anything less than exemplary individuals.

KATE: She didn't even crack a smile, which is sort of shocking.

DET. PIERCE: What I'm saying is, you've got one dead student and one of his classmates pulled the trigger, but we can't tell which one because they're either hiding what really happened or they were too drunk or stoned to remember. Most people at those parties are drunk or stoned. There's talk of sports betting and drug deals. And then there are the graphic pictures on the Internet of those three girls. And one of your parents came in to report cow manure in his daughter's air-conditioning system. And then there was the graffiti and the smoke bomb, and every person I talk to keeps coming back to this group of boys as possible culprits. So, Mrs. Flynn, when I say you've got a wild bunch here, that's putting it mildly.

KATE: *Her face is a shade of red I've never seen.*

MRS. FLYNN: If you have a specific question I can answer, Detective, please ask it.

DET. PIERCE: Tell me what you can about these boys: Grant Perkins, Henry Carlisle, Logan McCullar, Shep Moore, and John Michael Forres.

KATE: *She relaxes in her chair a bit but still looks really stern.*

MRS. FLYNN: They are good boys. I've known most of them since elementary school.

DET. PIERCE: From what I understand, they were inseparable.

MRS. FLYNN: *Inseparable* is a good word for it.

KATE: *She sits forward, resting her elbows on the desk. She raises her left eyebrow.*

DET. PIERCE: If you had to pick one who was quickest to get in a fight, who would it be?

KATE: *She leans back again, her eyes going to the ceiling like she's thinking about it.*

MRS. FLYNN: Logan was quick to use brute force, but the others were just a step behind him. If one had a problem, it became their entire group's problem.

DET. PIERCE: So was there ever a problem within the group?

MRS. FLYNN: Oh no. On the contrary. They never went against one another. But I bet everything has changed. They all loved Grant. I would guess that group is a ticking time bomb now that he's gone.

22

PRIVATE NUMBER: Oh Shep. I'm so sorry

I'm not the only one hanging around for a glimpse of the River Point Boys. The media is still here, as are Grant's parents.

Since I couldn't bring myself to go back to Stone's office, I've been hiding out in the small corner near the first-floor deli that sells sub sandwiches, snacks, and drinks. I've been texting Reagan throughout the afternoon, getting updates. They've been photographed, fingerprinted, and booked into jail while their parents work on getting them out on bail.

My phone dings and it's a text from Reagan.

REAGAN: Bail has been posted. Shep's parents put up some property as collateral, but the others just wrote checks. They should be out shortly.

KATE: Okay. Thanks.

It's only about thirty minutes more before Shep, Henry, John Michael, Logan, and their parents, flanked by lawyers, step out into the hall heading toward the parking lot. Reporters fire questions at them, but the lawyers hold their hands in front of the camera lens and repeat, "No comment," over and over.

I move closer, hoping Shep can see me here, when Mr. Perkins pushes off of the wall he'd been leaning against.

"You piece of shit!" he yells at the top of his lungs. Everyone stops—the River Point Boys, their parents, the media—and looks at Mr. Perkins.

He's pointing at Shep, and everyone, except his parents, take a small step away from him.

"You killed my boy!" Mr. Perkins yells, his face red with rage.

Shep's dad steps forward in front of his son, his hand out, and says, "Now, wait a minute . . ."

But Shep grabs his arm, stopping him. He moves in front of his dad and faces Mr. Perkins.

"I swear to you, I didn't shoot Grant," he says without breaking eye contact. Then he turns and looks at the other boys and adds, "He was my friend."

The other boys shuffle around and look everywhere but at Shep. It's quiet for about three seconds, then it's chaos again. The reporters' questions are louder, as are the lawyers' pleas for the boys to keep quiet.

The crowd starts moving again and I'm frantic to get Shep's attention. I want him to know I'm here for him when it seems like very few others are.

Keeping close to the wall, I pace the crowd. Just before they go through the doors taking them to the parking lot, Shep looks over his shoulder. And his eyes fall on me.

I give him a tight smile and he gives me a small nod. It's not much, but for now, it's enough.

Reagan comes up beside me. "You ready to get out of here?" she asks.

"More than ready."

The three of us stand in a circle, at a new spot . . . one we've never been to before.

"How did it get pinned on Shep?" one of us asks.

We were all shocked by the charges today, Shep more than anyone else. Even I was surprised they gave someone like Lindsey so much credit. She must have sold the shit out of her story.

Shep got hit hard . . . second-degree murder. There's a part of me that feels bad, but I'd rather it be him than me.

"I don't know, but we're screwed, too. I can't go to jail, man. I just can't. They think we've been covering for him, but I don't know shit! I've been telling y'all that for weeks!"

The other two are freaking out and I've got to calm them down before they do something stupid.

"Y'all need to relax. Let's find out what they have on Shep and see how bad it is. They must know something we don't," I say. "Second-degree means it wasn't an accident. Maybe Shep wasn't who we thought he was."

At this point, the other two will agree with anything to save their own asses.

"We all need to go home and keep our damn mouths shut. If we stick together, they can't touch us."

They nod and we all walk off to our vehicles. I think about Lindsey. I don't think she'll hold up long under questioning. And I'm screwed if she tells them what I said to her.

I check the glove box and see that the bag of pills is still where I left it.

23

Reagan and I are on the couch, an empty pizza box open in front of us. We're digging straight into the ice cream, no bowls needed.

"So you've been seeing him?" she says. I told her just enough to explain why I'm so upset, but I didn't tell her everything.

"A little. It's not what you think. It's not like we're dating. We're just trying to figure out what's going on. He wants justice for Grant as much as I do. Probably more." I don't tell her about the picture with the threat, because I know her. She'd go straight to them and threaten them right back.

"How do you know he's not using you for information? He got hit with second-degree murder today. That's not something they throw around lightly."

I dig another big scoop of ice cream out. "I know. I was in there. But it's wrong. They have it all wrong."

She's skeptical and I don't blame her. I'd feel the same way if things were reversed.

"I don't like it," she says. "And I don't want you hurt by this."

"Me either."

Reagan stays until she thinks I'm better. She's meeting Josh to study and it's hard not to be jealous that their relationship isn't bound by secrecy.

A few minutes after she leaves, I call Shep.

"Hey," he answers after the third ring.

"Hey," I say. "God, I've been so worried about you. Are you okay?" Of course he's not okay, but I don't know what else to say.

"No. What happened in there? Why is it all on me?"

I take a deep breath. I'm not supposed to tell him, but I know she's lying, and Shep needs to be prepared for what he's up against. It won't be long before the defense files a motion to get everything Stone has anyway. "Lindsey Wells was the girl who testified. She said it was you. Said she heard Grant say your name on the phone just before he was shot."

Shep's quiet for a long time. So long, I think he's not there anymore. "Shep?"

"I'm here," he whispers. "Why would she say that?"

The despair in his voice is like a punch in the stomach.

"I don't know."

I hear his mom in the background, and he gets off the phone quickly. I try to focus on my homework, my financial aid applications for college . . . anything to get my mind off of what happened today, but it's no use.

Even though it's risky, I need to see him. Need to make sure he's okay.

Shep's family lives on Old River Road, which is basically a long strip of old plantation homes on the bank of the Acadiana River. Since I can't park in the driveway, I pull into a small wooded area on the opposite side of the street from Shep's house.

The heavy clouds cover any moonlight that might light my way, so I trip and fall about every other step. By the time I get in the front of Shep's house, I've got dirt and leaves stuck to me in random places.

The yards are big on this street, so I'm a good distance from any neighbor. And no one is on the roads.

I work my way around to the backyard, keeping to the shadows. At least the big windows across the back of the house that look out onto the river make it easy for me to see inside. The house is dark and quiet.

Pulling out the burner phone from my back pocket, I send Shep a quick text:

I wanted to see you. I'm in your backyard.
Can you come outside?

It only takes a few seconds before a light turns on and the curtain is drawn back.

And then I see his face.

Even from here, I can tell it's bad. He's wrecked.

He pushes open the window and hangs halfway out.

I step out of the shadows and his face lights up when his eyes land on me.

Shep motions for me to come up, but I shake my head. He points to the side of the house, and I step through the yard and turn the corner.

On the other side of the house, there is a narrow staircase that leads to a balcony. Shep appears on the balcony and again motions for me to come up.

I take each stair slowly, hoping to avoid any creak or noise. I have no idea where his parents' room is, but obviously he feels like it's okay for me to be inside his house.

He meets me at the top of the stairs and I jump into his arms. Shep buries his head in my neck and we hold on to each other.

"You have no idea how bad I needed this," he says.

"Just as bad as I did."

He breaks away and pulls me across the balcony, toward an open door. Shep closes the door once we're inside, and the only light on in the room is a small lamp by his bed. His room is big, large enough that there is a seating area on the other side of it, with a couch and huge TV and gaming system. His bed sits closer to the windows; from up here, he probably has a gorgeous view of the river.

Shep hesitates a moment in the middle of the room—between the bed and the couch. I make the decision for him and pull him to the bed.

We stretch out, side by side, just like we have on the floor of the tree house, but this is a thousand times more comfortable. He rolls over and switches off the light, the room falling into darkness.

His hand reaches for mine and we lie there, in the dark, hands clasped together. My eyes haven't adjusted to the darkness yet, so I can't make out any details of him. I pull him closer. Our faces are just inches apart, but neither of us close the distance.

"I'm so sorry. I didn't know how to warn you. It all happened so fast." I'm crying and he finds my face in the dark and wipes away my tears.

"You did prepare me. Last night after you called, Dad and I had a long talk. The first honest talk we've had about this whole thing. I told him everything I knew. Something in my gut told me it was going to be bad today. You did warn me."

"Why do you think she named you?" I ask.

He pulls me even closer until we're touching from head to toe. "I think whoever sent us those pictures got to Lindsey somehow. And he's probably going to push the others to turn on me."

"So what are we going to do?" I ask.

"We?" he asks. "Not we, me. You're not getting mixed up in this more than you already are."

I take a deep breath and work up the nerve to tell him the last thing

I've been hiding from him. "I'm with you in this no matter what. It's my fault Stone went after y'all the way he did. The DA asked him to lose this case, but I convinced him to dig deep. To find out what really happened, because I thought you were Grant. I wanted justice for the guy I had fallen for. And I ran into Lindsey a few days ago. Told her if she knew something that would help Grant's case, that she should come in and tell Stone. I just wanted justice and for this to be over for you. But instead, you're the one in trouble."

His hands go to my face. "This is not your fault. There should be justice for Grant—no matter how big of an asshole he was, he didn't deserve to die. One of those guys shot Grant. On purpose. One of them is sending us threats and probably threatened Lindsey. This is on one or all of them—not you."

He kisses me quickly. Deeply. And I search for absolution, because no matter what he says, I feel guilty.

We lose ourselves in this moment, desperate to erase what happened today and to forget what will happen tomorrow.

His hands roam across my back, wrap around my sides, pull me in as close as he can. How many more moments like this will we get? Our legs tangle together and we press against one another. How many more midnights will we lie together, sharing our secrets, blocking out the rest of the world?

I pull back slightly and frame his face in my hands. Eyes adjusted, I can now make out the details of his face. The deep-set brown eyes, the strong cheekbones, the full bottom lip.

"We're a team, remember? We'll figure out a way to get through this," I say.

He nods but doesn't answer. Then we hear a noise downstairs that makes us both jump.

"I better go," I say.

It's hard leaving Shep, but I stayed longer than I should have.

I keep to the edge of the road on the way back to my car. Approaching headlights have me ducking behind an overgrown bush. I wait for the car to pass, but instead of speeding by, it slows down.

It's a truck I've never seen before, and the longer it idles there on the side of the road, the more my hands shake.

"Why are you hiding behind that tree?" a voice booms from the truck.

Crap. I'm totally busted. I peek my head around and find the passenger-side window is rolled down. It's dark inside the cab of the truck, so I can't make out who's inside.

"What are *you* doing here?" Before I have a chance to do or say anything, he's out of the truck and moving toward me. When he steps in front of the headlights, I can see it's Logan.

Oh God. Why is he in that truck and not his Tahoe?

I try to shrink back in the shrubbery.

"I asked why you're here. Snooping around? Spying on us? *Again?*"

I shake my head and try to find the voice that has totally deserted me.

"No, I . . . ummm . . . I was just driving around . . ." I've got nothing. No good excuse for being here at this time of the night, and by the expression on his face, he knows it, too.

Logan stops just inches from me. He's not as tall as Henry or Shep, but he's built like a linebacker. His hands are fisted by his sides as he glares at me.

"Why are you here?" he asks in a cold voice.

"I don't know. I was just driving around, thinking. Am I not allowed to do that?"

He pulls a phone out of his pocket and taps the screen.

"Hey," he says in the phone. "Come out here. I'm across the street in front of the Smiths' house. I found something you need to see."

And then he ends the call. I can't stay here. I'm not sure who he called, but I can't be here.

I try to move past him, but he holds an arm out, blocking me between him and the tree behind me.

"You're not going anywhere."

My heart beats so strongly, I'm sure he can hear it. "You can't keep me here," I say, hoping I don't sound as frightened as I am.

"Well, we can call the cops. Let them sort this out," he says with a smirk and a laugh.

"Call them. I'm not the one who just got bailed out of jail, though."

At this point, I'd rather answer to Mr. Stone than stay here with him one more minute. Using both hands, I push against his chest with everything in me. He's surprised for a moment, and I slip past him, but I don't get far before he catches up, pushing me against the bed of his truck.

"No, no, no," he says in a mocking voice.

I'm facing his truck and he's behind me, pressing me into the cold metal, his arms on either side of me. I can feel him against me and I'm terrified. He leans in closer.

All of those different self-defense moves rush through my brain. I should stomp on his foot or somehow kick him in the balls. I pull my arms in close, preparing for my attack, when suddenly, he's gone.

I scramble around, trying to determine where he went but find Shep instead.

Shep's here.

His back is to me and he's standing in between me and Logan, who is on the ground a few feet away.

"Are you okay?" Shep asks without turning around.

"Yes," I mumble quietly, wrapping my arms tightly across my chest. The adrenaline is leaving me, making me jittery.

Logan stands up slowly and moves toward Shep. "Man, I was headed home," he says, pointing down the street, "and I thought I was doing you a favor, letting you know she was spying on us, but seems like you already knew she was here. I guess there's more to all of this than you're telling us."

"Kate, you need to leave. Right now. Get in your car and go," Shep says to me.

Logan's eyes glance from me to Shep and back to me.

What's going to happen if I leave? Will they start fighting? "Are you—"

"Go. Now," Shep says, his voice urgent.

"Well, well, well . . . look's like my boy Shep's got it bad for the girl with the camera."

I edge away, my eyes never leaving the two of them. Logan blows me a kiss and Shep takes a step toward him.

Logan laughs and the sound knots my stomach. I turn to leave, but something stops me. I've never been put in a position like the one Logan put me in, and I hate him for scaring me. For making me doubt my ability to take care of myself. So I turn around slowly and stand next to Shep.

"Kate," Shep says under his breath.

Logan cocks an eyebrow at me, daring me to say something or do something, and before I can even think twice about it, I say, "Looks like that scar you got from 'shaving' is almost healed. Come near me again and I'll open it back up."

His hand flies to his neck, and if looks could kill, I'd be dead on the ground. I may have made this situation worse, but at least I stood up for myself.

I throw Shep a quick glance as I turn to leave, and I can't miss the pride in his eyes.

When I hit the pavement, I make a run for my car. Within seconds, it's cranked and I'm down the road, far away from Shep and Logan.

I grip the steering wheel to try to stop the shaking. I just threatened Logan. And showed him how much I know about this case. Whether or not he's the one who sent the picture, he knows there is something between me and Shep now for sure. If the others were going to turn on Shep—I've just given them a good reason.

I should have never come here tonight.

This could be over by the end of the week.

Some of us are feeling bad for Shep, but I remind them all of the evidence is pointing to him killing Grant. And when everyone hears Kate was with him tonight, it just proves how much he was keeping from us.

Life in prison.

I wonder how it will be at school tomorrow. The lawyers want us to go, keep up the façade. Look the part of the well-mannered sons of Belle Terre.

Will we be treated differently tomorrow than we were yesterday? Will the curious glances and whispers be replaced with outright stares and ugly remarks?

Whatever we get is nothing compared to what Shep will.

Right now, his mind has to be spinning. He has to be questioning why it all fell on him.

Or maybe he knows. Maybe he understands he lost the protection he had when he was our brother.

There are things he can say to hurt us.

But there are things I can do to remind him what can happen if he does.

Tomorrow . . . a whisper here, a rumor there. It doesn't take much for the tide to turn. And when it does, it will roll right over him.

24

NOVEMBER 19, 1:02 A.M.

PRIVATE NUMBER: I probably made things worse. I'm so sorry.

I look like a complete mess. I showered, dressed, and was out the door for school within thirty minutes of waking up. Mom brought home Mr. Stone's car last night, so thankfully, I have my own ride for today.

Reagan, Mignon, and Alexis are already there when I get to the media arts room, which proves how late I am this morning.

"Dang, Kate, are you okay?" Mignon asks. "You look like a truck ran you over."

"More like a bus . . . or a freight train," Alexis says with a laugh.

"Ha, ha, ha," I say in the most deadpan voice I can. "Had trouble sleeping last night."

Reagan arches an eyebrow at me. Thankfully, I'm spared from any further questioning when Miranda bursts into the room.

"The River Point Boys showed up for school today," she says in a rush. "They're in the office. Some parents already got word of it and are up here, complaining."

I knew they would be here. Their lawyers know this case is going to be played out in public just as much as it will be in the courtroom. Just like wearing the nice clothes every day makes them come across as well-dressed, respected members of the community, showing up for school today proves that they care about their education. Also that they aren't afraid or ashamed to be in public.

Mignon turns to me. "Kate, grab a camera and come with us. There's no way we're not doing a story on this."

I'm already reaching for it and heading to the door. I meant every word I said to Shep last night. We are going to figure out who really shot Grant, and to do that, I need to be the River Point Boys' shadow.

My friends are just steps behind me, but they have to almost run to keep up. There's a crowd in the main hall when we get there. I can spot all four boys through the window, just inside the office. Shep is a good three feet away from the other boys, and he looks as tired as I feel.

Reagan glances at him, then back at me. She's putting it together. I can see it on her face.

The principal is out in the hall, addressing the group of parents gathered there. I recognize one of the defense lawyers a few feet away. I pull my camera out and start firing shots.

Principal Winn holds his hands up. "Please, everyone, let's keep it down."

"If those boys are going to be here, then I'm pulling my daughter. There's no way I'm sending her to school with a bunch of killers," a woman at the back of the crowd says.

"I agree. At least send home that Moore boy. He's charged with murder!" a man yells out.

I can tell Shep heard what the man said, as anger flashes in his eyes.

The lawyer steps forward and everyone turns toward him. "My clients have only been charged with a crime, not convicted of one. In that grand jury, we weren't allowed to defend ourselves or show any evidence to contradict the prosecutor. Once we have our day in court, I am confident all four of these young men will be exonerated of all charges. Until then, they have every right to attend school and stay on track for graduation."

A loud murmur ripples through the crowd, and Principal Winn steps forward. "Look, this is a new experience for us." He gestures to the lawyer at his side. "Our policy is clear that any student convicted of a felony must be expelled, but as Mr. Baxter points out, they have not been convicted yet. I called the judge and he said until there's a conviction, they're allowed to attend school."

Shouts echo through the crowd, all expressing the same sentiment—they are not happy. Somehow, Principal Winn settles the group down and manages to get them out of the building. Once the hall is all but empty, Mr. Baxter pulls all four boys aside. Their heads bend toward him so they can hear his whispered words while Principal Winn waits patiently nearby. A few minutes later, Mr. Baxter turns toward Mr. Winn and says, "They're all yours now."

"If they so much as put one toe out of line, they're out of here. I don't care who their daddies are. You hear me?" Mr. Winn asks and jabs the air in front of him for emphasis.

"They are well aware that they will be watched more closely than any other student here, and they will be on their best behavior."

Mr. Winn storms back into his office. Mr. Baxter says his goodbyes and leaves while the River Point Boys shuffle off in the direction of the main hall. Shep is two steps behind, clearly not in the group anymore. He throws a glance over his shoulder at me, and my hands itch to touch him, to let him know he's not alone, but I can't.

And that kills me as much as anything else.

No English class today, so no chance of seeing him there. My group moves in the opposite direction, and I reluctantly follow.

For two hours, either walking down the hall or sitting in class, the only thing anyone can talk about is Shep.

"I heard Shep is gay and he was in love with Grant, but Grant was totally grossed out when Shep made the move on him so that's why Shep shot him."

"I heard Shep killed someone back in Texas and that's why his family moved here."

"I heard he does coke in the bathroom at lunch."

It will be a miracle if I don't go crazy before noon. Reagan and I meet up with Mignon and Alexis to head back to media arts, my and Reagan's last class of the day. Apparently Mignon and Alexis just got out of science, where Shep and John Michael were.

"I still can't believe they showed up today. I mean, if I was arrested for killing someone, there's no way I would show my face," Alexis says.

Mignon lets out a sharp laugh. "I'd be on the way to Mexico or Canada. Anywhere but here."

"Y'all. Just think about the media circus that this town will be when it goes to trial. We need some footage of Shep, here, before it gets crazy. If the national news picks up this story, we'll probably get credit. How awesome is that?"

They high-five each other and make plans to stalk him later this afternoon.

Reagan ducks her head and stays silent. Thankfully, she's not joining in.

A hollowness forms in my gut and grows every time they say his name. I want to scream at them to shut up, tell them that they don't know him or they wouldn't be talking about him like that, but I also know that if Shep hadn't told me the truth, I'd be thinking the same thing. I would be reveling in his downward spiral.

I feel sick.

Sick.

I drop down in front of the computer. Hopefully, drowning myself in work will make this last hour go by faster.

"Ugh," Alexis says. "That picture is circulating again." She's at the computer next to me, scrolling through social media. "Look at all these jerks reposting it."

I slide my chair next to hers and take a peek at her screen. It's that graphic one of Bree and the other two girls. There's something off about it. Something weird I can't put my finger on. All I can hope is that Bree doesn't see it making the rounds again.

Alexis closes the pic and I scoot back in front of my computer.

"That picture is awful," Mignon says. "It showed up on my feed too."

Reagan would know the most about this, since the complaints from the girls and their families came through Morrison's office. From across the room, she says, "It's a shame they can't figure out where it was taken. You can't see anything but the girls."

That's it. That's what's weird. "Pull it back up," I say.

"Ew. Why?" Mignon asks.

"I want to see something."

I shuffle my chair next to Alexis as she opens her feed again, pulling the image back up. I can feel Reagan and Mignon peeking over my shoulder, their curiosity piqued.

Mignon holds a hand over her eyes and is peering at the screen through slits in her fingers. "I'm never going to be able to unsee this."

We've all heard about this picture, and gotten a glimpse of it before, but I'm pretty sure this is the first time we've really studied it. There are three girls in it, all of them naked. And they are . . . posed with hands and body parts in very graphic positions.

"Are they asleep? They look out of it," Alexis says.

"I heard they were given that date-rape drug," Reagan says.

"The angle of the photo is weird. Like the camera must have been directly above them or something. And look right here. It's very pixelated. So the camera would've been either very low resolution or far away," I say.

I try to get past what's in the image and look at the image itself. It's cropped close, like there's probably more to the original shot. Whoever took it probably didn't want to show anything but the girls.

I pull back from the image, judging the angle.

"Where would you say the camera was in relation to the girls?" I ask. Since Alexis shoots a lot of video, she gets what I'm saying.

I can see the second she starts examining the image in a different way. Her head tilts and she stands up, her hands holding an imaginary camera as if she's thinking about where you would have had to be to have taken this. God, what if we can help figure out where this was taken? Or at least how it was taken.

"From above somehow—you're almost looking down on them," Alexis says as she sits back in her seat.

"That's what I think too. But almost more than what a normal height would be. Like, the camera would have been elevated, right?"

"I mean, they're on some sort of couch or chair or something. So if I'm standing on the ground and they're elevated off of the floor, then I can't be directly over them and get this angle, right?" I ask.

When Alexis zooms in, we can examine small, pixelated pieces of the image, much easier to stomach than the whole. We all lean in toward the screen.

But it's just bodies and not much else.

Reagan reaches past me and taps the screen. "Not sure what this is, but it's not part of her. That's a pattern, like something you would find on fabric."

It's next to one of the girls, right at the edge of the picture. It's a small, swirl-like design and it definitely would be more helpful if you could see what it was attached to, but this small section is all we have.

"Okay, I can't take looking at it anymore," Alexis says and closes the screen.

This is the stuff of nightmares. Now I know why these girls and their families are so traumatized by this. And Mignon is right—once you see something like this, you'll never unsee it.

"Okay, I think it's safe to say we're scarred for life now," Reagan says.

The screen is blank, but it's like the image is burned in my brain. Yes, I'll definitely be having nightmares over this one.

25

NOVEMBER 19, 12:24 P.M.

SHEP: I bailed. Can't stay in this school
another second.

I wait until Mom leaves for a smoke break before I approach Mr. Stone. I've thought about it for half the afternoon, and the sooner I can talk to him about Shep, the better. I'm still not willing to tell him I know Shep, have been seeing Shep, but I have to try to convince him that he's got the wrong guy.

I knock on his door and he swivels around in his chair, pulling the headphones off.

"Yes, Kate?"

"Ummm . . . can I talk to you a minute?" I ask.

"Of course," he says, and gestures for me to have a seat in the chair next to his desk. "What's on your mind?"

I pick at my thumbnail, tap my foot, do everything but actually face him. "You don't think it's weird that Lindsey said Shep's name in front of the grand jury yesterday but never mentioned that part to us the night before?"

His mouth turns down into a frown. "I believe once she really thought about that conversation, it's possible that more details surfaced. I'm just grateful she came forward, as should you be. From what I remember, it was as important to you as it was to me to make a case against one or all of these boys."

And now I'm drowning in the guilt because he's right. This is what I wanted. This is what I pushed for.

His head is turned to the side, so I know he's looking at me the only way he's able.

"I'm just not sure. I've been watching these boys at school and studying those interviews, and Shep was the last one I would have suspected of killing Grant."

He sits forward in his chair. "Were you leaning toward one of the others? You didn't mention that."

I don't want to throw a random name out and have another innocent person be accused of this crime. I mean, there's Logan and the guys in the woods, and Henry with his mystery girl. And I have pics of John Michael passing drugs out and getting in a car of a known drug dealer. But none of it is strong enough to go against what he has on Shep. While I'm gathering my thoughts, he says, "Is it maybe that you don't want it to be Shep? Maybe something about him appealed to you in the videos or at school. Maybe I shouldn't have asked so much of you."

I lean back in the chair and really consider what he said. Am I blind when it comes to Shep? No. I've never been so sure of anything in my life. Shep is innocent. I would bet my own life on it.

"It's not that. It's just a gut feeling I have. We're going off something one person said. And that's a pretty big part of the story she left out the night before. I mean, if there was something else pointing to him, that would be one thing, but there's just what Lindsey said. That's not a lot when you're talking about someone going to prison."

Stone leans back in his chair and crosses his arms across his chest. "I didn't ask that girl to come forward, nor did I put those words in her mouth. I'm bound to use any and every piece of evidence I have to win my case, and that's exactly what I'm going to do. And I'm not going to refute a piece of evidence just because you don't like it. Gaines is furious with me. To waffle now would all but push me out of the door, and I'm not quite ready to leave just yet. Mr. Moore has counsel and will get his day in court."

I can totally see where he's coming from, and if I were him, I'd be running with what we have too.

Left with nothing else to say, I nod and leave his office and settle into my space next to Mom's desk.

Mom scurries in a few minutes later, and from her expression, she doesn't have good news.

She goes straight to Stone's office and I follow her, dying to know what's got her ruffled.

"It's been leaked that Lindsey Wells pointed the finger at Shepherd Moore. I was walking back in from outside and a news reporter was on the front steps, filming a segment. She doesn't mention the girl by name but she reports everything else. How she was on the phone with Grant . . . how Grant said Shep's name . . ."

Mr. Stone's face gets bright red, and if this were a cartoon, smoke would be pouring out of his ears. He paces around the room.

"It wouldn't surprise me if Gaines himself handed over the transcript," he says, then storms from the office.

A few minutes later, I give Mom the excuse that I don't feel well and ask to leave. She's worried, checks my forehead for a fever before giving me her keys and letting me go. I must look terrible. The lack of sleep I've had in the last few weeks is leaving its mark.

. . .

Once I get home, I boot up my laptop, opening the folder where I copied every single picture and file on the River Point case.

Pictures of the woods . . . the trees . . . the back patio . . . the fire pit . . . the map inside with the tags . . . I scour every inch. I read reports on Grant, the crime scene, the coroner's report. Everything.

After a few hours, I feel like my eyes may start bleeding at any moment. I have been combing through the pictures, but there's . . . nothing. Nothing.

I slam the laptop closed and pull the covers up over my head.

What am I missing?

Just like I've done for weeks, I run through what I have on each boy that would make them want to kill Grant. It's not much.

I start with John Michael.

He's the hostess with the mostest. Parties at his place every weekend. Can get anything anyone wants—alcohol, drugs, whatever. Disappears for periods of time. Jumps in cars with drug dealers. He was mad at Grant that night . . . not his normal laid-back self.

But why?

Did Grant do something to him? Something bad enough that John Michael would shoot him over it?

Then I think about Henry.

And the girl. The one from the video. The one he saw downtown. He cares for her—it's obvious in the way he touches her, runs his hands through her hair. She was pissed at Grant. But why? Would Henry have wanted to get back at Grant for whatever it was?

And then there's Logan.

What am I missing on Logan?

He's a bookie. Did he bet Mark to dress up like Grant? And the money. The two guys in the white truck. I'm guessing the guys Phoebe saw at River Point are the same ones he met behind Pat's. They want the money. If Grant took it and Logan needed it back, how would he get it if Grant was dead? And why would Grant take it in the first place? He was rich. He had a nice car, a nice watch—even his class ring was made with a real sapphire instead of those imitation ones you usually get.

Then something starts itching around in my brain. What was it? Something with the watch. And the ring.

I bolt up out of bed and turn on my laptop once more. Grant's dad asked Mr. Stone about them when we were at River Point. He filled out a report that they were missing the next week.

I scroll through documents.

Finally, I find it. A claim was filed. Both items combined were worth over fifteen thousand dollars.

Would it have been enough to pay the bookies back? Would Logan have killed him over this? It's possible, if Logan was afraid for his life.

It's far-fetched, and the defense could tear it apart without trying, but it's something.

Something we didn't have five minutes ago.

$$\bullet \ \bullet \ \bullet$$

I call Shep on the way to school, since there's little chance I'll get to talk to him in person. I've thought about it all night, and I think there's a decent chance Logan shot Grant and that the watch and ring are the reason why.

"Hey," Shep says when he answers.

"Hey," I say. "I have a weird question. Did Grant always wear his watch and class ring?"

"His watch and ring?"

"They were expensive, right? Did he always wear them? Do you know if he had them on when y'all went hunting?"

"He usually wore them. He may have had them on. God, I don't remember. Why?"

"The watch and ring are missing. His parents filed a claim saying they believe they were on him when he died, but we have no record of it, and they weren't on him in the photos they took of him at the scene. He and Logan were fighting that night over money. Any chance Logan killed him and took his watch and ring to pay off what he owed to the bookies?"

Shep lets out a low whistle. "He'd have to pawn them or something—turn them to cash. He's smart. There's no way he would get caught with Grant's stuff. But yeah, I think it's a possibility. Logan isn't scared of many people, but he would do anything not to find himself on those guys' bad side."

"This is something. Every little bit matters."

"This is incredible. I'm going to tell Dad. He mentioned last night that we need to get our own lawyer. I'm going to ask Logan about it, too. See what his reaction is."

"Be careful."

"You be careful. This is really helpful, but I told you, I don't want you any more mixed up in this than you already are."

"I know. I won't be. Just going through what we already have."

We talk a few more minutes until I pull into the school parking lot.

"Okay, I'm here. I'll call you later," I say.

"You're already at school? I'm still in bed," he says with a quiet laugh.

"I like to get here early and have the media arts room to myself when it's quiet."

We get off of the phone, and the rest of the morning drags. Work is no better. I'm stuck back on the third floor with a huge pile of papers to be filed.

My burner phone vibrates and I see a text from Shep.

I called around to a few pawnshops. Told them I
was looking for a nice watch. The one on 2nd st
said they had a lot of them. It's a long shot but
I'm going by there this afternoon when I get out
of school

That's only a few blocks away from here. I could go there right now and see if it's there. While I don't think Logan would be stupid enough to pawn it locally, it's worth making sure.

Mom won't be looking for me until later, so she'll never know I left. I text Shep.

I'm going to check it out. Will let you know.

The pawnshop on Second Street is only three blocks away from the courthouse. I push through the door just as I get a text from Shep.

No. Don't go there. I don't want you to get
involved with this any more than you are.

Too late. I'm already inside. There are several glass cases showing off jewelry and watches, and I study each and every piece. I get to the last case and come up short. I knew it would be a long shot but one I had to try.

"Are you looking for anything in particular?" a man asks me.

"I was looking for a—" And then I stop cold. It's the preppy guy Logan met with in the wooded area behind Pat's. He's in a button-down shirt and khakis, just like before. I glance around the room, and I spot the tall guy who was with him before. The one who got a look at me before I drove away.

Preppy Guy tilts his head, waiting for me to finish my sentence, but I'm frozen. Tall Guy recognizes me, I can tell. I need to get out of here.

"Uh . . . a gift for my mom. Sorry, I need to go." And then I'm out the door, running the three blocks back to the courthouse.

I'm out of breath, so I lean against the side of the building until I'm ready to walk inside.

I text Shep.

> Watch was not there but those guys
> Logan met were. I'm back at work.

He texts back immediately.

> Oh shit. Don't go back there. I'll tell Dad.
> Please be careful. That was crazy for
> you to go over there.

I walk into Mom's office and she says, "Oh, good! I could use a break. Catch the phones for me."

She grabs her cigarettes and lighter out of her purse and heads down the hall to the elevator. I wait until I hear the ding before I go into Stone's office.

He nods and says hello when he sees me, and I drop down in the seat next to his desk.

I'm going to jump right in. "Do you remember when Grant's dad asked you about where his ring and watch were, since they couldn't find them at home and they weren't listed as being on him when he was shot?"

Stone tilts his head to the side. "Yes. At River Point."

"And then remember those pictures I showed you a couple of weeks ago, the ones of Logan with those other two guys?"

"The guys that you say assaulted Logan?"

"The tall guy, yes, he punched Logan in the stomach. We know from the interviews that two guys showed up at River Point looking for Logan because he owed them money."

"So we're making the assumption these are the same two men?"

"Yes. We know those guys are after Logan over money. And we know Logan was mad at Grant for not delivering it. And I don't know if Grant blew the money or what, but it's gone. So what if Logan shot him and then took his ring and watch to pay off the debt? But he'd have to pawn the stuff, right? So I popped inside a pawnshop not far from here, just on the off chance the watch and ring were there."

"Were they there? The watch and ring?"

"No, but I saw those guys. They were working there."

Stone leans back in his chair, his eyes going to the ceiling, and I know I've got his full attention. "We have testimony that puts Shep there with a gun at the exact moment of death."

"But . . ."

He sits up, holding his hand up. "But I think this is interesting. Something to think about."

He'll look into it. I let out a deep breath and get up to head back out to Mom's desk just as he says, "Good work, Kate."

The girl with the camera? Still a problem.

26

NOVEMBER 21, 6:51 A.M.

PRIVATE NUMBER: Are you coming to school today?

SHEP: Yes. But I'm coming as me, not one of the River Point Boys.

The second I turn the corner to the hall leading to the media arts room, I spot him. Shep is leaning against the wall and I can't help but sprint across the room.

Throwing my arms around him, I ask, "What are you doing in here?" We both scan the hall, but there's no one here. Classes don't start for at least a half hour.

"Seeing you before class starts. You said yesterday you love to get in here before everyone else, and I thought maybe we'd get a few minutes together."

One more quick glance up and down the hall and then I turn the knob and pull him inside. He backs me against the closed door and his lips find mine immediately. Without breaking contact, he lifts me up and carries me to the closest chair, sitting down with me in his lap.

"I can't believe you're here. I would have been here an hour ago if I'd known," I say between kisses.

"How early can you get here tomorrow? I may only have a few more days before the school board kicks me out. Someone started a petition to remove me. You know, because of the murderer thing."

I bury my head against his neck. "Don't say that. Don't talk like that."

He pulls me back, framing my face with his hands. "Sorry. Bad joke. I told Dad about the guys at the pawnshop. It's a good lead. I'm getting a new lawyer today—we're going to fill him in on everything this afternoon."

"Good. I mentioned it to Stone, too. He's looking into it. It's good he's still open to someone else being the shooter . . . not just you. So don't give up. It's not over yet."

"I won't. I'm not going down for something I didn't do."

And then I notice what's he's wearing. Gone are the button-down and dress pants, and in their place are a faded pair of jeans and a T-shirt that must be one of his favorites, given how worn in it is.

"What are you wearing?" I ask.

Shep looks down. "Umm . . . clothes," he says with a laugh. "I can always take them off if they offend you." His hand goes for the hem of his shirt and I burst out laughing as a blush stains my cheeks.

"No, I mean, why are you in regular clothes?"

He shrugs and throws me a smirk. "I've decided it's time to be myself, for better or worse."

"This is definitely better." I pull him back close. We kiss and talk and kiss a little more. Glancing at the clock, I give him a quick kiss and say, "You better go. This room will be packed soon."

Shep opens the door and peeks out before launching himself into the hall. I sit there with a ridiculous grin until people start filing through the door.

"You look happy this morning," Alexis says as she drops down in the chair next to me. "What's going on?"

I shrug and give her a confused look.

"Spill it," she says.

"What? I can't be in a good mood without something going on?"

She looks at me a few more seconds, then scoots her chair across the room. "I'm watching you."

. . .

I get started on the dreaded filing pile. Mom's out to lunch and Mr. Stone is listening to one of the recordings, so for now it's just me versus the pile of papers on Mom's desk. A knock on Mom's door startles me. It's a guy from the mailroom.

"I've got something for Mr. Stone that needs to be hand-delivered."

I show him into Stone's office. "There's a package for you," I say.

Stone takes the package and I go back to Mom's desk.

"Kate, I need your help," Mr. Stone hollers from his office.

"Yes, sir," I say, when I stop in front of his desk.

"Tell me what this is. It's hard for me to make out the details." He passes me the manila envelope that was just delivered to him, and there is a single item inside. I pull it out and it feels like the world falls out from around me.

It's a picture of Shep and me. It was taken from outside the media arts room this morning. I'm all but straddling him, and we're lip-locked.

The picture shakes in my hand as Stone waits patiently for me to describe what it shows.

"I can tell there are two people in it, and they seem to be in an embrace, but I can't make out who it is," he says.

I open my mouth, but no words come out. Do I tell him the truth or lie? Before I can even make a decision, Mom sticks her head inside his office.

"I'm back if you need me," she says; then her smile falls away when she sees the shock on my face. "What's wrong, Kate?"

She moves across the room and her eyes go to the picture. I can tell the instant she recognizes Shep and me.

Mr. Stone leans forward in his chair.

"I was just asking Kate to help me out. Apparently, there is something of great interest in the photograph that I'm missing. Please enlighten me."

Mom's expression changes to one of disappointment. "Kate, please tell Mr. Stone who is in this picture."

With my eyes never leaving hers, I answer, "It's me. And Shepherd Moore."

His gasp tears my gaze from Mom as I spin to face him. He's horrified. Snatching the picture from my hand, he tries hard to make out the details for himself.

"How could you do this? You are jeopardizing this entire case! I trusted you and you're kissing this . . . this . . . killer behind my back. Are you telling him what goes on in here? Does he know everything we have against him?"

Before I can answer, Mr. Stone turns on Mom. "Did you know about this?"

"She didn't know anything. It's all me. Just me," I say through the tears that are rolling down my face. Mr. Stone is looking at me with pure disgust and it's killing me.

"Why did someone send this to me? What do you think it means?"

I shake my head. "I don't know. Maybe it's Logan. Maybe he knows we're onto him about the watch and ring?"

"I sent someone over to that pawnshop with a copy of that picture you took of Logan and the two other men, and the owner has no idea who they were. Said he had never seen them before."

"He's lying! I saw them there yesterday."

"Get out!" he yells, making me jump. "Get your things and get out of here. You'll say anything to wreck this case and get your boyfriend out of trouble."

Mom is torn between standing up for me and not losing the job that keeps us afloat. I squeeze her hand to let her know I'm okay. There's no way I'm letting her get fired over me. I grab my bag on the way out and run down the stairs.

It's only once I'm almost to the parking lot that I realize I don't have the keys to Mom's car. I drop my bag and sit on the curb, my head buried in my hands.

No matter what I find to help out Shep now, there's no way Stone will ever listen to me.

Grabbing my phone out of my bag, I call Shep.

He answers on the first ring.

"Hey! What's wrong?"

I check my watch, forgetting he doesn't get out of school for another hour.

"God, I'm sorry. I should have waited until you were out of school. Hope I'm not getting you in trouble."

He's quiet on the other end for a few tense seconds. "No. It's fine. I'm not at school. My parents checked me out. We're about to go into a meeting with my new lawyer. We moved the appointment up. Henry, Logan, and John Michael were offered a deal. If they testify against me, the charges against them will be dropped."

The weight of his words settle over me, choking me. Suffocating me.

Hopefully, this is one of the last times we have to meet in private like this. By the end of the week, things could be back to the way they were.

"This feels wrong," one of us says.

By now, we all know about Lindsey and the phone call, but even though they think Shep killed Grant, no one really wants to see him go down for it. Though none of us would ever say it out loud, Grant got what he deserved.

"They're going to convict him. There's no sense in all of us going down," I say.

"What about the girl?" the other one asks. There are lots of things that we want to stay buried, and that girl is scratching a little too close to all of them. She works for that prosecutor, and now we're all going to be on her shit list.

"I don't think we need to worry about her anymore," I say. Kate's days in the DA's office should be finished once that prosecutor sees the picture I took of them this morning.

The other two nod in agreement with me.

One more nudge . . .

I look at the one on my left. "Did you shoot Grant?" I turn to my right. "Did you?"

They're both shaking their heads.

"I didn't either. That leaves Shep. If it's not him, it's one of us. And he's the one who's been hiding stuff from us. I don't know . . . it just feels like he's changed," I add.

There it is. They're with me. I can see it in their eyes.

"So we're taking the deal."

"Yes, we're taking it."

And as soon as the ink dries, I'll visit Lindsey.

No more loose threads.

27

REAGAN: Did I just hear you got fired??????

KATE: Damn, that news traveled fast.

REAGAN: KATE WHAT HAPPENED???

KATE: The River Point Boys.

That's what happened.

Before I have a chance to scream or cry or say anything at all to Shep, he's got to go. I want to fling my phone to the ground. Or to kick the car next me or tear something apart.

I'm furious.

Beyond furious.

And then I really think about what he said. The other boys are cutting a deal.

But Stone didn't make any mention of this. The deal would have had to come through him.

Gaines.

The DA is handling this for his "good ol' boy" friends. And I'm back to wanting to smash things.

"Kate," Mom says from just outside the courthouse doors, keys dangling from her fingers. I jog back up the steps to meet her. "I figured you needed a way home."

I hug her tight and she doesn't hesitate returning it.

"When I get home tonight, we will talk about this," she whispers in my ear.

And then she's gone.

I can't go to Shep, and I can't stay here, and I don't want to go home, so I head to the only place I've ever been able to really think.

The park.

There are a few small kids there with their moms, but for the most part, it's deserted. I sit on a secluded bench on the far side of the park and stretch out, my legs dangling over the edge and my eyes staring at the big blue sky overhead. It's cold enough that my breath makes those tiny little puffs of smoke when I exhale. I wrap my arms around my body and let my mind go.

I don't think about Logan. Or Henry. Or John Michael.

I don't think about losing my job or what this means for Mom.

I don't think about Shep or what it must be like for him sitting in that lawyer's office, listening to the details of his friends flipping on him.

I don't think at all.

I just breathe. In and out.

My eyes close and my mind goes to the pictures of River Point. I flick through them, shot after shot. I've seen them so many times, they're burned in my memory, and I can't get past the idea that I'm missing something.

I start at the beginning, just like I shot it—the walk into the woods, the trees, the leaves on the ground, the spot where Grant died, then shots in every direction. The image is clear in my mind, like I'm there.

What am I missing?

The walk back to the camp, the path leading to the back patio, the house, the windows, the board with the name tags still hanging to show the location of the hunters.

I stay like this until I've gone through the entire series of photos twice and I can't stand the cold anymore. My toes are numb. The tip of my nose feels funny. And I'm frustrated.

I'm just about to leave when my phone vibrates in my coat pocket. It's a text from Shep.

Just finished with the meeting. Hoping I
could see you if possible.

I text him back immediately.

I'm at the park. You know the one.

I sit cross-legged on the bench and wait for Shep, rubbing my hands together, trying to generate a little warmth.

It's not long before I see his tall form enter the park, looking for me. I wave him over and he walks toward me, head down and shoulders slumped.

I'm guessing the meeting didn't go well.

He drops down on the bench next to me and I don't waste a moment scooting close to him.

"You're freezing," he says, then takes my hands in his, trying to infuse his body heat into mine.

"I've been here a while just thinking. How did it go?" I ask.

He shakes his head and his face crumples. I feel like I've been hit in the gut.

"Gaines is going to have your guy offer them a deal tomorrow. It sounds like their dads told him their sons would be 'very cooperative' with enough incentive."

"Oh, Shep . . . I'm so sorry. What did your new lawyer say?"

"He's supposed to be one of the best—but he was clear that the evidence against me is 'very overwhelming.'"

His lawyer feels like he got a loser case. Just like Stone felt when he got the River Point case.

Shep hops up and starts pacing in front of me. He picks up a rock and throws it hard, hitting the side of the fence. "I'm so pissed!" Then he picks up another one and lets it fly. Shep spins around and says, "They were my friends. My best friends. And they're going to go in front of a judge and lie about me." He kicks a stick and then picks it up and throws it, too. "They're going to say I killed Grant."

I get up and move in close, wrapping my arms around him. He buries his head against my neck. Some parents on the other side of the park are looking at us, watching him fall apart, so I turn him where they can't see his face.

"I'm scared, Kate," he whispers in my hair. "I'm scared I'm going to jail for something I didn't do."

I squeeze him hard. Hearing the pain in his voice makes it hard for me to swallow. "Don't say that. It's not over yet."

He pulls back slowly. "You're not at work right now. What happened?"

I let out a shaky breath and tell him about the picture of us this morning, getting fired, and even about Stone sending someone to that pawnshop.

He moves away from me and picks up another stick, flinging it against the fence. "Fuck!" he yells, and a few moms whip around in our direction, shooting daggers at us with their eyes.

"What's going on?" he asks out loud, though I know the question isn't one he expects me to answer.

"I'm guessing those guys at the pawnshop told Logan about the guy Stone sent by. He knows I would do whatever I could to help you and he wanted to stop me. I guess mission accomplished."

"I don't like it. I can't stand that they're watching us and screwing with you." Shep scans the park, then moves away from me.

He throws his hands out and turns in a slow circle. "Get a good look! Here I am, asshole. Get a good shot of this." And then he holds up his right hand with only his middle finger raised.

Parents are now ushering their children far away from us, disgust on all of their faces. I pull him down to the bench and throw apologetic looks their way.

He leans forward, resting his elbows on his knees, and drops his head in his hands.

"Kate," he says. "What if there's no way to stop this? I can't go to prison for this. I can't."

His voice sounds hollow. I wrap my arms around him, pulling him as close to me as I can.

"It's not over. Do not give up on me, Shep. I won't let you give up. You didn't do this."

We stay like this for a while. He's holding himself together, but not by much.

"I'm not giving up," he says. "But I'm afraid my lawyer isn't even going to try. I've got another meeting with him tomorrow. I'm just going to have to convince him I didn't do this."

He sits up and scans the almost empty park. "We should leave. It wouldn't be good for us to be seen together."

I shake my head. "I don't care about that anymore. Stone fired me, remember."

He pulls me up until we're both standing. "But I haven't forgotten that someone, probably Logan, is watching us . . . threatening us."

We walk, hand in hand, stopping at the edge of the parking lot, in between Mom's car and his Jeep. It's by no means private, but we're hidden somewhat from view. He backs me up against his Jeep, his hands braced on the window on either side of my head.

He moves in closer, his body connecting with mine from my shoulders down to my knees. My hands snake under his jacket and wrap around his waist. His lips land on mine softly at first. Then harder. Shep invades all of my senses, and it's so easy to get lost in him. I want to cry when he finally steps back, the cold air slamming into me once his body isn't there to block it.

"I don't want to walk away from you right now," he says.

"Me either."

His hands frame my face as he plants tiny kisses, starting from one cheek and moving across the bridge of my nose to the other cheek.

"We're not giving up," he whispers.

"Not giving up," I whisper back.

· · ·

I don't expect Mom to be home when I get there, but she is. She's at the kitchen table with a mug of hot tea in front of her, as if she's been waiting for me for hours.

"Sit down, Kate."

I sit across from her. It's hard to look her in the face and see the disappointment there.

"Start at the beginning," she says in a quiet voice.

And I do. I tell her everything. She never interrupts, although her facial expressions and small gasps tell me she is completely shocked.

When I'm done, we sit quietly for a few minutes as she absorbs everything she's heard.

"That wasn't what I was expecting," she finally says.

"It wasn't what I was expecting either."

She nods. "Stone needs to know about the first picture. The one you got during the fire drill."

I shake my head. "Stone isn't interested in hearing any of this. I don't blame him for being mad at me, but I never thought it would be more important for him to win rather than to get it right."

Mom lets out a soft huff. "This isn't a normal case and you know it. And he thinks he is getting it right. And you've given him no reason to trust you now."

I don't reply.

"So you're still talking to him? Seeing him?" she asks.

I nod and pick at my thumbnail.

"I want you to stop. At least until this case is over. I know you believe he didn't do it. But we don't know for sure, and I still work for Stone. We can't afford for me to get fired, too. Someone is taking pictures of you with him, and, well, that's just more than I can handle. You are the one and only important thing in my life, and I'm not willing to risk your safety over this."

I duck my head, embarrassed by her words. We don't usually say mushy stuff to each other.

"I'm serious, Kate. This is not a game. One boy is already dead. Let Shep's family and his lawyer get him out of this trouble. If he didn't do it, the truth will come out."

I nod but have no intention of deserting Shep. And I don't know how she can still be so optimistic when it comes to the legal system after all these years.

I'm not.

It was easy, really. Almost too easy.

We all sat in the district attorney's office telling our story.

Yes, sir, we saw Shep pick up the gun.

Yes, sir, we were scared to admit it when we were first questioned.

Yes, sir, we're sorry for not coming forward earlier.

Easy.

28

DECEMBER 3, 11:53 A.M.

SHEP: If I don't get out of this house
soon I'm going to lose my mind.

The last week and a half has been torture. Thanksgiving break was depressing. Without school or work, I barely left the house. When we came back from break, I lost my work pass since I lost my job, so until I can find another one I'm stuck at school until three. And because I don't have any classes scheduled in the afternoon, I spend most of my time in the media arts room. I've edited all the images taken over the last several weeks, the website is up to date, the paper is ready a full day before it's due, and I've worked on all the ads that have been turned in for the yearbook.

At home, Mom is watching me like a hawk and Shep's parents have put him on lockdown after a blurry pic of him flipping the bird in the park found its way onto the news. There was no question who took it; one of those moms was happy to be interviewed about the entire event.

Luckily, I didn't make it into the shot, but Shep's new lawyer suggested it would be better for him to lie low for a while, so now he's being homeschooled. We still talk on the phone, but I haven't been brave enough to try to sneak over there at night. I don't want him to get in any more trouble than he's already in.

I've never felt so bored or useless in my life.

Glancing at the clock, I see there's still another hour to go before the final bell rings. God, it's been a long day. I pull out my phone and open the gallery, scrolling back until I get to the picture I took of Shep Halloween night at the football game. This is my favorite image of him.

I flip to the next picture and stare at the screenshot I took of Shep's post that shows Grant and Henry passed out on that chair at River Point. I laugh again when I read the caption, but then my brain snags on something, but I can't focus in on it. What is it?

Opening up my laptop, I scroll through the pictures until I get to the ones of the back patio at River Point I took the day I visited the scene. The furniture is an eclectic mix that somehow makes sense. A few rocking chairs next to an iron table and chairs and even a few pieces with fabric cushions. But there seems to be a space in the center of the area . . . like something is missing. Where's the chair?

Holding my phone up next to my laptop screen, I see where the chair used to be.

But it's gone.

I stare at the picture of Grant and Henry in the chair. There's something else. Something familiar. The chair is wide . . . wide enough for both of them to fit comfortably side by side and still have a little extra room. And they are reclined back somewhat. Not all the way, but enough. There's something there, but I can't put my finger on it.

And then I zoom in closer. I feel like what I'm looking for is just out of reach, like when you have something on the tip of your tongue but can't say it. What is it?

And then it hits me.

"Holy shit!" I scream, and a few people on the other side of the room look at me.

"Sorry," I call out. I look back at the screen, minimizing the image, then pulling up every social media account until I find that photo that keeps getting reposted. When the picture of the girls pops up on-screen, I can't stop myself from cringing.

This is why the one of Grant and Henry was so familiar. I zoom in quickly, focusing on the corner of the picture that caught Reagan's eye the first time we looked at it . . . the small swirl-like design. It matches the design on the chair in Shep's picture.

But it's more than that. Even though the picture of the girls is taken from a different angle, the size of the chair and the way it reclines back matches the one the boys are on.

This is where the girls were when this picture was taken. They were at River Point.

I zoom back out on both images and put them side by side, even though it's really hard to look at the one of the girls.

But I'm trying to figure out how it was taken. I'm assuming Shep was standing when he took the one of the boys, but the angle of the one with the girls is totally different.

It was taken from a higher angle, like that camera was looking down on the scene.

But how?

. . .

By the time I'm walking to Mom's car after school, I'm drained.

Reagan calls just as I'm about to pull out of the lot. She's been keeping me up to date ever since I got unofficially banned from the courthouse.

"What's going on?" I say when I answer.

She's quiet for just a second. "They're offering Shep a deal."

Ever since the others turned on him, I knew this was coming.

"What's the deal?"

"Instead of second-degree murder, he'll get manslaughter with a cap of twenty years in prison."

I hit the steering wheel so hard it hurts my hand.

"When does he enter his guilty plea?" I ask.

"Tomorrow. At nine. Everyone wants this over and done with."

"I gotta go," I say, and end the call.

Banned or not—I need to talk to Stone.

I'm a few blocks from the courthouse when I see the protesters. I have to give them credit for sticking with their cause. The local reporters have been all over John Michael's dad the last week since there's been a lull in the River Point case. I've enjoyed watching him squirm when they ambush him with questions.

And then I see her. Pulling Mom's car over, I watch her. The girl who attacked Grant in that video. The same girl Henry was with at the St. Jude's barbecue. She's walking toward the same coffee shop she was coming out of the other day, wearing the same T-shirt with the shop's logo. School just got out, so she must be headed into work. Her arms are wrapped tightly across her chest, her eyes scanning up and down the street.

And I look at her face. Really look at it.

"Oh God," I say quietly to myself.

I pull my laptop out of my bag. Still frozen on the screen are the side-by-side image of the picture of the girls and the picture of Henry and Grant. The girl on the right is Bree but the girl in the middle of the picture is walking down the street in front of me.

And she was at River Point the night before Grant was shot. And she was mad at him. And Henry pulled her away. And Henry told Grant, *"You better hope you didn't do what I think you did."*

Change of plans.

She's half a block away when I pull Mom's car to the side and jump out. I catch her just before she goes inside. "Excuse me?"

"Yes?"

"Hi. I'm Kate Marino and I work for the district attorney's office. Can I ask you a couple of questions?"

She hugs herself tighter and squints her eyes at me. "What do you want?"

"We're handling the River Point case and going over some of the evidence we found in a video from the party the night before. You were in it. You were really angry with Grant Perkins, and Henry Carlisle had to intervene. Can you tell me what was going on?"

She shifts back and leans against the side of the building, scanning up and down the street before turning back to me. She drops her backpack on the ground beside her.

"You're here to question me about this. You're basically my age. I call bullshit."

Was not expecting that.

"I work for the assistant—"

"Look, I'm sure you know who I am. I'm sure you've seen the pictures. *Everyone* has seen those pictures."

"And that's why you were angry at Grant," I say. "The pictures. Right?"

She crosses her arms in front of her again and stares at me to the point of being awkward.

"What are you trying to do?" she asks, her eyes narrowing on me.

"I'm trying to figure out what happened at River Point that morning . . . and the night before. Why were you so mad at him?"

I don't think she's going to answer until she says, "Grant said something to me at the football game earlier. Something that, when I thought about exactly what he said later on, made me believe he was the one who took that picture."

"What did he say?"

Her cheeks go pink. "Let's just say he mentioned something that even those who have seen the pictures wouldn't know."

I nod and swallow hard, trying not to let my imagination run away with me.

"So I went there to confront him. Of course, he denied it. But I know it was him by the way he smirked at me."

Great. She knows it was him but has no proof of it.

I can see her getting impatient. "And we noticed Henry came to your rescue . . ."

She leans forward and says, "Yeah, because he's not a dick like the rest of them."

"But it's more than that, isn't it? I mean, the way he is with you. It's obvious in the way he touches you, looks at you. He cares for you. And you care for him."

She tucks her lips together, her mouth forming a straight line. I can see I've thrown her.

"Henry was as angry with Grant as you were. Did he realize Grant took that picture of you and the others? What did Henry say to you that night?"

She dips her head. "What Henry said to me is none of your business."

I gnaw on my bottom lip, trying to think of anything else I can ask her. "Why don't you go to the police and tell them you suspect Grant took those pictures?"

She looks at me like I'm stupid. "Why would I? He's dead. And I'm not sorry he is. I just wish I could have been the one to blow him away."

I'm momentarily speechless. But I have to get to the bottom of this. "So who was? Was it Henry?" I whisper.

She swings her backpack up, nearly hitting me with it. "Do you know how many people act outraged over what happened to us, then turn around and say that we probably knew what was happening, or that we did something to deserve it?"

I shake my head. She's trembling, she's so angry.

"Hardly anyone tried to figure out who did this to us—most just talked about us. How we looked naked. How we were touching each other. How we probably liked it." She takes a deep breath and says, "*If* Henry did it, then he was the only one with the guts to actually do something about it."

I keep telling them it's almost over. Everything will be back to normal soon.

I glance at the picture again. My daily reminder.

But there's still one loose end . . . a mystery to be solved.

One that I may never be able to figure out. One that Grant took to his grave.

29

DECEMBER 3, 3:29 P.M.

PRIVATE NUMBER: Need to talk to
you. Urgent.

My phone rings instantly.

"I guess you heard," he says when I answer. "I'm still at my lawyer's
office, looking over everything, trying to make a decision." He sounds
broken.

Taking a deep breath, I say, "I may have found something. I'm not
sure."

"What did you find?" Suddenly, there's hope in his voice.

I tell him about noticing the chair in his post was missing from
the back patio and how it's the same chair in the picture with the girls.
Then I tell him about the video from the party and the girl on the street
with Henry and John Michael.

"Lori. She was one of the girls in that picture. Henry has had a
thing for her for years," Shep says. "He was furious when those pictures
came out."

"But I thought they were part of the prank war? Those girls are seniors, so why would Grant have done that?"

"Grant probably thought it was the perfect way to get the juniors in trouble. Prank them by making everybody think *they* were the ones taking things too far. He was twisted like that."

"Was Henry furious enough to kill Grant if he thought he was the one who took it?" I ask.

"Hell, I don't know."

"But just knowing this is an option could be enough, right? I talked to her."

"Lori? What did she say?"

"She wouldn't come out and say it, but it sounds like she thinks Henry did it. Maybe if your lawyer questioned her. Or something."

"Maybe this will be enough," he says, but I can hear the anxiety in his voice. "And Kate, thanks for this."

"This isn't over," I say.

"I'll call you later."

. . .

It's really late when Shep calls. "Want to go for a ride?"

I don't hesitate a second. "Where do I meet you?"

This may be our last night. If he accepts the deal tomorrow, he'll immediately be taken into custody. I haven't talked to him since this afternoon, and I'm dying to find out what his lawyer thinks about Lori.

"I'll pick you up."

"I'll be waiting out front."

I don't care if one of the others is watching us. I already lost my job. He could possibly be losing his freedom tomorrow. Whoever shot Grant is getting what they want.

I hop into the Jeep the second he stops. He says quietly, "I'm really glad you're here." He pulls me in and gives me a quick kiss. It happens so fast I don't think I even kissed him back.

The top is still off and it's a little cold outside. Shep reaches behind him and pulls out a thick blanket.

"Here. This should keep you warm."

I bundle up and recline my seat back so I can look at the sky overhead. It isn't long before I pull a ponytail holder out of my bag to get my hair out of my face.

We leave town, driving down a narrow road with empty fields on both sides until we stop at a side road that's blocked by a gate.

"Just have to open it," Shep says, then jumps out.

I sit up a little straighter, trying to get my bearings, but I have no idea where we are.

Shep hops back in the Jeep and pulls through. He leans closer and says, "My dad brought me here a few days ago. His company just leased this land for oil and gas exploration, and the owners live out of state, so I knew no one would be here."

We drive down a gravel road for a mile or so, then stop at the edge of a small pond. Shep turns the Jeep off, and the quietness of the night settles around us. The full moon shines down across the water, chasing away the darkness.

"My lawyer and I went to see Lori at work. He thought there might be a better chance that she would talk to me, since we were friends."

I turn my head to the side. "What did she say?"

"She said she called the district attorney's office after you left, and they told her you'd been fired. She reported you for harassing her. She also denied everything. Said she has no idea who shot Grant, but there was no way Henry could have done it. Said you were making it all up so I wouldn't be in trouble."

"What! I didn't make any of it up! She's the one who's lying!"

He laces his fingers through mine. "I know. But there's no way she's going against Henry. Lori is a dead end."

I throw the blanket off of me. I'm so pissed.

"I can't believe she reported me!" Whatever credibility I had with Stone is completely gone now. Why do I always make things worse?

"What did your lawyer say?"

"He 'strongly suggested' I take the deal. He's looked into Logan and the missing watch and ring and those two guys. Dead end. Henry and Lori are a dead end. John Michael and his drug deals are a dead end."

"What about Lindsey? We know she's lying!"

"Yeah, but the other three are taking a deal in exchange for swearing under oath that they saw me with the Remington that morning! That only makes her testimony that much stronger. If this goes to trial and the jury finds me guilty—I'll get life."

It feels like my heart drops right into my stomach. I lace my fingers through his.

"So what are you going to do?"

"I don't want to take the deal but I'm afraid to risk life in prison." He bangs his head against the back of his seat. "Hell, even after twenty years, my life would be basically over."

"You can't give up. You have to try," I say.

Shep turns sideways in his seat so he's facing me and pulls his hand away from mine. "Try what? This isn't a game, Kate! I'm out of time. My deal is good for twenty-four hours. I know you're trying to help, but every lead we have is a dead end. I'm not giving up. I'm trying to figure out how to salvage a small piece of my life. If we had something— anything—I'd be the first one fighting. But we have nothing."

I brush away a tear that's sliding down my cheek. "I'm with you through this, no matter what."

He's shaking his head. "No, you're not. Think about it, Kate. My life is over. What, are you going to stick by me for twenty years, wait until I'm out of prison?"

"So this is goodbye? You brought me out here to say goodbye?" The tears are flowing now, and I don't try to stop them.

He pulls me close, his hands framing my face.

"Don't cry. Please don't cry. I don't know what else to do. I'm scared. And I'm mad. My life is ruined. There's no reason for yours to be, too."

I'm sinking. Drowning.

"I don't want to talk about the case anymore. Or what will happen tomorrow. This is our last time alone together. Can we stay here a little while?" he asks.

"I'll stay as long as you'll have me," I answer.

• • •

It only takes about twenty minutes to get to River Point. My hands are shaking as I pull into the familiar driveway. It's early, the sun is barely up, and it wasn't that long ago that Shep dropped me at home. I haven't slept, because I can't get past the idea that there's something else I'm missing. And I refuse to believe every lead is a dead end. I know the picture was taken here, and I know Grant was the one who took it. There's something really off about that picture of those girls and the angle, and I have to try to figure it out.

What if I'm wrong in thinking they wouldn't be here since they're all due in court in just a few hours? What if someone is here?

There are a few vehicles in the carport, but they seem like the kind that stay here all the time. I pull in close to the house but then go ahead and turn the car around. At least if I have to bolt, the car is pointed in the right direction, ready to go.

I grab my camera from my bag on the passenger seat and walk toward the house just as my phone beeps. It's a text from Shep.

I'm sorry I was angry last night. Thank you for
believing in me. Thank you for fighting for me.
You deserve someone who can be there for you
in every way. More than anything I wish it could
be me.

His words energize me. Now, more than ever, I'm determined to find a way to clear his name.

I duck when I pass in front of a window, although I'm pretty sure no one is here. It only takes a few moments to get to the back of the house.

And there is the empty space where the chair used to be, according to Shep's post. I pull another chair to this spot as a placeholder, then set my laptop on a nearby table, open to both pictures.

I take a shot of it and compare it to Shep's. Shep is several inches taller than me, but basically, we have the same angle.

Then I hold it above my head and point the lens down toward the chair and compare the angle again.

Direction is right but the camera's not high enough.

Grabbing a chair, I scoot it across the patio until I get it where I want it. Once I'm standing in the seat of the chair, I fire off another shot.

It's close. Still not high enough.

But why would Grant be standing on a chair? I turn around and look at what's behind me. There's a low brick wall separating the patio from the woods. There are several trees on the other side of the wall. I search the trees through the lens, zooming in for a closer look. There doesn't seem to be anything unusual . . . just some trees, bare limbs, a few birds, an outdoor spotlight pointed toward the patio, and an old weathered birdhouse.

And then I zoom in a tad closer on the birdhouse. There's something inside the hole, something shiny.

I jump down and drag the chair to edge of the patio, using it so I can climb up on the wall. When I'm right in front of the birdhouse, I turn around carefully and snap a picture of the chair the girls were on.

It's almost a perfect match.

Turning back to the birdhouse, I find a hinge on one side. A hinge on one side means the front must open. It's not hard to find the latch when you know what you're looking at. When the front of the birdhouse swings open, I almost fall off of the wall.

There's a camera inside, one very similar to the wildlife cameras Mr. Forres has scattered throughout his property. But this one is different. I take a picture of it, making sure the make and model are in focus.

I glance at the light right above the birdhouse. It's brilliant. If the lights are on, even at night you would be able to get a usable photo.

From what Mr. Stone found out about the other wildlife cameras here, I know that if I open it there will be a media card inside, but I'm afraid to touch it. I don't want my prints to show up here and give Stone any reason to throw out this evidence.

I wish I had a glove or anything to put over my hand so I can open it up. I could grab my laptop from the car and load the images directly onto it.

My sock. It's gross but it will do the job. I sit on the wall and remove my shoe, then my sock, putting it over my right hand. I rub off the latch, hopefully removing any fingerprints I put there.

It's not hard to get the camera open. I hit a small button on the side and the front pops open. There is the lens, the batteries, but not much else. Where's the card?

I fool around with the camera until I'm completely frustrated. How can there not be a media card?

But there is the name of a website printed just inside the door, along with a camera number and password. I take a picture of it and hop down, moving all of the furniture back to its original place.

I check my watch and realize I've been here too long. Once everything is back the way I found it, I jump in the car and speed away from River Point.

I dial Reagan's number and it takes several rings for her to answer. "Help!" I shout into the phone. "I need you." I'm scared about what I'm going to find. And scared about what I won't. I need her with me when I look at the images from that camera.

"What is it?" I can picture her sitting up in her bed, her black hair sticking out in every direction.

"I just did something crazy."

"What did you do, Kate?"

I give her the short and dirty version and she gasps about every other sentence.

"Oh my God, Kate! You have to go to Stone and tell him about the camera."

"I've tried to talk to him. He won't listen to anything I have to say. I need to see what pictures are on there. And I need to do it quickly. Can you meet me at the media arts room? I'm hoping I can log on to the site there and check out how to view them."

"Yes! Holy crap! I'll meet you there."

I end the call and drive to school like a crazy person.

By the time I get parked and inside the media arts room, I get a text that Reagan is pulling in too. When she walks through the door minutes later, I've never been so happy to see my best friend.

I can't get the website up fast enough.

"Okay, so what's it say?" she asks when she sits in the chair next to me.

The website for the wildlife cam boasts of the camera's remote-viewing capabilities and ease of use, enabling all members of a hunting lease to view images anytime, from anywhere.

"It looks like all I need to do is log into that camera using the ID and password I found inside the door."

I enter all the information and wait while the site processes it. I feel like I'm going to pass out. What if there isn't anything there? What if this is a dead end too?

And then images start filling the screen. There are thousands of them. The camera's settings are on the dashboard at the top of the screen and the camera is set to go off when there is movement, one picture every ten seconds until there is no movement for five minutes. It uploads through the Wi-Fi at River Point.

"It's going to take forever to go through these," I say.

I glance at the clock. It's almost seven thirty. The morning is flying by.

"Well, maybe not," Reagan says. "Look, you can filter by date. What date was Grant shot? We can look for whoever went hunting with that rifle."

"October fifth," I answer. "I thought about that, but they all said they left through the garage to go hunting. That's on the other side of the house. I'm trying to see if there are pictures of Grant and those three girls."

Reagan scoots me out of the way and sits down at the computer. "We got the first complaints about those pictures around the first of October, so let's look at the weekend before that all the way until the morning he was killed." She clicks the filter-by-date button and puts in *September 27–October 5.*

It takes a second for the screen to load. Once the pictures are there, we start browsing. Lots of party shots. And I was right about the spotlight. Even at night, everyone in the images is fully illuminated.

We scroll through until we're at Saturday night, the week before the game. There are tons of people there, including all of the River Point Boys. My heart skips every time Shep is in one of the frames. It's not until much later, after most people have left the party, that you see the girls. They are clearly drunk or drugged, stumbling around and falling on the ground. Grant leads them to the chair, and then he starts removing their clothing. It's choppy seeing everything happen in ten-second intervals, but it's easy to get the gist of what was happening.

When he gets them just like he wants them, he steps back and lets the camera take over. There are several shots of just the girls, and then he's back, dressing them and leading them back inside.

It's so disgusting.

"They had no idea," Reagan says.

"I feel sick."

I keep flipping forward, hoping like hell there is something else here. Something that can help Shep, because at this point, I hate that anyone gets in trouble for killing Grant.

We scroll through Sunday, then Monday, with little activity until we get to Tuesday afternoon.

"Wait, what is this?" I ask.

It's two men, their backs to the camera as if they are looking out into the woods.

The next shot, they're sitting down at the iron table and chairs, a briefcase between them.

"It's Gaines," Reagan says.

"And John Michael's dad," I add.

Ten seconds later, the briefcase is open and it's full of cash—nice, neatly bundled piles of it.

"What's this about?" I ask.

Reagan leans closer to the screen. "No. No, no, no."

It's clearly a payoff.

"We've had complaint after complaint come through Morrison's office about Forres and his construction company overcharging the city for those renovations downtown. I guess this is why Gaines hasn't done anything about it," she says.

"This has been on the news a lot. Reporters keep showing up at his office asking him about it." I continue to scroll through the images. "And this is what those people are protesting every day."

Reagan leans closer to me and says, "Yes."

I'm nodding and checking the clock every few seconds.

"Wait. Grant told John Michael, *'Don't forget, I've got the trump card.'* Do you think he was talking about having dirt on his dad and the DA?"

"This is some serious dirt. I'm afraid to see what's next," Reagan says.

"At least we know why Gaines was so eager to help the River Point Boys," I say. I'm confident now, because even if there isn't anything else, this may be enough to cast immediate doubt on the case against Shep.

Not much else until we get to the party the night before Grant is killed. It's like catching a glimpse into everything I heard about that night. Shep and Grant fighting over me. Logan and Grant getting cornered by the bookies. The girl, Lori, showing up, mad at Grant, and Grant and Henry getting into it.

And then the early-morning hours with them around the fire. It is just as Shep described it. They all get up just as the sun is rising and they head into the house.

"I guess that's it. They went in to get their stuff to go hunting," Reagan says.

I keep clicking through, knowing there's probably not much more to see, until all of a sudden, someone returns to the patio. Checking the time-stamp, I see it's about six minutes after they all left. It looks like he's running back into the house—then he comes quickly out again.

Carrying the Remington.

His face is framed perfectly in the image, his hands on the gun.

It's John Michael Forres.

We walk up the steps to the courthouse, ready to enter our pleas and make everything official.

Dad shakes Mr. Gaines's hand when he meets us at the door and they speak quietly to one another.

I haven't told Dad about the picture yet.

But I will.

I'm going to use it to my advantage, just like Grant was going to use it to his.

I peek at the image hidden in my coat pocket. I've looked at it every day since Grant handed it to me at the party and said, *"It sure would suck if this made it out into the world."*

I still haven't figured out how he got this. I've been to River Point a dozen times, searching for some hidden camera or something.

Grant would have milked this for all he could, for as long as he could, although I don't know what more I could have given him.

But he crossed the line that night. With me and everyone else.

It was time for Grant to go.

And now it seems like it's Shep's time, too.

30

I pick up the phone to call Mr. Stone. He's got to know what we have. The call goes to voice mail.

I try Mom and then Shep, and it does the same.

"Shit! They're probably already down in the courtroom getting ready." Because of the problems with Stone's sight, he likes to get in there early so Mom can help orient him in the room.

Reagan stands up so quickly her chair almost falls over. "We'll just let the pictures speak for themselves. The control room for the audio-visual stuff is in the office next to the courtroom they're going to be in. We sneak in there and hook up your laptop and let the images play."

"We need to make sure Gaines can't bury the part he played in this. Let's take the shot of him and Forres with the money and let everyone see it. We'll let our paper break the story on the corruption that's happening downtown," I add. "Are you okay with that?"

Reagan drops down at the desk. "Just give me a minute. My parents will be pissed, but you're right. He's corrupt and everyone should know it." She starts dragging images around. "I'm choosing the images we need to tell this story. I'm putting a ten-second delay at the front so we'll either have time to get inside the courtroom and watch the show or run like hell away from there. Your choice. I'll write the story for the paper, with the shots of Forres and Gaines, in the car on the way. What about the one with John Michael with the rifle? Want that one in the piece? If we're going to do this—go out in the open with it—we should do it right."

I think about those threatening pictures he sent Shep and me. I think about how willing he was for Shep to go down for this in his place. I think about how Shep thought of him as a friend.

"Let everyone see that one too."

Reagan burns a copy onto a flash drive, while I throw my laptop back in my bag.

I stop mid-motion and turn to her. "I can't thank you enough for this."

Reagan pushes me toward the door. "We'll hug it out later."

"You should stay here. I'll probably get in a lot of trouble. There's no need to go down with me," I say to her.

She laughs as she jumps in the passenger seat. "I wouldn't miss this for anything."

It's straight-up nine o'clock when we pull into the parking lot. We run like something is chasing us.

We run like Shep's freedom depends on us.

Curious stares and startled cries follow us as we barrel down the hall. A quick glance through the window of the courtroom door lets us know everyone is inside. We cut into the office next to the courtroom and open the side cabinet that houses the controls for the courtroom. We nearly drop the laptop in our haste to get everything plugged in.

My hand hovers over the control pad. "Are we ready to do this?" I ask.

"Yes. Do it."

I tap play and we race out of the room, into the hallway, and throw open the double doors to the courtroom. Everyone stops what they are doing and turns around to see what the commotion is about.

My eyes find Shep immediately. He's standing at the defense table with his attorney. The other River Point Boys are there along with their families, since they have to put in their pleas for the deals they're making as well. They are in the gallery chairs behind the defense's table. Grant's family is sitting behind Mr. Stone along with the team of investigators.

The judge smacks her gavel just as the screen on the right side of her starts to lower from the ceiling.

Everyone's attention leaves us and goes to the screens. Everyone's except Shep's. He's worried, his forehead scrunched up, and I give him a big smile that I hope lets him know it's going to be okay.

Reagan has her laptop, and the second the video starts playing, she uploads the story she just wrote to the school's online paper.

Now it's time for the show.

Reagan wasn't playing around when she said the pictures should speak for themselves. The room is quiet as image after image flashes across the screen.

I watch the River Point Boys, especially John Michael. He's antsy, glancing from the screen to us and back again.

When the pictures of Grant and the girls come across the screen, you could hear a pin drop. Mr. and Mrs. Perkins drop down in their chairs, and they both start crying quietly. Then pictures of Gaines and Mr. Forres begin appearing and the crowd visibly cringes. Mr. Forres starts screaming to turn it off, and Gaines sinks down on the bench on the side of the room, his face ashen.

The pictures cycle through the party. Since most everyone in the room knows the evidence in this case, it's not hard to follow the story being played out. When the five boys head off to hunt, the room becomes silent.

And then there's John Michael, back for the Remington. The slide show ends with the frozen image of him with the gun, the picture time- and date-stamped from the morning of Grant's death.

John Michael sits down in the chair next to his mother, lays his head on her shoulder, and starts crying.

31

It takes a while for the judge to get control of the room. Another bailiff is dragging John Michael away from his mom as she clings to him. The other boys are yelling at him and at each other. Grant's dad looks like he's seen a ghost. I'm sure it was hard to stomach the pictures of Grant with the girls.

I hated to do that to him, but when you want the truth, you have to take the whole truth. And poor Mr. Stone. He's sitting at the prosecutor's table, his head in his hands.

But Shep's face makes it all worth it. He's all smiles, relief radiating from him and his family, and they stand together, wrapped in each other's arms. He eyes find mine and I'm overwhelmed by what I see there.

The judge pounds her gavel until finally it's the only sound in the room. "I will have order in this court!" she screams.

Shep's lawyer stands in front of the judge when she gives him permission to speak. "Obviously, in light of what we've witnessed here today, we will not be taking the deal offered by the prosecution."

The judge looks back at Reagan and me and motions us forward. "This all started when you two entered the room."

We both nod and she slams the gavel down once more. "Bailiff, take

Mr. Forres and his son into custody, please. I would like Henry Carlisle and Logan McCullar detained for questioning. I believe they were here today to swear they saw Mr. Moore with that Remington. And you," she says, pointing to the district attorney. "I'm giving you the chance to surrender yourself for questioning. I suggest you take it."

Gaines looks physically ill but manages a quick nod, then follows the bailiff out of the courtroom.

The judge directs her attention back to us. "You two come with me."

I peek quickly at Mom, who is sitting at the table with Mr. Stone. She gives me a nod of encouragement, and that's all I need.

Reagan squeezes my hand, and then we follow the judge through one of the back doors to her office.

She shuts the door behind me and instructs us to have a seat.

"What in the world just happened in there?"

Reagan and I look quickly at each other, and then I turn back to the judge and say, "Your Honor, like most everyone at my school, I saw that picture of those girls. And then when I was doing research for Mr. Stone, I found bits and pieces that connected Grant to that picture but didn't put it all together until very recently. I didn't know anything about what Mr. Forres was up to until I stumbled on the images from a hidden wildlife camera at River Point. All of the images you just saw came from that camera."

I pause for a moment and then say, "And I didn't think it would be a good idea to contact the district attorney's office with what I found. I just wanted to make sure the images were shown before Shep pleaded guilty. I just saw the pictures for the first time about an hour ago. I guess you could say I thought this was the fastest way to get the information in your hands."

"Well, you certainly accomplished that," she says. "Is this the only place you've shared these images?"

Reagan takes a deep breath and says, "As journalists, we felt it was important to make sure our readers know what happens in their community..."

"You wanted to be the ones to break the story?" the judge interrupts. "This is going to be a nightmare to unravel."

"We just shared the images of Mr. Forres and Mr. Gaines. And the one of John Michael with the gun. We didn't want to hurt those girls any more than they have already been, so those were only shown here."

The judge leans her head back against her chair. "There's more to this that you're not telling me. Why didn't you see the pictures until this morning?"

I take a deep breath and tell her everything. About following the boys, taking pictures of them, how the camera works, and that the photos are actually stored on the manufacturer's site.

She leans back in her chair and studies me.

"But I didn't corrupt any evidence," I add. "The images are all still there on the site, time- and date-stamped. No one would listen to me when I said Shep didn't do it, so I had to resort to drastic measures."

"Drastic measures, indeed," the judge says with a smirk on her face.

"Am I in trouble?" I ask.

She runs a hand through her hair. "I think they will be dealing with the fallout of those pictures for a while, but for sure, your employment here is at an end."

I nod. No reason to tell her I was fired almost a week ago. I feel bad for Reagan, though.

"And you need to assume you will be called in to testify in these other matters as to how you obtained the pictures and be ready for them to tear you apart."

I nod again. At this point, as long as Shep is out of trouble, I'll do anything.

"And thirty hours of community service wouldn't hurt either one of you."

We both nod and answer, "Yes, Your Honor."

"You're excused for now," she says, and we bolt from the room. Gaines, Mr. Forres, John Michael, Henry, and Logan are gone, as are most of their families.

Shep moves away from his family and meets me in the middle of the room. He pulls me in close and swings me around in a tight circle.

"I cannot believe this just happened."

"I told you it would all work out," I answer with a relieved sigh.

He brings me back to the ground, then gives me a kiss that should embarrass me in front of my mother and his.

But it doesn't.

I kiss him right back.

32

SHEP: I'm surrounded. They're out for blood.
You may have to rescue me.

A huge smile breaks out across my face. I walk into the other room, and there's Shep with about six four-year-olds on top of him.

He makes a loud roar sound and the kids giggle so hard they start rolling off of him. He stands up slowly, only the most tenacious ones still holding on. Shep does a monster walk across the small room, kids hanging from every limb.

Mrs. Weis comes into the room, laughing. "Shep, do you need rescuing?"

"Please," he says desperately.

It takes both of us to untangle the kids from Shep, but once Reagan pokes her head in and mentions the popcorn and movie are ready, they can't get away from us fast enough.

Shep lies on the brightly colored carpet as if he's too exhausted to move.

"Y'all are done for the day. I'll go tell Reagan once she gets them settled in front of the movie that y'all can leave."

Once Mrs. Weis leaves the room, Shep reaches up and grabs my hand, pulling me down with him.

"How many more hours do we have left of this?" he asks.

I don't let his words fool me. He loves this more than he'd ever let on. When Reagan and I got assigned to do our community service at Providence House, a shelter for homeless women and children, he volunteered to do the hours with us. Today was our first day, and he's already the favorite of everyone under four feet tall.

"We've got a little ways to go."

I stand up, then pull his arm until he's standing. "Don't get lazy on me now. You owe me a date."

In the craziness that followed that day in the courtroom, we're just now getting around to having that very public date in that very expensive restaurant, flaming dessert and all.

At last check, the school's online paper has had over a million views. And *Good Morning America* even interviewed us via Skype a few days after everything went down.

Grant's case isn't settled yet. There are lots of motions and appeals and pleas concerning John Michael, Mr. Forres, and the district attorney, but none of that is our problem now.

Shep stands up and pulls me close. It's still so scary to think how badly things could have gone.

"I owe you more than a date," he says quietly.

I squeeze him tight.

"You two are getting on my nerves," Reagan says.

"Please. You and Josh aren't much better." I move away from Shep, but he doesn't let me get too far. "Want to go to dinner with us since Josh has practice tonight?" I offer, and Shep pinches me.

"So I can sit across from y'all while you make googly eyes at each other all night? No, thanks. See y'all tomorrow," she says, then leaves the room.

Shep and I walk hand in hand to his Jeep. Once we're inside, a text comes over his phone. Henry's name flashes across the screen.

"Are you ever going to talk to him?" I ask.

Sadness crosses his face. "Maybe. But not today."

Henry and Logan were able to re-enroll at St. Bart's, but Shep stayed at Marshall. They were both put on probation and have about three times the community service hours we do. And they've both been trying to talk to Shep for a while, but he's not ready to listen just yet. He may never be.

I turn in my seat, facing him, and say, "I'll make you a deal. We'll go eat at that fancy restaurant because for some reason it's a big deal to you, but how about we get our dessert, fire and all, to go, and take it to the tree house?"

His hand moves to my face, then runs through my hair. "That's the best idea I've heard in a long time."

I lean forward and he meets me halfway, kissing me softly on the lips.

"How about we get the entire meal to go and head straight to the tree house now?" I ask softly.

"Even better."

I watched Grant walk into the woods that morning. And then I thought about his gun, his beloved Remington that was still in the gun cabinet inside.

The one I wanted to shoot him with when he first gave me that picture of Dad and Gaines. The picture he was holding over me.

I sighted him in. He turned around. I was just going to scare him. I wanted him to know he'd gone too far. Then he asked me what I was doing there, like it wasn't my right to be anywhere I wanted to be on my own damn land. He wasn't scared. He was annoyed. So I pulled the trigger.

It felt better than I thought it would.

I waited until I saw my friends coming from the other directions. Then I started running toward Grant too. Everyone was freaking out. They dropped their guns and I made sure the Remington was on the top of the pile along with the gun Grant had. Then we surrounded Grant. They were scared. And upset. But I felt things could be better between us with Grant gone . . . just like it used to be. There had been a lot of trouble at River Point lately and most of it was because of Grant.

He was like a cancer in our group, killing us slowly from the inside.

I kept waiting for someone to point at me. Accuse me of shooting him, but no one saw me with the Remington.

I knew we'd all used his gun, knew our fingerprints were all over it. And since I had those pictures of the DA with the money, I knew he would make sure we didn't get in trouble. Grant wasn't the only one who could use that picture.

So we made a pact in those woods. There over Grant's body, we agreed to stand together. We say we didn't use the Remington. We say we don't know anything about it. If we all say it, none of us will be in trouble. No one knows anything. Silence was the only thing that would save us.

But I was wrong. Instead of making us stronger, it pulled us even farther apart.

The truth found a way.

When the new district attorney asked for my statement when I pleaded guilty . . . this was my story.

awkward as it was, I asked him how my River Point Boys could get away with murder. Mike was kind enough to take my calls and answer endless questions as I hammered out the first draft. I'm pretty sure I called him once a week for months. Thank you so much for all of your help!

And thank you to every other lawyer friend who I bugged with questions at parties and lacrosse games and anywhere else we may have been, especially Sonny Huckabay and Craig Smith.

To Dr. Baron Williamson—thanks for all the info on macular degeneration. It was so helpful! And again, any and all mistakes made are fully on me.

I had tons of help with the hunting side of this book as well, especially from my husband, Dean. Thanks for listening to every "What if . . ." I threw at you. And thank you to Bubba Salley, for all the info on wildlife cameras, and to Mary Cecile Hancock and Buzz Hancock, for the bow-hunting demonstrations. They were so helpful!

To Frances Kalmbach, thanks for helping me name Camille! And good luck with your writing!

To my amazing friends: Elizabeth Pippin, Christy Poole, Missy Huckabay, Aimee Ballard, Ashley Hancock, and Lisa Stewart. Thanks for being there for me when I freak out.

Thank you to every reader for all of your e-mails, tweets, blog posts, and Facebook posts! And a special shout-out to: Stacee (aka Book Junkie), Rachel Patrick, Jaime Arkin, Amelie Fleming, and Gray Hodges—you never fail to put a smile on my face!

To Miller, thanks for being my go-to when I have a high school–related question and for setting me straight when you say, "No one does that." To Ross, thanks for always being my first reader and loving this story as much as I do. To Archer, thanks for being so excited when I talked to your class about writing. It was the best first-grade school visit ever.

And always, the biggest thanks to my husband, Dean. Twenty-five years together and looking forward to twenty-five more. So glad you are mine.

Acknowledgments

To my agent, Sarah Davies—thank you for the continued support and guidance. And thank you for introducing me to Megan Miranda and Elle Cosimano, who were first my critique partners and are now my dear friends. I couldn't do any of this without y'all.

To Laura Schreiber—thank you for loving this book. Seriously—in every edit letter and conversation we had, I could tell how much this story meant to you and that means the world to me. Thank you for pushing me to make it better. And to Mary Mudd, thank you for your incredible insight. This was definitely a group effort! The support and guidance you both gave me are so appreciated.

To Polly Watson—thank you for your careful copyediting and your humor. You made this part more enjoyable than it should be. To the entire team at Hyperion, thank you for all of your support.

To Maria Elias and Tanya Ross-Hughes—words cannot describe how I feel about this cover. It is so amazingly perfect that I cried when I first saw it. Thank you!

This Is Our Story wouldn't have been a story if my mom, Sally Ditta, hadn't been summoned for jury duty and Elle Cosimano hadn't been in my kitchen when she called to complain about it. Somehow that combination led to the idea for this book and to both of you, I'm so grateful for your inspiration and support.

Since I'm not a lawyer, I had a ridiculous amount of help making sure I got the legal part right. Any and all mistakes made and liberties taken are fully on me. I'm lucky I could call my dad, Tony Bruscato, and say, "Hey, I have this idea but not sure it'll work . . ." Dad handed the phone to Assistant District Attorney Michael Fontenot, who was sitting right next to him on a bench in the hallway of the courthouse, and as